Busting
Loose

More from Kat Murray

Taking the Reins

Bucking the Rules

Busting Loose

KAT MURRAY

BRAVA

KENSINGTON PUBLISHING CORP.

www.kensingtonbooks.com

BRAVA BOOKS are published by

Kensington Publishing Corp.
119 West 40th Street
New York, NY 10018

ISBN-13: 978-0-7582-8108-1
ISBN-10: 0-7582-8108-0

First Kensington Trade Paperback Printing: January 2014

10 9 8 7 6 5 4 3 2 1

Printed in the United States of America

First electronic edition: January 2014

ISBN-13: 978-0-7582-8109-8
ISBN-10: 0-7582-8109-9

Chapter One

Morgan Browning, DVM, stared his archenemy down. "You can't beat me."

His enemy blinked.

"I'm smarter. I'm stronger. And I can think."

Blink. Blink.

"I will take you down."

The phone blinked again, signaling that this little intimidation exercise had not, in fact, helped solve the problem of how to get the voice mail off the machine to make the light go off.

"Dammit." He pushed away from the desk in disgust. Why had Jaycee left for the day already? It was only three. She was the only one who knew how to make the stupid machine behave.

She'd given him a month to find a replacement for her as she trained to move up from receptionist to vet tech. And in reality, he agreed with her choice to become a tech.

But why, God why, did she leave him alone for the afternoon without teaching him how to make the ugly thing stop blinking?

The bell above the door swung open, and Morgan summoned up the friendly smile he always pasted on for paying customers. But as he turned and caught sight of his patient, the smile broadened naturally.

"Bea, hey. What's going on?"

"I—" She glanced at the phone as it rang, then at the empty chair. "Do you need to get that?"

"No, it's fine." He reached for Bea's Boston terrier, Milton, whom she'd adopted a few months ago. "Did you have an appointment?" The dog licked his face, smudging one lens of his glasses more so than it already had been.

The phone stopped ringing, and blissful silence—but for the dog's snuffled breathing—filled the waiting area. He sighed in relief, then his body clenched again when the phone rang once more.

"No appointment. I just . . . okay, are you sure you don't want to get that?" She pointed a finger at The Devil. "We can wait a few minutes."

"Ignore it." He was. Morgan held the Boston up to eye level, squinting through the smudge. "Hey, dude. What's up?"

"He keeps scratching." Bea puffed and blew some baby-fine white-blond hair out of her eyes. Her hair reminded him of a pile of feathers, it looked so lightweight. And she wore it in a short style that framed her face, too short for pulling back like most women he knew. But a face like that deserved a frame.

"Dogs scratch, Bea." He hid a smile behind Milton's back. To Bea's mind, every whimper and whine was a new health scare for her pup. "But let's go take a look at—"

"Okay, that's it!" Bea swerved around the desk on heels so high they had to be a danger to her health and plopped down in Jaycee's old chair. Picking up the phone and pressing two buttons he never would have considered pressing together, she chirped, "Morgan Browning's office, how can I help you?"

Morgan's eyes nearly bugged out as far as Milton's. The flighty, sometimes ditzy-acting Beatrice Muldoon had just sounded like a true professional. Fascinated, he leaned over the desk to observe.

"Yes, of course. Oh, the poor thing," she cooed. "Let me check for you, please hold just one moment." Pressing another two buttons, she glanced over at him quickly. "Appointments this evening?"

He shook his head. "None so far. Who is it?"

"The Peckinpaughs. Their family dog is throwing up. Do you want to . . ." She motioned to the phone.

"Yeah, just a minute."

He picked up the receiver, then stared helplessly at The Devil. "Help."

"Men," she muttered, then pressed a few buttons and waved for him to continue.

"Thank you," he mouthed and pointed toward the open exam room behind him, holding up a finger to indicate he'd be there in a moment.

She nodded and scooped Milton up, walking to the room and closing the door behind her.

God almighty, those legs of hers made his mouth water more than any medium-rare steak ever could. The things he would give up in life to be able to watch her kick off her shoes under his exam table and crawl up there for—

"Hello?"

Shit. "Yes, hello, Mrs. Peckinpaugh. I hear Toby's having some trouble."

Legs could wait. At least for now.

"No, Milton, stop that." She bent down and placed her fingers between his scratching paw and his neck, earning an unintentional swipe over her knuckles for her trouble. "Ow, that hurt."

"Did he get ya?"

Morgan's voice from behind startled her, and she

straightened so fast, the blood rushed from her head. His hands went around her biceps to steady her and ease her into a chair.

"Whoa now. Didn't mean to scare you. Just sit a second. Standing up at that altitude might really get ya."

"Altitude?" she asked, bringing her hand up to inspect the scratch. Just a red scrape, no broken skin. She eyed the dog, who looked innocent. A look he'd been perfecting for a few months now.

"The heels," he said with a smile. "They're tall enough to have you ducking low-flying aircraft. Need me to check your pulse?" He was watching her eyes from behind hopelessly smudged glasses, and she knew he was taking stock of whether her pupils were dilated. Or not dilated. Whatever it was those medical types looked for.

Cutie. Dr. Cutie. Wanting to save the world, one forlorn case at a time.

"I'm fine. But Milton needs help."

Morgan looked skeptical at that, but he sat back on his haunches and called the dog over, who trotted toward him with ease. Morgan removed his collar to inspect the skin under. "Where is he scratching?"

"His shoulders and neck, mostly. Sometimes at his ears."

"You're using a flea and tick prevention?"

"The one you recommended, yes."

"Bathed him in anything new?"

"No. Same stuff since I got him."

"Hmm." Morgan picked up the dog and checked under one leg, then the other. "Any other problems? Not eating, not drinking?"

"He's fine, other than the scratching."

"Well, then I think you're gonna make it, my man." He roughed up the top of Milton's head with two knuckles in an adorable gesture of manly affection for the small dog. "I think he's got allergies."

"Allergies? The dog?" She rolled her eyes. "It would figure I'd get a high-maintenance canine. Allergies."

He refrained from making any sort of joke about a high-maintenance dog for a high-maintenance woman. It was a softball, even she could admit it. She appreciated the restraint. But he did smile and hold out a hand to help her up.

"I'll get some samples of allergy meds. But really, you can give him the human stuff. I've got a paper around here somewhere that gives you the dosing instructions based on his weight."

He walked back out to the front desk and started opening file cabinets at random, peering in, and slamming them shut again quickly. Milton escaped deep under the desk, in a dark corner, as if sensing something bad was coming.

The phone rang again, and Morgan completely ignored it.

After the third ring, she asked, "Should I get that again?"

"No, I can do it." His voice was muffled in a drawer.

Uh-huh. Right. Since he didn't know how to take a call off hold, he could obviously answer the complex office phone system. To soothe his male ego, she said, "You're busy—I'll just answer this one." She slid around him, her thigh brushing against his shoulder.

And okay, wow, her nerve endings stood up on point for that one. Clearly, if she was getting hot for the vet, she'd been in Marshall too long. Finding him adorable in a distant, *sure, he's cute* sort of way was one thing. Getting hot for the good animal doctor was another thing entirely.

"Morgan Browning's office, how can I help you?" She listened, scribbling the message down on a pad of paper to pass to him when he was through. "That's wonderful, I'm so glad you're considering a dog from our shelter. I have to tell you, I just got my Milton from there a few months ago and it was the best decision I ever made."

Morgan turned to watch her, but she shrugged. How hard could this be?

"What kind of dog were you looking for? Mm-hmm, yes, okay . . ." She scribbled down the qualities the family was hoping for on a pad of paper. "I'll have Dr. Browning give you a call back in a bit after he's had a chance to think about it. How does that sound? In the meantime, there's a form online you can print off and fill out to bring in with you. That would save you some time when you come in. Yes, just go to the vet website, then click on the tab up above for the shelter. Yes, that's right. Well, thanks to you, too. I hope you find what you're looking for!"

She hung up and smiled, then caught Morgan's stare. "What?"

"How did you do that?"

"What?" She looked at the phone. "Answer it?"

"No, know how to do all that . . ." He waved a hand around like he was swatting flies. "All that talking crap. Know all the right things to say."

Bea rolled her eyes and patted his cheek . . . which was easy to reach because he was squatting by another file cabinet. "Sweetie, talking is what I did for a living. Acting on a soap is ninety percent talking. And when I was still auditioning for gigs, I was night receptionist at a twenty-four-hour pharmacy."

"But even with the adoption stuff . . ."

"I just went through this process a few months ago. It's fresh in my mind. They're looking for a small dog, more of a lap dog than anything. No kids, just the wife and her husband. Empty nesters." She pushed the pad toward him and stood. "That's their number. I told them you'd check what's available now and get back to them."

He grabbed her arms again, like he had in the exam room, but it had nothing to do with catching her before she fainted. His hands were warm against her chilled, bare skin, the pressure just a little insistent.

"You can answer the phones."

She nodded slowly at his wild-eyed gaze. "Yes."

"You can talk to people."

"I manage to use real words and everything," she bit off.

"Can you use e-mail and figure out a calendar program?"

"Morgan, who the hell doesn't know how to use e-mail anymore? What's this all about?"

"You're hired."

"I'm what?"

Bea walked into the big house, dropped her keys and bag on the floor by the row of boots, flipped her heels off out of habit more than any desire to please their housekeeper, and set Milton down on the floor. The dog, as if to make up for all the trouble he'd caused her that afternoon, had the good sense to go hide somewhere. Likely wherever little Seth had been earlier, dropping crumbs. Kid left a trail of Cheerios in his wake like he was inviting ants to a picnic.

"Bea?"

And shit. Peyton's voice. Darting upstairs would cause too much noise. Maybe if she quietly walked toward the office, she could slip away unseen. Her sister might just assume one of the hands was dropping something off in the office. She might—

"Miii-mon!"

Seth's delighted shriek—Milton's butchered name—had her closing her eyes in resignation.

"Bea, we're all in the dining room."

She sighed and headed that way. As she turned the corner and saw everyone sitting down, she bit back a second useless sigh and propped her shoulder on the doorjamb. "Yes?"

Her brother Trace patted the seat next to him. "Sit. We're eating, and there's plenty, as usual."

Milton hopped up into the chair, tail wagging excitedly at the idea of being invited to dine with the big people who had the good food.

"Oh no. No, no, no." Emma walked around the table and used a napkin to shoo the dog back down to the floor. "I tolerate that barking cat in the house, but I won't have him sit at the table."

"Calm down, Emma. He was just confused." To placate the housekeeper, she sat and grabbed a plate. Nothing made Emma happier than people eating her food. Emma nodded her satisfaction and headed back to the kitchen— her kingdom, over which she reigned on high—and left the siblings, plus their mates Red and Jo, to eat. "Pass some veggies, please."

"Try protein," Peyton suggested, handing over the platter of fried chicken instead.

Bea's mouth watered, but she used one finger to nudge the platter of fried trouble to the side. "Thank you, no. The vegetables if you please."

"Here." Peacekeeper Red, who'd moved in with Peyton that spring, handed over the mixed veggies with a smile. Over the clatter of silverware and Seth's excited babbling from his high chair, he asked, "How was your appointment? Everything okay?"

Bea scooped a heavy serving of vegetables on her plate, debated a second spoonful, then decided no. They were likely cooked in butter and oil. She'd grab an apple on the way back to her garage apartment across the ranch. "Milton has allergies and I have a job."

The screech of a fork over a plate made her cringe.

When she glanced up from her forkful of green beans and carrots, she stared into four identical shocked faces.

Peyton, naturally, was the first to break the silence. "A job? Like, where you're actually going to work?"

"No, the other kind, where I do nothing and get paid for it," she bit out.

"So your old job," her sister replied.

"Acting. Is. Work." Her jaw ached from clenching.

"How exciting!" Trace's girlfriend, Jo, exclaimed, a little louder than socially acceptable. "Doing what?"

Just to piss Peyton off, she answered, "Working at Harem Ladies."

"You," Peyton said dryly. "Working at the strip club outside city limits."

"Oh, sure. They have the cutest uniforms." Warming to the idea of annoying Peyton, she continued. "Of course, I'll have to order my pasties from online. There's bound to be a pitiful selection here in town."

"Jesus, Bea-Bea." Trace flushed and looked like he wanted to escape, or maybe rip something apart with his bare hands. "What the hell?"

She threw a piece of her uneaten roll at him. "Oh for God's sake, Trace. No. Morgan Browning asked me to fill in for his receptionist at the vet clinic."

Silence greeted the statement.

"Answering phones, checking in patients, that sort of thing."

More silence, broken only by the sound of Jo's water glass clinking on the table in front of her.

"Oh, come on, guys. It's not like I'm neutering dogs or anything. It's sitting in front of a computer for a few hours a day." God, how inept did they really think she was?

How inept had she let them think she was? Maybe she really was a better actress than she'd ever thought.

"If you wanted money," Jo said slowly, "you could have asked me for a job at the bar."

"Or just pulled your weight around here," Peyton added.

"Right. Like you would even give me the chance." She didn't look up, didn't care to see the scorn in her older sister's face. Okay, so mucking out a stall was about as high on her to-do list as swimming in shark-infested waters. And her sister certainly had never asked for her help.

Maybe that was her own fault.

Morgan walked in the back door of his parents' home and wiped his boots on the mat.

"Morgan?" His mother's voice filtered into the mud-room.

"Yeah, Mom." He hung his jacket on the hook by the door, next to his father's heavier coat meant for his days in the fields.

"Boots off."

He thought to argue they were his good, clean office footwear, not his barn shitkickers, but didn't bother. Instead he sat down on the wooden bench his grandfather had made his parents as a wedding gift and pulled off his shoes. The cement of the mudroom was freezing cold, the chill seeping through his socks as he hopped his way onto the marginally warmer worn linoleum of the kitchen.

Cynthia, his mother, set another plate on the table. Without looking up, she pointed at the kitchen sink. The now-familiar routine served as a good reminder why he had built the house at the edge of their property for himself, rather than live with his parents. Plenty of room, but plenty of rules. At thirty-three, he should be able to wash his hands when he wanted.

But under his mother's roof, he washed when Cynthia said.

Over the rushing water, he said, "It's quiet. Where are the little demon spawn?"

"If you are referring to your niece and nephew, they're in the den with your father, watching some God-awful show they insisted was fantastic and they couldn't miss." Cynthia rolled her eyes and handed him a towel to dry his hands on. "They watch too much TV, but I swear I was going crazy with them underfoot while I made dinner."

Morgan wasn't fooled. He set the towel on the counter and leaned down to kiss his mother's cheek. "You love every noisy minute, and you know it."

"Of course I do. Having little ones in the house is a nice change from the quiet."

"When do Meg and Simon get back again?" His sister and her husband had taken themselves off on a cruise to celebrate their tenth anniversary and left the kids with Grandma and Grandpa Browning.

"Four more days." She looked up to the heavens, as if exasperated and begging for relief. But the minute those kids left, Morgan knew she'd be sobbing. Even living only ten minutes away, she'd be heartbroken to part with them.

"Uncle Morgan!" Six-year-old Andrea bulleted out from the den and ran smack into his legs, nearly taking him out. Small, but mighty. "Did you bring any puppies home? Did you? I want to bottle-feed a puppy!"

"No, not today. Sorry, short stuff." He ran a hand down her messy ponytail, which tilted crazily to one side.

"Did you cut anything open?" Brent, at eight, was more interested in guts and gore than fuzzy puppies who wanted to snuggle.

"Brent. We're about to eat dinner. That's not appropriate. Now, go take your seat. Bert! We're eating!"

Morgan's father shuffled in, slippers already on, paper tucked under his arm. The man loved his paper. And he winked at Morgan before asking, "So, any operations to-day, son?"

"Honestly." His mother yanked the paper from under his arm and whacked him with it. "Go sit."

Morgan watched with amusement at the short fight for who would sit next to whom at the table, before both Brent and Andrea were satisfied. Sitting in the exact same seats they had been yesterday for dinner, naturally. But the bickering never got old. He'd done the same thing with Meg when they'd been children.

"Anything interesting at work today? Not operating room–related," his mother qualified quickly, with a scolding look at Brent.

"Not too much. A couple might stop in for a dog later this week. And I found a temporary replacement receptionist."

"Really?" His mother glanced up from cutting Andrea's asparagus. "Who?"

"Bea Muldoon." He took a sip of water and waited.

Cynthia froze in the middle of a cut. "Beatrice?"

"That young Muldoon gal?" his father asked, just as puzzled.

"She's pretty," Andrea said, ignorant of the undercur-rents. She spooned up a piece of potato. "I saw her at the grocery store once. Mama said she was an actress. You have to be pretty to be an actress."

"That's not what's important," his mother said quickly, resuming her grandmotherly duties.

"But she is pretty hot," Brent acknowledged with a grin.

"You're eight, what do you know from hot?" Morgan asked, biting back a smile. Christ, kids were growing up too fast these days.

"I know it when I see it." Brent shrugged, then dug into his casserole.

Uh-huh. He turned to his dad, hoping for a little backup.

Instead, he got a wink. "She is definitely a cute one, no denying it."

"Okay, so she's attractive." Sexy, sassy, with mile-long legs and a slender neck that made him want to take quick, nipping bites all along that elegant curve . . . "But that's not all. She's good at the job, as she showed me today. She can handle it."

His mother snorted, then winced when Andrea looked up. "Sorry, dear. That was rude. We don't snort at the table."

Andrea giggled, but said nothing more. Brent smiled down into his plate.

"But really, Morgan. I don't mean to tell you how to run your business . . ."

"Which is to say, she's going to tell you how to run your business," his father muttered out of the corner of his mouth.

Cynthia shot him a Look. Capital *L*. "But," she continued more sternly, "I have to say I think this is unwise. You know I adore Peyton."

"Didn't you think she and Morgan would make a cute couple at one point?" Bert asked.

"Jeez, Dad." Morgan winced at the thought. He loved Peyton, like a sister. She'd been a good friend, as had Trace, and he'd hated how hard she had to work the past few years under her mother's thumb. But she'd triumphed with Red's help, and they were a solid duo, both in business and as a couple.

"I'm merely warning you. Beatrice is not long for here. She's told anyone who would listen for more than five seconds, she has big plans to head back to Hollywood and continue her career. Don't depend on her."

"She's a temp, not a full-time employee. She's filling the gap until I can find and train someone new. I'm lucky she's willing to help out. I was drowning and she just walked in like a life raft at the perfect moment." When neither of them said a word, he blew out a breath. "You'll be eating these words. I believe in her."

"Sometimes," his mother said quietly, not looking up from her plate, "one should be wary of perfectly timed life rafts."

He attacked his meal with a vengeance, eating fast enough to get out of there quickly but not so fast his mother's feelings would be hurt. Andrea and Brent's good-natured squabbling helped keep the mood light, but he needed his own space.

On the short walk back to his own house, a half mile down the road, he wondered why his mother was so insistent on his not thinking about Bea being around for the long haul. Did she suspect he'd been struck dumb by her since the minute she'd come into town?

He winced at the thought of his own mother contemplating his love life, or current lack thereof. Not a good place to go.

It didn't matter, really. Bea was a temp, and he had no desire to force her to stay. But if something should just happen to nudge her into thinking about making Marshall her permanent home again . . .

Well. He wouldn't argue.

Chapter Two

Bea placed a hand on the door handle, then dropped it and stepped back. Not ready yet.

"This shouldn't be so hard. Right?"

Milton, looking quite dapper in his morning sweater and booties, just stared at her.

"I'll go in, tell him, 'Thank you for thinking of me, but I'm not in the market for a job.' That's all."

Milton cocked his head, one of his ear tips winging up momentarily before flopping over again.

"No, I really don't think I should reconsider this."

He lifted one front paw, then the other, like a little dance in place, as if to say *If you're not reconsidering, why am I standing on cold pavement instead of warm linoleum?*

"You're wearing your booties. Get over it." She pushed the door fully open this time, and the little bell above the front door tinkled.

The main area was empty of patients, but she was also an hour early for opening. He'd never specified a time to come in, so she'd merely guessed. And she wasn't about to have this conversation within earshot of customers. That would just be embarrassing.

"Morgan?"

No answer. Bea took a few steps in, her heels clacking

unnaturally loud on the worn, scuffed floor. "Hey, it's Bea. Can we talk?"

She didn't hear his voice, but an answering distant bark, followed by several meows, led her behind the desk, down the short hall of exam rooms, and to the door that led to the adjoining shelter. She pushed through and paused at the row of cats, sticking her fingers through to rub friendly kittens behind the ears.

Milton waited patiently behind her heels, backed as far away from the cage containing reaching, curious kitten paws as possible.

"Scared, Milton?" She laughed and gave him a quick rub. "You're bigger than they are, you know."

He eyed them warily, but didn't advance. Either he didn't believe her, or he wasn't willing to chance it.

"Let's go find Morgan." She wandered farther, past the few empty cages left open for overnight guests of the vet clinic. Nobody here, so he must not have had any spays or neuters the day before.

She found him another thirty seconds later, scooping food into multiple silver dishes. He looked ridiculously adorable, standing there in his nice khakis and his dress shirt, sleeves all rolled up, with his tie slung back behind him. His glasses, those sexy thin wire frames, slid down his nose, and his hair was falling into his eyes. He probably could barely see what he was doing. As she edged closer, she heard him muttering to himself.

"Cage two gets a half feeding. Cage three is three-fourths feeding, cages five through seven are full . . . no. Seven's a half."

"Seven's a full," she corrected, then clamped a hand over her mouth to stifle the laugh as he yelped and scattered food.

He straightened, then stared in exasperation at the mess. Milton left her side to play vacuum.

"I'm sorry," she said between swallowed laughs. "I thought you'd heard me calling out before now."

"I've been too damn busy trying to figure all this out." He let the scoop fall back into the massive tub of food. "You should get him out of here before he eats it all and gets sick."

"Milton, come." Bea patted her thigh, but he ignored her. "Come now."

He sucked up another piece of kibble, tail wagging so fast it could churn butter.

"Dumb dog," she muttered, but picked him up and cradled him against her shoulder. He groaned in response.

"He's not going to think of himself like a dog if you keep carrying him around like a baby. He thinks he's a person. And . . ." Morgan took a step, slipping a little on the kibble, and pushed his glasses up over his nose with one finger, squinting. "Are those shoes?"

"Dog booties." She held up one paw. "Aren't they cute? They keep his little paws warm on the cold sidewalk. He doesn't like to be cold."

"I'd guess he doesn't like to be embarrassed either, but it's too late."

She scowled, then turned on her heel. "I'll just leave you to play cleanup, then."

"No, wait. I'm sorry. He looks cute in booties. Just come back and help me, please, I beg you."

He sounded so lost and frazzled she couldn't say no. "Scoop some of that up and then I can put him down."

Morgan reached into the closet and grabbed a broom and dust pan, then haphazardly swept up stray kibble kernels until the floor was passably clean. Bea set Milton down. Without the food to inhale, he stuck to her like glue.

"Can you just go down the row of cages and read out what the cards say on each one, so I get the serving sizes right without running back and forth?"

She headed to cage one, which held a duo of what looked like basset hound mixes. "Oh, aren't you two cute?" She reached in and scratched one behind its long ear. The other bounded over and flopped on his brother, scrambling for her attention. They licked at her fingers, rubbed against the metal fencing, jumped, and pounced on each other to gain the advantage.

"Bea, the card?"

"Oh, sorry. This one is two half servings." She glanced down at Milton, who sat patiently at her side. "Not jealous of the attention I'm giving these guys?"

Milton stared at the two pups in what could only be canine disgust. His look all but shouted *have some dignity, fools.*

"That's my boy," she murmured, then moved down the line, reading out cards. At each cage, she had to stop and share some love, though she didn't open anyone's door. Too risky with Milton. All dogs that were up for adoption were temper tested before being considered. She remembered that from reading the paperwork that came with Milton. But still, it was never a great idea to mix two dogs on short notice. And some of these guys were three times his size.

After cage ten, the last one not designated for vet clinic patients, she looked around. "I think some of these guys are still here from when I adopted Milton. How sad."

"Yeah. It's getting harder to handle the influx. We're the only shelter for nearly forty-five minutes. And now that my hopes of having a partner fell through—"

"Partner?" Bea's head snapped around.

"Yeah." He rubbed a hand over his neck, a weary gesture that made her want to walk over and rub his shoulders. "I had set up an interview with another vet, and she was supposed to come in and help pick up some slack. Would have given me a chance to expand the shelter work a bit more. But she balked at the rural area." He grinned at her, but his eyes were more solemn. "Some city girls just can't adapt like you."

"Please," she muttered, but was stupidly pleased at the compliment.

Morgan brought over the last dog's food, then slipped it in the small slot designated for food delivery and headed back to clean up the food prep area. "So we're back to where we started, just me and my merry band of helpers, doing what we can to save the world one fuzz butt at a time. And so many ranches still don't bother to spay or neuter their dogs. They figure it's no big deal if they have pups, since every ranch needs a working dog. But when you get a litter with twelve pups . . ."

"Not all are going to be needed." She sighed, understanding his frustration. He had such a great mission started, and she loved his caring heart.

And now she was going to squish him by turning down the job, just like the unknown vet who had stood him up on the partnership. Dammit. How was it, no matter how hard she tried to avoid being cruel, life seemed to set her up to be the Coldhearted Bitch anyway?

"Morgan, I . . ."

He grabbed her hand, cutting her off. "Bea, you have no idea what your help means to me right now."

"Oh." *Do it now. Rip off the bandage.* "I—"

"I know the pay sucks, and it's not easy work necessarily. And this isn't your life's ambition. But your jumping in to take this job makes it easier for me to keep up with the shelter responsibilities."

"But I'm a screwup," she said automatically.

His eyes held hers, mesmerizing her through slightly smudged lenses. "You're the right person for this job. I know it. You're going to be a blessing for me. I mean *us.* The shelter and the clinic."

Pow. Right in the kisser. She looked around at the poor, sad dogs all stuck behind their bars. Heard the begging pleas of the kittens behind her to let them out to play. Milton, almost on cue, leaned into her leg for a quick reassuring snuggle.

The cosmos was against her.

"I can't stay forever."

He nodded.

"I'll help find my replacement, though. I can interview them or . . . something."

His smile was all boyish hope.

She sighed and reached up for his glasses. He blinked in surprise as she removed them and used the corner of the cute new tank she'd ordered from Marc Jacobs online— on clearance, naturally—to clean the smudges off. "There." Without thinking, she replaced them. Her fingertips brushed back behind his ears as she straightened the glasses.

His body heat poured off him from the morning's exertions. She'd had to step in close to reach up his tall frame, despite being five-ten herself. And only now did it occur to her she was all but slathered to the front of him like some horny teenager at the homecoming dance. She took a healthy step back, her heel sliding just a little on the concrete floor.

He caught her at the elbows, though she'd already steadied herself enough. "Careful. Might want to rethink the shoe choice from now on."

"Oh. You don't like them?" Almost automatically, she popped one foot out to the side and pouted, a face that seemed to drive men crazy when she pulled it. "I thought they were cute."

He frowned at her a second, then shook his head. "They're impractical. I won't tell you what to wear, but I'd prefer you didn't break your ankle. That's just going to make more work for everyone."

Then, with a pat on her shoulder, he just brushed past her and toward the clinic side of the building.

Well. That was a first, in many respects. And wait a minute. Did she still have a job?

"Milton?"

The dog peeked up, offering a paw as if to say *you can take these booties off now. I have a feeling we're gonna stay.*

"Yeah." She squatted down, the heels giving her an advantage. "We're gonna stay. For now, anyway."

Morgan slipped into his tiny office and shut the door, leaning his head back against the cold wood and shutting his eyes. His fist clenched and unclenched, and his mind focused intensely on the contraction of the muscles in his hand and forearm. A tactic he'd learned early in his hormonal years to stave off an ill-timed boner.

She was going to stay, though he'd sensed she'd been about to quit before even getting started. Shaking his fist out, he wiped his wrist over his forehead, then grimaced at the sweat staining the top of his cuff. Some verbal tiptoeing and cutting her off had done the trick, at least for now. But it bothered him to hear her call herself a screwup. He could appreciate and laugh at self-deprecating humor. But that didn't strike him as humor so much as just stating what she considered to be obvious.

And that little pouty act with the practiced pose, modeling her shoes? What the hell was that? The simple manbeast in him had appreciated the way she'd looked, like a perfect combo of sweet innocence wrapped in a sexy as sin package. But the thinking part realized immediately it'd been too effortless, too smooth. Like it was just another trick in her arsenal.

Somehow, somewhere she'd gotten the idea she had no value other than her looks. Her acting likely hadn't done anything to discourage the notion, but he had a feeling the roots ran deeper than that.

He stood still, listened as Bea and that dog-baby she loved so intensely walked back through the doors to the clinic area and up to the reception desk. Likely she'd brought the dog because she hadn't thought she'd be here long. He didn't care if she brought him daily. He was well-behaved enough—and chill enough about other animals—to not be an issue. One of his techs often brought her own massive golden retriever, because he was too old to stay home alone now, and the sweet thing curled up on a bed in the back storage area most of the time.

Part of him couldn't help but wonder . . . had he hired her because he'd been struck dumb by her since the day she'd shown up at the M-Star? He could barely remember her as a child. She'd just been too far below him age-wise to make an impression. If Peyton had been Trace's younger sister, Bea had just been "the baby" to his boyish train of thought. Hardly worth a second glance. But now . . . she was worth a lifetime of glances, as far as he was concerned.

Maybe he wanted to see her succeed more than she did. Maybe the job would be a disaster. He immediately shook that thought off, as he heard Bea coo to Milton for performing some trick or another in the front lobby. She'd proven herself in those few moments the day before; at least she was more capable than he of handling the phone and customers. She could do this. He hadn't imagined her skills.

And if his mother was right, and it turned out to be a disaster, he'd figure out a way to fix it. Morgan was fairly certain he wasn't so blind with lust that he would risk the reputation of his clinic or the shelter just to make a pretty woman happy.

They'd see how it went. And he had a feeling, come hell or high water, Beatrice was going to prove herself a worthy partner. She was a Muldoon, after all. They never did say die.

How the hell did this stupid scheduling system work? Bea clicked around, opening the scheduling system several times on the ancient desktop, but each time the schedule showed no patients. She knew that wasn't the case at all, since the backup handwritten schedule had markings all over it. Code, that is. The former receptionist must have had a system in place. She'd just have to check about that later, when Jaycee came in after classes. Maybe there was a different program she couldn't find. She would ask Morgan, but he hadn't come out of his office since they'd finished feeding the shelter dogs.

The bell above the front door rang, and she gave one final click before sighing in exasperation and turning to greet her first customer.

"Hey there." Bea smiled brightly at the sweetheart with a bright purple shirt and coordinating shorts standing in front of her desk. "And who might you be?"

The little girl, maybe nine or ten years old, grinned, showing off a missing tooth, and whispered, "Alice Stevens." The name came out as a lisp thanks to the missing front tooth.

"Hi, Alice. I'm Bea. It's nice to meet you." She held out a hand, which the girl shook quite seriously. "Who have you brought in for us today?"

"Sampson," she lisped, still barely audible. Kid couldn't catch a break with the *S* words today.

"Sampson, huh? Is he new?"

Alice shook her head, the long tail of carrot-orange hair slinking to and fro.

"Does your mommy or daddy have Sampson in the car?"

Alice nodded, grinning.

"Well, bring the handsome man in. I'm new, so I'm playing catch up here and meeting all the patients." Bea couldn't help but smile as the little girl skipped out the front door. Kids. So much cuter in their natural habitat than on a sound stage. The few children she'd observed through her years on *The Tantalizing and the Tempting* had been . . . challenging. Either their intense stage-crazy parents made it all but impossible to deal with them, or they'd turned into royal brats far too soon. Bea could appreciate bratty behavior; she spoke brat fluently. But these kids put her tantrums to shame.

Not to mention, as a rehabilitated prostitute, her character, Trixie West, hadn't had that much contact with the kids firsthand.

But little Alice was a doll. Bea scooted her chair out from the desk and smiled at Milton, who was camped out by her feet. "See? This is going to be easy." Milton raised his head, blinked one sleepy eye at her, then rolled over and ignored her. Typical.

Now, if only she could figure out the scheduling system. She tried one more time, looking under the program's saved files—of which there were apparently none—and sat back in the chair.

Defeated before nine in the morning. Great start to her first day.

The bell rang again and Alice raced up to the desk. "He's here," she mouthed, pointing to a small plastic crate.

"So he's a small guy. Well, bring the little one here." Bea patted the top of the desk and waited.

"Alice?" A woman—Bea could only assume it was the little girl's mother since her hair was only a shade or two darker than Alice's carrot coloring—stepped in through the door. "Alice, no, don't—"

But the carrier was on the desk, and Bea was face-to-face with a massive green snake, staring at her with one beady eye that blinked up rather than down.

Other than a short intake of breath, Bea was rather proud of her lack of hysterics. At least outward hysterics. She merely pushed back from the desk and stood up. "He's . . . lovely. How, uh . . . handsome?" When she looked to the mother for assistance, the woman hurried over and grabbed the handle on the crate.

"I'm so sorry. Alice loves this guy and forgets not everyone's into reptiles like she is. Alice, remember when I said it's not nice to surprise people with Sampson? And how if you did it again, you were going to be in trouble?"

"But she asked to see him," Alice said, lip wobbling.

"It's true, I did," Bea confirmed. "She was only doing what I'd asked."

The mother glanced over her daughter's head skeptically. "You wanted to see the snake?"

"Oh, yes. Of course." *Until I realized it was a snake, anyway.* "I'm new at the clinic, so I'm just meeting all the patients as they come in."

Sighing with reluctance, the mother held out her hand. "Janine Stevens. And I apologize again. We normally are in here early, before other patients, for obvious reasons. Not many people can handle sharing a waiting room with Sampson."

"Of course." When Alice looked at her, her lip wobbling a little at the insult to her beloved pet, Bea added, "Because they're so jealous. I mean, he's very . . . lovely. I have a pair of shoes that same color and they're one of my favorites."

Alice seemed pleased with this, and grinned widely. "I can't take him to show-and-tell. The teacher said no."

"More jealousy, I'm sure. The other kids would cause a

riot, because they would all want to take him home." Bea shook her head, not able to hold back a smile. "I'll tell Morgan you're here."

She watched mother, daughter, and reptile take a seat and hurried back to the office door, Milton's nails clipping along with her heels. She knocked quickly. "Morgan? You've got a patient."

"Already?" He opened the door quickly, faster than she'd expected. "Walk in?"

"Uh, I don't think so." *I'd know if the darn schedule wasn't in code.* "Alice Stevens and her sweet Sampson?"

He stared for a moment, then winced. "Damn. When they're coming in, Jaycee warns me early so I can be out there to greet them. I'm sorry, I hope the snake didn't startle you."

It had, but she was annoyed—in a contrary sort of way—that he didn't think she could handle a single snake. Not her favorite pet, sure. But still, what was she, a toddler? "No worries. They're out front. Where should I put them?"

"Room two— it's got the best table for all those sort of animals. The small ones," he explained when she gave him a confused look. "Hamsters, gerbils, birds, so on."

"Oh, right, right." Ick, ick. *Time to get over it, Beatrice. You've got a sister to prove wrong.* "I'll show them in right now."

"Thanks." He grinned and winked. "You're made of sterner stuff than I might have thought. I'm impressed."

She showed Sampson and his handlers into room two, closing the door behind her, and headed back to her desk. The compliment warmed something inside her. Something she hadn't realized felt so cold before now.

She ran a hand through her hair, then pulled the strands behind her ears rather than letting them hang in front like a swoop bang. There. More practical already.

Let the day begin.

Chapter Three

Bea pulled her sweet convertible drop top onto the M-Star property, and almost veered left to head to the main house. Most nights, she would have done just that. But tonight, she was too exhausted to spar with Peyton, even verbally.

Besides, she had a date to get ready for. Turning to the right, she wound her car around the many potholes that pitted the dirt driveway until she reached the back garage where the main ranch vehicles were stored. Above the garage was her apartment. Okay, *apartment* was a bit of a loose term. But it sufficed for her purposes, which were mainly privacy and . . . privacy.

"Come on, Milton. Let's head home." She opened her door, and he launched himself onto her lap and down to the ground before she could even unbuckle her seat belt. He trotted over to the nearest patch of grass to relieve himself. Crazy dog. He was going to hurt himself pulling stunts like that.

Of course, Morgan would likely have some pithy re-mark about how dogs shouldn't be allowed to just do whatever they wanted. Ride in the back with the cargo, follow orders, blah blah blah. She rolled her eyes as she walked up the outside stairs to her door, Milton clamor-ing up behind her. His short legs struggled a little on the uneven, rough stairs, but the exercise was good for him. Plus, his feet were protected by the booties Morgan had mocked.

Maybe she could talk to Trace or Red about refinishing the stairs . . . *and oh my God*. That was a permanent thought. No. No, no, no.

As she opened the door to the main horse training quarters, she breathed the first sigh of relief. The second was when she toed off her heels and let them fall carelessly to the floor in a pile, along with her purse and keys. She'd pick them up later. Or not. Her place, her choice. Just another reason she had to get out of the main house.

She walked on the balls of her feet to the kitchen for water, stretching her insteps and then curling her toes under to regain some circulation. She'd rather burn at the stake than admit it, but Morgan was right about her shoes. When he'd said he needed a receptionist, she'd thought she'd be sitting all day, looking cute behind the desk while answering phones and using the computer—which still didn't operate at a speed acceptable in the twenty-first century. But no. She was up, she was down. She was back and forth to different exam rooms, into the shelter to let the dogs out for their afternoon run, scrambling back to the desk to answer calls because the crappy phone system kept eating voice mails and she didn't trust it.

This wasn't a cute little side hobby. This was a real job. He could have warned her.

She sipped her bottle of water and walk-stretched herself over to the small kitchen table where she kept her laptop, opening it and pushing the power button. While that started, she grabbed a plate of fruit and cheese. She was too tired to make a sandwich or heat up soup, and she didn't have enough time to head to the main house for some of Emma's cooking and a delightful lecture on proper eating habits.

She just had a few minutes to change out of her office attire. Which was another thing she would need to reconsider. And okay, she'd started the day thinking she was turning the job down. But it occurred to her a few hours into the day that seated behind the desk, the modest cleavage visible in her mirror was much more lascivious when a man was standing up looking down at her from a three-foot advantage.

She smirked at the memory of a few bug-eyed men, and the one wife who had actually slapped her husband's arm for staring too long. The male species really was too predictable.

As she tugged her worn jeans on, kicking her feet to get the soft denim over her knees, her computer quacked with a FaceTime call. She shuffled over, buttoning the fly as she went, and answered the call with a click of the mouse.

"Hey!"

"Hey, girl. Okay, what's going on with the outfit there? Are you getting into the Howdy Doody spirit? Did someone steal your entire wardrobe?"

"What?" Bea sat, then realized her friend had gotten a good glimpse of her old jeans and worn denim shirt while she'd been standing. Whoops. "Oh, you know. It's so gross out here, I hate for my nice stuff to get messy."

Keeley Corbin nodded, her perfectly highlighted brunette bob swinging around her chin. Bea's best friend was more of a ponytail kinda gal, but her character on *The Tantalizing and the Tempting* had recently decided to make a life change and chop off her long hair, so Keeley was suffering the consequences. "You growing the hair out?"

Her friend scowled. "Don't I wish. Apparently Desdemona"—she said her character's name with scorn— "has decided this suits her. Which is to say, Marc in hair and makeup made a call to the producers and said it flatters my fat face better."

"Your face is not fat. But it looks good. Makes your eyes pop." The whiskey color, which normally looked ordinary brown, almost reflected the highlights in the nearby strands and shone a little.

"Don't you start too." She ran a hand through her hair, blowing out air when it settled back into place, framing her face. "I miss my ponytail, dammit. Now all I can do is bobby-pin it back or wear a headband. And those things hurt my ears."

"Whine, whine, whine," Bea teased. She'd chopped her own hair off without consulting anyone at the studio. A bold move, and one that hadn't won her any fans in the production team. They could have chosen a wig, but instead they wrote it into her character's story arc. Easier to beg forgiveness, she thought with a small smile.

"So what are you doing out there? I thought you'd be back ages ago."

Bea scrunched up her nose. This part would be tricky. "Well, I got a job."

"From long distance? Did you do a Skype interview? Holy hell, your agent must have worked miracles to pull that off! Tell me everything!"

Bea hid a grimace behind her hand as she fake coughed. "No, I mean, a job here." Keeley blinked. "Like, a nine-to-five job."

Keeley stared at her, frozen. Bea checked her Internet connection, but they were still up and running. Then her friend shrieked, "A job? A job!"

Bea winced. "It was an accident."

"An accidental job." Keeley rolled her eyes. "Only you could manage to pull that off. So spill. What's this job that's keeping you from your bestest friend ever? It must be something amazing. You haven't even mentioned once about coming back."

Bea chewed her lip, then whispered, "I'm a receptionist."

If Keeley hadn't blinked, Bea would have again thought
they'd lost connection.

"At a vet clinic and shelter," Bea added. As if that was
somehow going to make it easier to understand.

"The place you got Milton?" Instead of shock, Keeley's
eyes went speculative. "The one run by that cute vet."

"Yes, the place I got Milton. And how do you know
he's cute?"

"You told me. Repeatedly."

"I did not!" Oh God, had she?

"Something about glasses, and how he talks fast like he's
nervous. And something about how he always seems to
dress up, and then ruin it with animal hair everywhere."
Keeley's grin grew. "You're totally crushing on the nerdy
vet."

"That's ridiculous. He's a family friend, and I'm merely
doing a favor."

"You totally want to bang the vet."

"That's gross, Keeley." And now she couldn't erase the
video playing in her mind. A video containing Morgan,
putting his hands on her to steady her in the shelter. Those
long fingers, that strong grip. How adorable his glasses
were when they were smudged, and how he always looked
like he was shocked by how awful they were. Like he
never realized he was looking at the world through a blur.

"Beatrice and Vet Man, sitting in a tree," Keeley sang
softly.

Oh hell. "Not true. And if you keep that up, I won't let
you see Milton."

Keeley snapped up. "Not fair. Where's the little guy?"

She reached under her chair and drew him out. This
wasn't getting any easier, now that he was gaining weight

and filling out from his previous skin-and-bones physique. "Here he is. Say hi to Auntie Keeley, Milton."

He stared blankly.

"Hey, Milty. Are you being a good boy for your mommy?" Keeley cooed. She leaned forward in the frame, likely to look closer at Milton. Her hair flopped over one eye and she brushed it back with an aggravated swipe of the hand.

His ears flicked, but otherwise, he was completely uninterested.

Bea sighed. "Fine. Go." She set him down. He ran for his stuffed frog and came back to sit under her chair, frog in mouth.

"So when are you really coming back, Bea?" Keeley looked serious now, and a little worried. "You've been saying it was a quick trip this whole time, but it's been nearly a year now. I thought you'd be back long before now. Are you . . . are you there to stay?"

"Hell no!" Bea laughed, but it sounded a little hollow. Luckily, Keeley wouldn't be able to tell, or she would attribute the off sound to the speakers. "There's not even a decent freaking mall in this area. I have to drive two hours to get to a mall with a Dillard's. A Dillard's, Keeley."

Keeley gasped, eyes wide. "That bad? Honey, come home."

I am home. No, wait, that wasn't right. "I just have . . . a few more things to settle. I'll be back soon. Promise."

"In the meantime, are you watching *T-and-T*?" Their abbreviation for the show's mouthful of a name.

"Every day." Except now she'd have to DVR it and watch marathons on the weekends. Jobs were a lot of bother. "Desdemona's great. But watch out for Angelo. I have a feeling he might be in cahoots with his current girlfriend, Cassie, to give you the boot."

Soaps were a cutthroat business, both on the screen and off.

Keeley nodded. "I'll keep an eye out. Thanks, sweetie. Love you!"

"Love you back." She blew a kiss and disconnected the call.

After leaning down to scratch Milton's head—the ungrateful brat actually jerked the frog out from her reach, as if she wanted the slobbery thing—she stood and found her old riding boots.

In an hour or so, it'd be late enough she could sneak over, saddle Lover Boy, and head out. She needed to clear her head like she needed air.

And there was no way in hell she'd let Peyton know she used riding to do it.

Morgan watched as Bea's snappy convertible pulled up to the side of the vet clinic and screeched to a halt. The woman even drove like a maniac. But she stepped out of the car in those candy pink heels—sky high again, naturally—and white Capri pants with some navy top, and he had to roll his tongue back up in his head before she caught him drooling.

Milton pranced alongside his beloved—and aggrieved—owner, happy as a clam without his damn booties on. Booties for a dog. Hell.

"Good morning, Morgan." She pushed her oversized sunglasses up and shot him a dazzling smile.

"Looking good, Bea." He glanced down at her shoes and raised a brow.

She waved that off, as if his commentary on her footwear wasn't required. "You look different. Where's your suit?"

He smiled, slow and sure now. She was going to kill him. "Today's rounds day."

"Rounds day," she mouthed silently. His eyes strayed to watch her lips form the words, and he wanted to reach behind her, pull her in, and kiss the hell out of her. "I'm going to need a bit more, Morgan."

"Did you look at today's schedule?"

She scoffed. "I was so busy yesterday trying to keep up with yesterday's schedule, there was no time. I figured I'd play catch up this morning."

"Instead of fifteen-minute or half-hour appointments, you'll see big chunks of the day divided up. It's the day of the week where I head out to do big livestock checks. So I'm out of the office the entire day, basically, unless there's an emergency. One of the techs stays in to handle walk ins that don't need me or to make consults but otherwise, I'm out all day."

"Oh." She took that in for a moment, nudging Milton to the side a little with the side of her foot when he pressed into her. "So I man the desk and the shelter, and help out whoever's scheduled for today?"

"Nope. You come with."

Her mouth dropped open, giving him those unreasonable kissing fantasies again. "But shouldn't one of your vet techs go with you? I'm useless. I can barely answer the phones. I ruined yesterday."

"You did great yesterday, being thrown in the deep end. Give yourself some credit." He watched as a blush stained her cheeks and she glanced down at Milton to hide it.

She'd handled his compliment about looking good without a bat of an eyelash. But mention her work ethic and she flushed like a shy girl being asked to dance. He risked the bold move and brushed a finger down her nose, pulling back before she could even register. "You were a big help. And it'll get easier every day. You'll be running this town before we know it."

He almost laughed when she blushed harder, then bent

down to adjust Milton's already straight collar. "I don't have to, like, do anything medical, do I?"

Now he did laugh. Pushing his glasses back up, he said, "You don't have to give vaccinations or anything. I just need you to take good notes and help keep things straight. Jaycee would come with me, but she's got class today and so for the next few weeks, you'll have to come with me. Then her schedule shifts and you're off the hook."

"Well, then I guess I'll just go set the voice-mail system. At least I got that part fixed yesterday." She walked past him, the faint scent of something floral tickling his nose. Then she glanced over her shoulder. "It might take me a few minutes to do that."

"You're fine. There's a set of office keys by your computer. Lock up on your way out. Lydia is coming in to open at the regular time and she's got her own keys."

She nodded and headed in, her small companion right beside her the whole time.

He bit the inside of his cheek to keep from grinning. She likely had some cute secretary fantasy running through her mind, where she stood off to the side and looked adorable while he did all the dirty work.

Oh, she'd learn.

"Morgan Browning, that is the most horrible thing you have ever said to me."

Bea sniffed, then immediately regretted it as the smell of manure nearly caused her to gag.

"Bea." Morgan sighed and ran a hand through his already-disordered hair. "I didn't criticize you. Just your shoes."

She angled one foot out the truck door and rotated her ankle to show the high pink heels off. "I keep telling you, there is nothing wrong with my shoes."

"There is today. Just take these. They're boots. Who cares what they look like?"

"I do, if I'm going to be in public."

"It's a barn."

"It's a barn with other people in it. I cannot be seen in those horrible things." She pushed away the boots, using his forearm instead of his hand, which was holding the pair of nasty wader-style boots that looked like they'd already seen the inside of a pigpen. Repeatedly.

"So maybe next time, you'll wear proper shoes. I can't help it. I warned you yesterday your heels were impractical."

Bea rolled her eyes. He was playing with words and he knew it. "I can hear you just fine from the truck. Just call out what you want me to record and I'll get on it."

"No." He stood firm now, his mouth set in a grim line. A line that reminded her how sexy his lips usually were, when they weren't all pursed with pissiness and attitude. Hmm. Had she noticed his mouth before now? Apparently, if she knew the difference. Just look at the way it moved. She nearly purred when his lips closed, opened again, formed a few words and . . .

"Bea!"

"What?" She snapped back to reality and blinked. "Sorry, what was that?"

"Is the smell that bad?" he said, smiling a little.

She shook her head, then gave him her best pout. "Morgan, please? Just pull the truck up a little more."

"Bea." He said it quietly now. "You can do better than this."

His eyes were glued to hers behind those dirty lenses, and she couldn't look away. It was like he dared her to prove him wrong. To prove everyone wrong who would say she'd never in a million years be caught dead in a pair of nasty waders in a pigpen. A silent dare, unspoken, but all the more powerful for it.

She could play more games, or just downright refuse. Quit on the spot.

A year ago, she would have.

"Give me those," she muttered. Then grimaced when her fingers touched the cold rubber. "And if you tell me where these have been before today, I will find a gun somewhere and shoot you."

"Lips are sealed." But she caught a hint of a twitch before he stepped back and waited. While she removed her heels—gently, and with all the reverence her Choos deserved—he went to greet the owner. She slipped on one, then the other boot. The tops came up to just under her knees, covering a good bit of her white pants.

And hell, now was so not the time to envision what this little field trip was going to do to her white Capris.

A few testing steps had her realizing the boots were a bit big, and she walked like an idiotic duck with a limp. But then again, fashion wasn't the point.

Fashion wasn't the point? Oh God, she really had changed.

She grabbed the clipboard Morgan had given her back at the clinic and followed him over to the owner.

"Chuck," Morgan said, "this is my new receptionist, Bea Muldoon. Bea, this is our first hit of the day, Chuck."

Chuck seemed amused at her plight, and watched her waddle/limp over with a grin. "Something wrong with your leg, Ms. Muldoon?"

"Not a thing."

"Might not be used to the pig-shit waders, huh? I don't think those are very Hollywood," Chuck joked.

"I hear rubber boots are all the rage in Europe." She stood as straight as she could in the embarrassing footwear and held out a hand to shake his. "Nice to meet you. I'll be . . . assisting Dr. Browning today."

"Might need to open up a clinic of my own one of these days," he murmured, holding her hand a little longer than she wanted.

Typical. She smiled thinly and pulled harder, her hand slipping out of his this time. "You'd be hard-pressed to beat Morgan at his business. He's the best."

Morgan glanced at her, surprise clear on his face. But what did he expect from her? Insults? Probably, after dumping the boots on her.

"Well, let's get to it. Bea? You're with me." He cocked his head, then walked straight through the muck and the mud, into the dimly lit barn.

Deep breath. Deep breath. Soak in the clean air now, and . . . "Hold up, I'm coming!"

Chapter Four

Trace's mouth dropped open in astonishment. "Just walked right in? Into the mud? No pushing or pulling required?"

"None." Morgan's mouth curved in pride. "Well, maybe a little verbal pushing, but minor. She's got spunk. People don't give her enough credit." He set his empty beer down on the table. He'd met up with his longtime friend Trace and his new friend Red for drinks after work, and couldn't resist sharing his day.

"And she likes it that way." Red shrugged when both he and Trace stared at him. "What? I watch, I observe. It's what I do. And your sister"—he pointed at Trace with the neck of his beer for emphasis—"likes to be underestimated. She's not what she seems, but she never wants anyone to know."

Trace winced. "No, Bea's helpless. Always has been. I love her, and she's a good person, when she stops gossiping and talking about clothes. But even as a little kid, she was determined to have everyone else do for her what she could have done herself. She was Mama's little doll. Perfect in every way, but almost sad at the same time."

And was probably raised to act as such. Morgan filed that one away for later. "Suffice it to say, she's working out at the clinic. I don't see any reason to change things up. She's got the job as long as she wants it."

Trace sighed and leaned over to pull his wallet out from his back pocket. Rifling through, he pulled out what Morgan saw was a twenty and slid it across the table to Red. Red nodded and stuffed it into his own wallet.

"You bet on your own sister?"

"Hell yeah, I did. Seemed like easy money," he muttered into his beer.

"How's that dog of yours?" Time to move away from Bea before he embarrassed himself with the subject. "Still no name?"

"No Name," Trace said.

"Why can't you name him? Just pick something."

"That's it. No Name. It just sort of stuck. He's a barn dog, through and through. Seth likes to look at him and wrestle with him on the front porch, but he's definitely learning the ropes working. Not really a pet. Shoulda thought that one through better."

"Who needs a pet on a ranch?" Red asked, waving over their server to signal for another round. "You're surrounded by animals."

"Bea certainly loves her pet. And that thing is so not a working dog. I caught him stealing Seth's toys last week, the little shit. Watched the dog look around, see nobody down there, and yank one of Seth's toys from his toy box and go stuff it under the damn couch, like he was saving it for later. If I hadn't been watching from the stairs, we never would have found it again."

"Dog's smart." Morgan grinned. "I don't think you guys give that little guy any more credit than his mama."

"Maybe if his mama didn't dress him up in sweater vests, I could take him seriously," Trace retorted.

"Now, now, girls. If you start pulling hair, I'll have to

separate you." Red smiled as their server, Amanda, set three new bottles on their table. "Thanks."

"No prob. Jo says these are on the house, long as you make it your last, Trace." She winked at Morgan, then sauntered back to the bar.

"She's got her eye on you."

Morgan blinked. "Me?"

"Yeah. Of course, you're not alone in her sights. Amanda's not picky. But if you're interested . . ." Trace made a "go right ahead" gesture with his arm. "I'm sure you'd receive a warm welcome."

"Yeah, I'm gonna pass." The days of enjoying sex for the sake of having a warm body were over. He wanted a wife, kids, a little annoying shit of a dog hiding the baby's toys. Not someone to pass a few nights with before she found something else shiny and moved on. Not his style. He didn't judge others for it, but it wasn't for him.

"You're like a monk. I think even Red got more action before he found my sister, and part of the time I thought he was a eunuch."

Red threw a coaster at Trace and hit him in the chest. "Fuck off."

"Just saying."

"*Just say* yourself upstairs. You've got a warm reception of your own coming."

Trace pumped his fist. "Daddy's night off. Thank Peyton again for babysitting," he added, clapping Red on the shoulder.

"Yeah, yeah." Red shrugged him off, but smiled.

Morgan waited until Trace was through the front door, heading around the side where Jo's apartment stairs were. His girlfriend, and the owner of the bar, lived on the second floor. When he had a free night off from his son, Trace was with Jo, without fail. After Jo was done pulling bar duty, Morgan knew she'd lock up and head upstairs herself. It was a comfortable routine they'd developed, and one he was surprised to see his friend so at ease in.

"You don't mind babysitting?"

Red snorted. "Hardly babysitting. By the time I get home, Aunt Peyton will have the kid in bed and asleep. He's down for the count, and won't wake up until after Peyton's already out the door in the morning."

Morgan watched the amber liquid swirl in his bottle as he tilted it back and forth. "You and Peyton thinking of getting married and making a few kids soon?"

Red sputtered a little on his beer, then used the back of his hand to wipe his chin. "Damn, man, could you at least wait until I'm not drinking?"

He never understood why other men were so sensitive about the subject of settling down, getting married. He'd known since he was ten he wanted to be a family man like his father. Maybe that made him boring, but it was true. It never occurred to him that he would be in the minority.

Red took another, smoother sip of beer and cleared his throat. "To answer your question, we've talked about it. Some. Nothing concrete, but it's . . . we'll say it's come up in conversation."

"The making kids part, or the getting married bit?" He laughed at Red's flush. "Both, then."

"Peyton wants to give the ranch another year or so under her personal care before she thinks about adding in marriage. I know I wouldn't take over running things, and she knows that, too. But other people don't. And she's still just a little touchy on the subject of how others view her work with the ranch. Something about cementing the Muldoon brand before adding Callahan to the mix legally or some such thing."

Morgan could see that. Enough scorn had been thrown her way when it'd come out she was sleeping with her horse trainer. Less than she'd probably expected, though. People respected Red, and more people than she knew respected her for picking up the pieces left by her mother's incompetent handling of business affairs after their father passed. There had been negative talk, but not as much as she'd feared.

"It doesn't bother you to wait?"

"Wait for what? The way I see it, marriage only changes one thing. Piece of paper we both sign. She's with me every night, and we're together working every day. It's exactly how I want it."

Another thing Morgan just couldn't agree on. Marriage was special to him. He understood the sentiment behind the whole "it's just a piece of paper" thinking. Intellectually, he agreed. But the emotional attachment to that ritual still meant something to him. Enough that he wanted it, with the right woman.

And more and more, he wondered if he'd already found her, or if Bea's desire to get back to California and not give Marshall a fair chance would halt things before they could begin.

Bea struggled into her newest online purchase: a pair of adorable peep-toe red wedges that looked great with her denim skirt. Maybe the peep-toe wasn't all that practical for around the ranch. But in the office, on that tile floor? She'd be fine.

"Milton? Thoughts?"

Milton snorted and set his underbite on top of his favorite frog.

Everyone's a critic.

She'd started to put the shoes back in the shoe box when a knock sounded on the door. She looked at Milton, whose ears perked up. "You expecting someone at seven in the morning?" On instinct, she closed her robe over her pajamas, which were merely a thin T-shirt and an old pair of boxers some long-forgotten lover had left at her place years ago. She still had bedhead and no makeup on. In other words, absolutely not fit for company. Maybe if she just ignored the summons, they'd think she was asleep.

Milton trotted over to the door and gave a quick sharp bark.

Well, there went that idea. "Coming." Bea slid her feet back into her ratty slippers—the floor was ice-cold in the morning, thanks to being over the garage—and shuffled to the door. No peephole, so she called, "Who is it?"

Her brother's laughter vibrated through the door. "Who the hell else would it be besides family?"

Bea rolled her eyes, unlocked the door, and opened it. "You say that like either you or Peyton have been making regular trips over here to say hi." She hugged him and let him in. Milton jumped up on Trace's jean-covered leg, whining like an infant for attention.

"This dog is pathetic," he grumbled, but he lowered to his haunches to give the Boston some love anyway.

"You adore him. He's charming, if flawed. Probably more charming for his flaws." Bea headed into her small kitchen area and called back, "Coffee?"

"Wouldn't say no."

Bea poured two cups, leaving his the way he liked it, black. In hers, she dumped several packets of sugar substitute and some low-fat creamer. Tasted like hell, but that was the price she paid for being in an industry that cared what she looked like.

"So what brings you over here?" Bea sat down at the small table across from him and smiled. "You had your date night last night with Jo, if I'm not mistaken. Didn't feel like staying in for an early morning—"

"Nope. Not even going there with my baby sister," Trace said easily and took a sip.

"Drop the baby, Trace. I'm twenty-six, if you can count that high." She blew a piece of hair away from her eye. When was the last time she'd had it cut?

And when was the last time she'd ever had to even think about that? She shuddered a little at the dangerous hygienic path she was treading. First it was skipping regular trims. Then clipping her nails back until they didn't exist. Before long she'd be forgetting to shave her legs and walking out of the house without her eyeliner. God.

"I'm just having some quiet time with one of my sisters, whom I haven't seen for years. Is that a crime?" He watched her with that same easy patience as Morgan and Red. It was like a bred-in-the-bone Marshall way of managing females.

"You haven't seen me for years because you didn't come visit."

"You didn't visit either."

Touché. "I stayed in one place. You were rodeoing all over the damn country. Easier to find me than you."

"True." He eased back in his seat, crossed one boot over his knee. The small coffee mugs she used looked tiny in his big hands. "But then again, we both could have met up for Christmas back home. And neither of us did. Wonder why that was."

Bea's hand tightened around the handle of her mug before she set it down. "Let's not be cute about it. This place sucked when Mother was alive."

"For Peyton, yeah. For me, sure. For you?" He took another calm sip. "You were her favorite."

Bea looked away, out the window, toward the open fields beyond the barn tops. It was a view so many might call typical Americana. The peaceful fields, the simple, family-owned ranch, the grazing cattle.

She used to call it a prison. Now she didn't know what to call it.

"Bea?"

"Hmm?" She glanced back. "What?"

Trace's lip quirked a bit. "Nothing. I've been thinking."

"Don't hurt yourself," she said automatically, then grinned. "Wow, the whole sibling thing really does come back to you, doesn't it?"

"Cute. But I've been thinking. We might want to get you a saddle of your own to have around."

His eyes watched her closely, and she fought against the rising panic. Had he seen her? Did he know? Had she left some sort of clue around his tack when she'd borrowed it during one of her nightly rides? *Play it cool. Play it calm.* "For what, a lawn ornament? What in the world would I do with one of those things?"

Her brother sat quietly for another moment, then shrugged. "Just thought it might be nice to have something around. You know, in case you decide to go riding with us one morning."

Bea snorted, back to her familiar façade. "Don't hold your breath, big brother. You won't catch me dead on one of those huge, smelly animals." She shuddered delicately for effect.

"Just a thought." He stood and took his coffee cup to the sink and rinsed it out. Emma had trained them all. Setting it in the drainer to dry, he walked by and kissed her cheek. "Thanks for the coffee. Have a good day at work, Bea-Bea."

"See ya," she said after he'd closed the door behind him. Then she stared down into her half-finished coffee. Okay, that was weird. Not just the impromptu morning chat—because she would often see him in the morning at the main house. Or at least, she used to, before she started working and couldn't afford the time to head over there before getting to the clinic.

But the mention of a saddle . . .

So, she'd just give up her rides for a week or so. The thought made her want to shriek. But it was for the best. Playing the helpless city girl was the only way she was going to be able to leave without any problems this time around. So she'd play it to the fullest, and that meant foregoing a midnight run with Lover Boy.

Dammit.

A knock sounded, bringing Morgan out of the paperwork he was finishing up. "Just a sec," he muttered without looking up. If he looked up, he'd lose his place. If he lost his place, he'd be doing this for another hour. If he was doing this for another hour, he'd have to stab himself with a pencil.

"Almost . . . there." He finished with an overexuberant period and shoved the file to the side. "Now, what's up?" He looked up and found Bea watching him from the doorway to his small office, one shoulder propped against the frame. Her long legs were crossed at the ankles, one red wedge tapping impatiently.

"Morgan, I've got a few questions about the shelter."

"Hmm? Shelter? Something wrong?"

Bea shook her head, then must have thought better of it and nodded. "Yes. I mean, nothing immediate. But you've mentioned before there aren't nearly enough spaces for all the dogs in this area that need a place to go."

"That's true." He laced his fingers over his stomach and stretched his back a little. *Thank you, God, for the break.* Nobody—absolutely nobody—became a vet for the paperwork and charts.

"So I'm realizing it's great and all that the shelter is here. I know it's pretty new. And it's very nice, for the dogs it can hold." She chewed on her bottom lip a little, and he wanted to smooth the mark away with his thumb. Damn, she had too pretty a mouth to worry it like that with her teeth. Full, but not in a fake, collagen-filled way. They were soft looking. Expressive. Kissable.

"Morgan."

"Right. The problem?" He blinked, then took his glasses off when he realized they were smudged. As usual.

Bea sighed and reached for the frames. He handed them over without a word, and she polished them on the sleeve of her shirt as she spoke. "The problem is, those dogs aren't moving fast enough. There are some awesome dogs, but nobody knows about them. I just had a patient ten minutes ago tell me she didn't know there was a shelter connected to the clinic, and she's been coming here for years."

"Hmm." He took the glasses back and put them on. The world became clearer. And Bea's beauty only became brighter, more well-defined. "I can't exactly do a whole lot about that, you know. If people don't pay attention—"

"Make them."

Morgan blinked. "Beg pardon?"

Bea smiled a little. "You're too sweet for this. You make them pay attention. That's all advertising is. Thrusting something under someone's nose often enough they can't ignore it any longer."

"I don't think I understand what you're getting at."

"It's like this." She walked in, closed the door, then opened it again as a whine penetrated. "Well, come on then." She shooed her dog inside the office. He pranced in like the fuzzy chaperone he was, and she closed it again. Then, perching her tight little butt on the edge of his file cabinet, she started again. "When I was auditioning for soaps, I had to make a nuisance out of myself. They didn't want to give me the time of day. Why? Who the hell did I think I was? I was nobody. One toothpaste commercial and a handful of catalogs do not an impressive résumé make." Bea's eyes went a little dreamy, as if remembering fondly those early days. Then she snapped back to the present. "I badgered. I bothered. I snuck into auditions and callbacks I wasn't invited to. And finally, someone no-ticed."

"And you got the part," he finished for her.

"No, I got kicked out by security." She grinned. "But on my way out, I delivered a stirring monologue—that might or might not have been laced with profanity. It caught the casting director's ear. Something about overt passion and whatever. Case in point, I caught their eye based on persistence and tenacity . . . and a little bit of cre-ative sneakiness. That's what the shelter needs." She thought for a moment. "Not sneakiness. But the tenacity part."

He sat for a minute, absorbing. Advertising. He hadn't really considered it, past putting a small flyer in each of the exam rooms. Clearly, even that wasn't getting people's at-tention. Decision made, he swallowed a smile and pointed at her. "Okay then. Let me know how that goes."

"Great! So . . . wait. How what goes?" Her face was a study of confusion.

"The whole advertising thing. Tenacity, persistence, the whole bit. That's what you were talking about, right? I'm too sweet to make a nuisance out of myself, but you're not? You were volunteering to take over advertising, weren't you?" He grinned widely. "That is such a relief, I can't even begin to tell you."

"But I . . . that's not quite what . . . I just don't . . ." Bea sputtered. "You can't trust me with this."

"Sure I can. I mean, let's face it. How much worse could it get, right? Nobody knows about us now. So any word out there would be better than nothing."

Bea nodded slowly. "You sure you trust me with this?"

"Of course I do. You're perfect. And it'd be a huge

help." He stood, and risking her scorn, wrapped an arm around her shoulders and squeezed in a platonic sort of hug. "Thanks for volunteering."

"Volunteering. Right." She opened the door, Milton at her heels. "Sure thing." As she closed the door behind her, Morgan laughed a little to himself.

Step by step, she was doing most of the work for him. Before he knew it, she'd be a permanent resident and be wondering why she hadn't moved back years ago.

Bea cursed the pitted, dirt-packed driveway that led from the main road to the ranch. Maybe she could convince Peyton to pave this sucker. It couldn't hurt to ask, right? When she came to the Y at the heart of the ranch, she debated for half a second before turning left instead of right to go to her apartment. She was starving, and all she had at her place was a suspicious apple and the remnants of a peanut butter jar she'd stolen from the big house a week ago.

"We're gonna go get some food, Milton." He nosed her arm in agreement, and she drove up to the main house, parking in her old spot.

She let Milton out, then just stood and looked for a minute at the ranch. The end of the workday was long past, and only a few men remained to finish cleaning up and settle the livestock down for the night. She watched the sun set over the land her parents had passed on to the three of them, and couldn't hold back a little smile.

This wasn't something she could find on a Hollywood sound stage. No replicating that clean view, or mimicking the way the wind gently moved the wheat and corn beyond the barns. There were some things no amount of Hollywood magic could re-create.

She watched Milton find a nice spot on the grass and water the lawn. That snapped her out of it. Wow, was she getting sentimental about land she didn't even want? Yeah, a third of it was hers . . . which was a shocker in and of itself. She'd felt sure, after their mother had passed, the entire thing would go to Peyton. The sister who stayed and kept up with the running of the ranch. The one who truly wanted the responsibility of owning all that . . . vastness.

But instead, it'd been split into three equal parts. And when she'd suggested her sister buy her out, Peyton had informed her that just wasn't happening. Not yet, anyway.

Would she have stayed, Bea wondered, if she'd had the check in her hands that day? Probably not. She'd have hightailed it back to LA and never looked back. She wouldn't really know her nephew—drooling slobber monster that he was—or get a front-row seat for the spectacle of her sister and brother meeting the loves of their lives and falling head over heels. She would have missed so much.

She *would* miss so much, she corrected, as she opened the front door and let Milton prance in ahead of her. "We're home!"

Only Emma's voice greeted her. "Kitchen!"

She toed off her shoes and left them on the mat by the door, following her dog. The boy had a keen sense for food, but a horrible sense for a weak target. Emma was no more likely to give the dog a scrap from her kitchen counter than she was to jump off the roof and fly. Tough old bird, their Emma. But more motherly than their own mom ever had been. Scraped knees, hurt feelings, and spilled juice were Emma's domain. Perfect children who kept their outfits spotless and their mouths shut were their mother's.

"Hey, Emma. What's for dinner?" She kissed the shorter woman on the cheek and nabbed a slice of green pepper from the cutting board.

"Stir fry, and don't be eating all the vegetables." Emma shooed her off and went back to chopping. The knife gleamed as she made quick work of the stack to be cut. "We'll eat in an hour. You're lucky I even have enough to cover you. You've been absent so many times these past few weeks, I almost forgot you exist."

"Aw, Emma." Bea hopped up on the counter, crossing her legs and letting the top foot swing. "I don't have any groceries at my place."

"Saunter in, saunter out. Steal food when you feel like it," Emma grumbled. All an act. Feeding people was her favorite pastime. Her second favorite . . . complaining.

"It's not stealing. It's . . . borrowing without the intent of returning." Bea considered grabbing another slice of pepper, eyed the fast-moving knife, and decided against it. "Besides, I'm entertainment. With me at the table, there's never any want for conversation."

"Your mother used to say that," Emma said, then winced when Bea froze. "Not that you're anything like her."

Bea sighed. "It's okay. I know I am. I hear it enough from Peyton. Trace, too, though he's more . . . subtle in his disappointment."

"They're not disappointed. They're confused. You just turned out different, is all. They need to figure out how to relate to you. Your mother—I know," she cut in when Bea scowled. "I know you don't like talking about her, but I'm gonna do it anyway. Your mother drove the wedge between you as children as surely as if she'd taken a sledge-hammer and pounded it there. She might not have intended to do it, but she did all the same. Thoughtless, as usual. That was your mama."

"And I'm just like her." No point in keeping the bitterness out of her tone. Emma wouldn't pop her for it.

"No. You're not thoughtless. You're out of practice

with considering others." Emma slapped at her hand when she reached quietly for another slice. "You'll ruin the stir fry for everyone else."

"I'm the only one in this family who appreciates a vegetable that isn't a starch." But she smiled and thanked her when Emma held up one more slice.

"Rabbit food," Emma grumbled.

"And I'm not out of practice. I'm just not prone to it, period. It's genetic. I like looking out for myself. I'm the most important person in my life, aren't I?"

"There's that fake junk again." Emma rolled her eyes and reached into the fridge for the chicken. "You have more soft spots than you want to let on, for God knows what reason. The point is, you think about others far more often than you want people to believe. I'm on to you."

Bea scoffed, but watched the housekeeper closely.

"You wouldn't have gotten that worthless dog if you didn't think of others." Emma pointed at Milton—situated right by her feet—with the tip of her knife.

"Small dogs are hot right now. Everyone has a purse dog."

Emma's eyebrows drew together. "He's not a working dog, he's not important. Sure isn't a pampered purebred purse dog either."

"He's a Milton, and I love him." Bea hopped down and rubbed the top of his head. "Yes, I do."

"There." Emma smiled, satisfied her point had been made. "Exactly. If you spent less time holding up this ridiculous helpless city girl façade and more time thinking about your family and what they need, you might actually turn a corner somewhere with them."

Bea sat on the kitchen floor for a while, quietly entertaining the idea. "But I am a city girl."

"I note you left out the word 'helpless.' "

Dammit. "I'm going to watch some TV before dinner. Come on, Milton."

"Think about it," Emma's voice sang out as she walked through the kitchen door and into the dining room.

"Pass," Bea mumbled.

Chapter Five

Morgan caught up with Trace in the barn, barely. He was hanging up his tack, staring at it like he was memorizing the placement on the peg board and table where he settled all the equipment.

"Problem, Trace?"

He rested his hands on his hips and shook his head. "Just giving everything a once-over. I like to see if elves have moved anything overnight."

"Elves?" Morgan glanced at his friend in the dim light. "Been drinking already?"

Trace laughed and shook his head again. "Nah." With a brush of his hands on the thighs of his jeans, he turned and smiled. "So, what's up? It's not normal rotation day. Peyton call you out?"

"Nope. Stopped by to talk to you, actually."

"Okay. Shoot." Trace led the way out of the equipment area and into the long row of stalls. Equine heads poked out over several stalls to say hello, and the men stopped to give a rub or a quick word of hello to each one.

"I'm going to be dating your sister."

Trace stopped short, hand frozen over a sweet mare's forelock. "I think you should talk to Red about that one, since I'm pretty damn sure he's gonna have—"

"Not Peyton. What the hell?" Morgan rubbed the back

of his neck. "Bea. Your youngest sister," he clarified, though he wasn't sure why. When Trace stared, he added, "Long legs, short blond hair, Muldoon blue eyes? Ringing any bells?"

"Yeah, it's ringing bells all right. Alarm bells." Trace scratched the filly and moved on. "But okay, so what's there to talk about?"

"I figured I owed you the heads-up, seeing as you're her big brother. Might be feeling protective. Wanted to let you know I have the best intentions there."

Trace laughed again, and Morgan relaxed a little. At least this wouldn't decline into one of those soap opera things where Trace defended his sister's honor with a punch to the jaw. Morgan could fight back, but being honest, Trace would kick his ass in the end. And he needed his hands to operate.

"I think you probably mean that."

"Then what's so funny?"

"Because," Trace said between chuckles, "I have a hard time seeing any of her intentions as being honorable in return."

Morgan's hands clenched into fists at his sides. "Are you saying something about her moral character?"

"I would rather not comment on my sister's moral character. I just think she'd run you in circles and leave without blinking." Trace shrugged. "It's her way. Doesn't make it wrong, it just makes it distinctly Bea."

Morgan had to work to keep his voice relaxed, when his jaw wanted to clench and his teeth threatened to grind. "So your only objection is for my benefit, not hers."

Trace paused and looked behind him for a second. His blue eyes, so like Bea's it was a little odd, narrowed. "Maybe I'm not saying it the right way."

"Ya think?" Morgan said under his breath, and had the mare nearest him whickering softly back. He rubbed her velvety nose and let her sniff his arm in return for the support.

"I just see it as an unbalanced match. Not in the whole 'one is better than the other' way. Just that . . . it doesn't seem to fit."

"You and Jo didn't fit at first," Morgan pointed out.

His friend's mouth quirked a little. "Got me there. Took more than a little convincing to get her to even think twice about a single dad. But we got around to making everything fit."

Trace shrugged and headed toward the house. "Coming to dinner?"

"Nah. Gonna head up to Ma's and eat. She's been chewing my ear off about not coming by recently." He waved as Trace walked on toward the main house, past Bea's car parked out front. Maybe he shouldn't have been so hasty in saying no . . .

But his family came first. And so he'd fulfill his obligations there and enjoy the time with his parents. And eventually, he'd get back to the goal of making everything fit for him and Bea.

Bea took her turn to clean up after dinner with the minimum amount of bitching. It was amusing to see both Peyton and Trace's jaws drop when she did something unexpected. But mostly, she wanted to avoid The Love Nest, which was what dinner had turned into recently.

She'd been avoiding meals for several weeks now, and her job had become a handy excuse in recent days. But mostly, she was starting to feel more than a little left behind. Not that they went out of their way to make her feel like a fifth wheel. But she could add up numbers, and since Seth didn't count as a formal date, she was definitely the odd man out.

After stacking the dishes in the sink for Emma—

who had a dishwasher loading system and refused to be budged—she wiped her hands on the towel and headed back through the dining room. Milton abandoned his post by Seth's high chair, where he diligently waited for the inevitable oopsie snacks, and followed her over to the living room.

If Bea had had a TV and cable in the apartment, it would have been much easier. But alas, no hookups. So she had to do her channel-surfing in the big house. She clicked on the TV, waited for the DVR to register, and started the most recent episode of *The Tantalizing and the Tempting*. But after five minutes, she turned it back off. Her stomach couldn't handle the cheese. Lord, had she ever been that obvious?

Of course she had been. That was the point with a soap opera. You were cheesy and overdramatic, to fit with the music and dialogue. Which was why the entire gig fit her like a glove.

"Bea?" Peyton walked in behind her, footsteps soft on the thick carpet. "Watching anything interesting?"

She snorted, and answered honestly, "Nope. You want?" She held the remote up.

Peyton shook her head. "No. I just thought we could . . . talk." Her mouth twisted as she said the last word, like it tasted funny.

Bea snorted again, this time with laughter. "Did you lose a bet? Or did Trace put you up to it?"

Peyton sank down into the gilt-framed Victorian replica chair opposite the couch, her back straight, butt barely touching the cushion. "I hate this chair."

"I hate everything down here."

Peyton nodded slowly, looking around the lower level of the house. Their mother had redecorated the home back when they were teens. Some theory about looking wealthy to attract wealth. Only she'd had worse taste than

Elvis, and just turned the entire first floor into a palace of gold gilt crap. Bea liked the finer things in life, but this wasn't fine. It was scary-hideous.

"Uh, how about my office instead?"

"Oh, sounds so official." When Peyton just stared, she shrugged. "Why not?" And followed her sister into the office that had once been their father's domain.

Only, not quite. Yes, his presence still rang true in the space. His desk, the thick, scarred hunk of wood, took up the majority of the room. A framed black-and-white photo of him as a boy on his first pony hung behind the chair. And some of his books were still on the bookshelves. But Bea was pleased—and surprised by the pleasure—to see Peyton had really made the space her own. Her own photos, her own books, just her, everywhere.

Peyton sat down and rocked a little in the chair. "You enjoy working at the clinic?"

Bea settled down on one of the soft chairs across the desk and crossed her legs. Milton pawed at her lower leg, whining to be picked up. She shooed him down again. "I don't mind it. It's something to do."

"Something to do," Peyton murmured, shaking her head. "You haven't asked about the ranch's financial situation recently."

Bea said nothing, only scratched the top of Milton's head.

"I still can't cut you a check worth anything decent."

She watched, fascinated, while her sister flushed with . . . what? Embarrassment? Shame? Anger? She couldn't remember the last time she'd seen Peyton flush. She was cool as a cucumber, always. No drama, no tantrums.

"Things are turning around, but the turnaround is slow. It's not going to be an instant fix. If you're hanging around waiting for a big payout, it's not coming anytime soon."

Bea waited a little to see if she was done, and when Peyton remained quiet, she sighed. "Am I a burden?"

Peyton's eyes widened a little. "No."

"Am I getting in the way?"

"No . . ."

"So, it's fine that I'm here. I'm not ruining your hopes and dreams by sticking around?"

Peyton's eyes narrowed. "Why would you say that?"

Bea stood, jarring Milton's head back. Dammit. She'd actually thought—for one stupid moment, really believed— they'd started making some headway. And now Peyton was hinting she could leave anytime. Why didn't she just shove her out the door with her suitcase? "If it's a big deal that I'm out in that apartment over the garage, I can find something in town. Or I can just leave."

"Sit down, Bea."

"I don't need to—"

"Sit."

Bea's butt hit the seat before she could even think twice; then she immediately scolded herself for following orders like a hired hand. She wasn't the damn help. She was a sister. A part of the family, much as Peyton would like to claim otherwise.

"I don't want you to leave. You don't have to go." Peyton rubbed at her forehead, tugged a little on the dark, sleek tail of hair she always had tucked up under a hat or pulled away from her face. They shared the same eyes, the clear Muldoon blue coloring distinctive enough there was no way to mistake their connection. But in every other way, they were as physically different as night and day.

"So if this isn't the boot, what is it?"

"Call it checking in. We don't see each other all that often. Less, now that you're not underfoot with that mutt. Your job and the garage apartment keep you pretty busy."

Milton made a sound, a mix between a whine and a growl that indicated he knew slander when he heard it. "It's okay, baby. She didn't mean it."

"I probably did," Peyton said, but in a cheerful voice and with a smile. "But either way, the point is, I just wanted you to know . . . it's okay. If you want to stay, it's okay."

The simple words, however stark and void of emotion, tugged a little on her heartstrings. "I'm not here for good, sis. Don't get any crazy ideas."

Peyton laughed. "I'm definitely not assuming that. But just . . . there's no rush. That's all."

Bea stood, feeling a little more off balance than she had been not ten minutes earlier. "Okay. Thanks."

"But if you wanna earn your keep," Peyton called out as she walked through the door, "we'd never say no to another pair of hands mucking out stalls."

"Spiteful bitch," Bea muttered, but smiled as she waited for Milton to prance through. Then she slammed the office door behind her, merely on principle. Peyton would expect it, and she'd hate to disappoint.

Bea stepped into Jo's Place and immediately wished she was there for pleasure instead of business. But instead, she scouted out her targets and locked in. Oh, this was fun. She tugged a little at her top—skimpier than usual, but one that looked fine when paired with the cardigan she'd removed ten minutes earlier—and made sure her top button was open. Just enough skin to provide the shadow of cleavage for anyone who was looking.

And she'd yet to meet a man who wouldn't look whenever possible.

After waiting a beat, as if scanning the crowd, she walked over to the bar and smiled at Jo. "Hey, girl."

"Hey, yourself." Jo smiled and draped a bar towel over the shoulder of the black polo she wore. All the servers wore the same simple uniform, with *Jo's Place* stitched where a pocket would go. Simple, understated, and something that made it clear this wasn't a yucky titty bar. Good food, great drinks, and a warm, inviting place to meet up with friends. Jo had taken the disgusting hovel of a cowboy honkey-tonk and turned it into a wonderful, classy but not overreaching bar. "Taking a break from work?"

"Lunch hour. Normally I bring something with me, but I decided to live dangerously."

"Need to be back fast? If you eat at the bar, it's quicker than a table." Jo pulled out a menu, then rolled her eyes and put it back under the bar. "Rabbit food and water?"

"Yes on the water, but . . ." She trailed off, then turned to scan the lunch crowd again. "Oh, look over there. Isn't that Bill Jeffries?"

"Yes," Jo said slowly. "Why do you care?"

"And he's sitting with Stuart Wilde, right?"

Jo set a glass of ice water by her elbow. "Bea, what are you up to?"

"Up to?" Bea drummed her fingertips on the top of the bar once and gave her the best *trust me* smile she could muster. "Jo, that's rude. You shouldn't assume the worst of a paying customer."

"Thus far, you've ordered water, which is free." Jo's eyes narrowed. "This doesn't have anything to do with that whole petition to close me down a few months ago, does it? Because that's in the past now, and I want it to stay there. Those two men are in here once a week, and they tip the servers well. Don't ruin that."

"Jo, not everything is about you." Bea took a sip of water and fluffed out her hair. It'd been a pain to deal with all morning, constantly falling in her eyes every time she bent over her computer keyboard or answered the phone, but she knew it was the most flattering way of framing her face. "Give me a ten-minute head start, then order a salad to go, please? I'll swing back by the bar and pick it up in a bit."

"Bea," Jo warned, but she was already off and hunting her target. Some hunted animals for sport, or for food. Bea hunted opportunities, and men were her desired target. Much easier to read and manipulate.

She drifted easily through the crowd, smiling and waving at a few faces she recognized. And when she brushed the upper part of her arm against Bill Jeffries's arm, she pulled back with a gasp, placing a hand on his shoulder. "Oh, I'm so sorry."

"No problem." He turned to acknowledge her apology, and Bea watched the flush rise in his cheeks as his seat put his eyes directly in line with her breasts. His gaze quickly jerked up and he stammered, "Ah, uh, yes, no problem."

"So clumsy of me." Bea put a hand over her chest and grinned. "You're Bill Jeffries, aren't you?"

"I am." He held out a hand, all elected-official smooth now. "Beatrice Muldoon, nice to see you once again."

"Have we met?" Bea took the opportunity to slide into the open seat across from Stuart Wilde.

"Oh, not officially, but my wife watches *The Tantalizing and the Tempting* and was always tickled pink that one of Marshall's own was a star on the show. And I do remember you a little from back in the day. My youngest was between your brother and sister in school."

"Ah, of course." She had no clue who his youngest was. She smiled then, across the table at Wilde, as if just realizing Bill wasn't alone. "I'm so sorry, I didn't mean to crash a meeting."

"No problem," Mr. Wilde said, extending a hand easily. "Stuart Wilde. I was friendly with your father. And I'm sorry about your mama, God rest her soul."

"Yes," Bea murmured. Soul? What soul? Cynthia was likely down in hell, seducing Satan for better accommodations. "It's nice to meet you. I'm sorry for intruding. I'm sure you men have things to discuss."

"Oh, just some boring city council chatter." Bill waved it off, but she could tell he wanted to sound important. So, she'd give him exactly what he wanted.

"Are you two on the city council?" She used her best *I'm so flustered to be in the presence of great men* face. Judging from the flush on their faces, she nailed it. "And to think, I've been meaning to get ahold of someone from the city council, and here you two handsome men are, and I nearly tripped over you! It's like fate."

They both laughed with pleasure. "What can we do for you, Miss Muldoon?" Bill asked.

"Oh, it's just this silly thing, really. I don't know if you're aware, but I started working at Morgan Browning's vet clinic recently."

"I'd heard that," Stuart said.

"And attached to that wonderful clinic is a shelter that Morgan runs all by himself. Did you know that?"

Stuart nodded, as did Bill, who added, "We had to approve the plans for the addition when he built the shelter."

"I'm so glad you did. It's a wonderful place. That's where I got my sweet Milton." She dug into her small purse and pulled out her phone. She swiped her thumb over the lock, then showed them the screen saver of Milton's favorite expression . . . bored. "Isn't he a doll?"

"He's a little guy," Bill said, smiling. Stuart looked unimpressed. He must have no soul.

So she'd now identified the tougher nut to crack.

"As you can imagine, it's just so heartbreaking, seeing those little faces behind the cages day after day. And the shelter, well—" She tisked sadly. "It's on a shoestring budget, of course. We need to get the word out so we can help more animals in need."

Bill nodded. And while Stuart nodded as well, she could tell she was losing him.

Big-guns time. Which, of course, meant breasts. She

leaned in just a little, so the table supported her minimal chest like a shelf.

"I had the most brilliant idea the other day, to hold an adoption fair. Just a few hours long. Get the little darlings all polished up, and have a wonderful time matching them with excited new families. And I was wondering what it would take to have our adoption fair in that nice building where you hold town meetings."

The men stared at her—drinking in her face and her boobs—with their jaws a little loose.

"It goes without saying we'd be doing all the cleanup and such. It would just be so difficult to have it at the clinic. And the town hall would make it a lot easier to handle that sort of crowd." *Please, God, let there be a crowd.* "So what do I need to do to make this happen?"

"Well, Ms. Muldoon . . ." Stuart cleared his throat and took a sip of water. Bea used her straw and took a quick sip of her own water, which seemed to only dry the man's throat up once again, as he gulped another time for good measure. "That would require a permit."

"Oh, a permit." She put on her *my IQ is only as high as my shoe size* face. "And what do I need to do in order to get one of those things?"

"Apply to the city council, wait for the next meeting, state your reason for wanting the building, and then answer any questions. And then there's the rental fee for the building itself."

Bea chewed her lip, but this time it wasn't an act. Crap. All that? They didn't have time to jump through hoops. "When's the next meeting?"

"We just had one last week, so three weeks from now."

"Oh." She thought for a moment. "And there's no way of getting around it? I was hoping to have the fair a week from this Saturday. The lull between sports seasons means most families won't be preoccupied with athletics, and—"

"It's just the way things go." Stuart's brows slashed together. "Fill out the application and wait your turn. That's how we do things here."

"Of course." She stood, then sat back down. One more shot, then she'd call it done. "Look, I'll level with you. There's an epidemic right now of strays. They're everywhere, and the shelter can't handle them all. Not by a long shot. Morgan is doing the best he can, but even he isn't Superman. He's got finite resources, both with money and space, and moving a lot of pets to good homes in a single day, while raising awareness of the shelter, would be huge. And from my estimates, a week from Saturday is the perfect day for this fair. Now I'm going to ask again. Is there no other way?"

Stuart looked close to shaking his head, but he caught a sidelong glance from Bill and stalled. Bill settled back a bit and motioned for her to continue.

"Oh. Uh . . ." She searched for a good monologue. One to really bring the audience home. "It would improve community relations, especially when we profusely thank the city council for allowing us to host this wonderful event. And the possibility of getting more spayed or neutered pets out there in the community means we can take in more strays. Fewer strays on the streets improves everyone's quality of living, both human and animal."

"Good points all around," Bill murmured, nodding slowly. "How about this? We'll take it to our fellow councilmen and work on getting them to agree. If they agree to the last-minute aspect, the place is yours. With the fee, of course," he added.

Bea granted them a gracious smile, completely sincere. "That would be wonderful. Thank you, Bill. Stuart, nice to meet you both." She stood and waved a little, weaving her way through the slightly heavier lunch crowd and back to the bar.

Jo glared at her and set a sack on the bar top. "Do I have to apologize to my customers?"

"Of course not. I was just introducing myself to some important men of the community." Bea slapped down some money and pushed it at her friend. "Honestly, Jo. Why does everyone just assume I'm up to something?"

"Because you usually are!" Jo called at her as she walked out the door.

"Yeah," she said quietly, pushing her sunglasses on and walking down the sidewalk toward the clinic. The bag swung easily from her fingertips, and there was a lightness in her step she hadn't felt on the walk to lunch.

And it felt good, knowing she was doing something for the community and not just herself for once. Maybe she should try it more often.

Chapter Six

Morgan opened his office and nearly tripped over the boxes piled high in front of his door. What the . . .

"Bea?"

"Just a minute!" she called, her lyrical voice echoing in the still-empty clinic. "I've almost got . . . yes!" She let out a cry of triumph so amusing, Morgan's throbbing shin receded in his mind, and he smiled at the sound. "I did it!"

"Did what?" He leaned against the wall outside his office, smiling at the fact they were having a conversation ten feet apart, but couldn't see each other.

"I figured out this stupid appointment program, and got all the month's appointments in there. Did you know Jaycee never even tried to get it to work? That's why it was empty. She just had the physical appointment book."

"No, I did not. I figured if the schedule worked, then it didn't matter how." Morgan nudged a box, but it didn't budge. What the hell was in these things?

"It wasn't easy starting from scratch, but I've got it all transferred over. I've even got it set up to send e-mail reminders of appointments to the customers who gave us e-mail addresses. I am woman, hear me roar."

Impressive. He never could have done it, and clearly Jacyee either hadn't been able to, or hadn't even tried.

He heard the sound of the desk chair wheels slide over the tile, heard Milton's nails click in time with his owner's own heels, then prepped his body for the inevitable.

She rounded the corner, looking sexy as sin, as usual. In a snug red tank and a denim pencil skirt, she was completely appropriate for the casual work environment he strove for.

Which did nothing to cool the lust firing through his system every time he caught sight of her. Even the fact that her pet-slash-chaperone was staring at him with those unnerving bug eyes did nothing to negate the fact that he would rather open his office door, pull her in, lock the dog *out,* and pull up that skirt so—

"Morgan?"

He blinked. "Yeah?"

"I said, did you know you were averaging an eleven percent no-call, no-show appointment percentage? That's horrible. Hopefully the e-mail reminders will change that for the better." She stepped up to him, smoothing a cool hand over his forehead. "You're flushed. Are you feeling okay?"

"Yeah." It came out a little strangled, so he cleared his throat and repeated, "Yeah. Sorry. It's a little hot in the back."

As was becoming her habit, she reached up for his glasses, then polished them on the corner of her tank. The movement showed off a good hint of skin above the waistband of her skirt, and he swallowed the excess saliva building up.

"So, what's the problem that has you hollering at me?"

He grinned and took his glasses back. "Did you just say 'hollering'?"

"I did," she said more primly. "I like to adapt to the local climate whenever possible."

"Or you're just showing your roots." He tugged on a lock of bright blond hair, which was held back today with a simple headband. He'd noticed when she came in to work, it seemed to be more back than forward. No more sexy sweeping bangs for work time. The gesture, whether it was intentional or not, pleased him.

"My roots are in LA," she said testily, slapping at his hand. "Now what's wrong?"

He opened the door to his office halfway, which was all he could do before it hit something and stuck. "This would be the problem."

"Oh!" Her face lit up, and he swore the hallway brightened with the force of her smile. "I totally forgot. The flyers came yesterday after you left for that emergency call. I didn't want to take up an exam room, so I just stuck them back in your office."

"Flyers?" He nudged the door a little harder with his shoulder, pushing at the box he'd hit with his shin earlier. "Flyers for what?"

"The adoption fair we're having." Bea's tone said he was an idiot if he hadn't put those two together. Like a student in the back of the classroom still asking how to do long division in the tenth grade.

"Oh, for the . . . the what?" He paused and looked at her. "Did you say 'adoption fair'?"

She smiled, a slow, sly smile that did interesting things to his libido again. Which was crazy, given it was likely a smile that indicated she was up to no good. He should be running like hell, and instead his dick was ready to offer him up as a sacrifice. "You did say I should take out advertising for the shelter and run with it. Were those not your words?"

They were, but it seemed foolish to admit to anything just yet. "You might have wanted to clear it with me first. I could have appointments that day."

"You don't."

He thought fast. "We don't have enough time to set up."

"We do."

"There might be permits and—"

"Taken care of." She grinned, as if realizing she had him completely trapped in a corner. "I spoke with the town council, and they agreed to waive the normal fee and application this time, since it's our first trial run. But in the future, we'll need to be more prepared."

Town council. He mentally flipped through his calendar. "There hasn't been a council meeting since we talked last. The next one isn't for almost three weeks. How did you manage that?"

Bea grinned, then tried to look serious. "I just located all of them individually and fixed it right up." She batted her lashes. "They just couldn't say no, after I explained how sad all the sweet puppies and kitties were in their cages, all alone."

Uh-huh. He'd just bet that was what they were thinking when they agreed. Bea could wield those baby blues with more accuracy than a Marine Corps sniper. With resignation, he asked, "So when is our adoption fair anyway?"

"Next Saturday." She clapped her hands once, then picked up Milton and held him to her shoulder. "Milton and I are going to be making the rounds later on, telling everyone about it. He's so charming and handsome, I'm sure he'll just inspire everyone to get a dog of their very own."

The charming, handsome dog looked at Morgan for a moment, then farted audibly.

Morgan waved his hand and pushed farther into the office with all his might. Talk about motivation. "Just . . . just figure out where these can go in the meantime, because I need my office."

With her blue eyes watering from the smell, Bea nodded and coughed delicately. Then she put Milton down and blinked rapidly. "Will do," she squeaked, then hustled around the corner. The stink bomb on four legs followed her.

Morgan took five healthy steps away and breathed in deep. Jesus, were his glasses fogging again or was some paint peeling from the ceiling? That black-and-white, bootie-and-bow-tie-wearing thing was a menace.

But when the smell cleared, and he heard her answer the phone in her chipper voice, he couldn't help but smile a little. Yup, giving her that project had been the best idea he'd come up with to date.

And soon enough, he'd take the next step and make a move. A romantic move, that was. One she couldn't mistake. As soon as he could find the right opening.

Benji—poor dog of the unoriginal name—yapped excitedly as Bea entered the shelter early Thursday morning. Most of the dogs, after a week or so in the shelter, calmed down and didn't get excited when people came in. But yapper Benji, he was another story.

She smiled and waited for Milton to make the rounds examining the inmates, as she'd come to think of the poor sweeties. She'd already released Mara, the overnight tech, for the day so she could head home and get some rest. Well, after Mara had checked on the one patient staying overnight from the vet clinic, that was. Bea could feed and water, walk and watch, coo and clean. But there was no way she was changing a bandage. No. Way.

Bea walked over to Benji's cage and gave him a quick scratch through the gate. "You really need a better name, bud. We're working on it. I bet some third grader is just going to fall in love with you and snatch you right up. Here's hoping you get a better moniker. Killer?"

Benji's tongue lolled out and he smiled.

"Or not. Maybe Brutus." She gave him another look. "Too small. Well, as long as it's not Fido, you're golden. Anything's an improvement."

She greeted all the dogs individually, bracing herself for the larger ones that liked to jump up and startle her back a step. Milton was really much more her size preference when it came to canines. Maybe it didn't make sense that she disliked seventy-pound dogs, but she loved her twelve-hundred-pound gelding. But horses were just . . . different. For one thing, none of them ever tried to jump on her and hump her leg. She glared at Rover—yes, Rover, for the love of God—in cage three. He drooped his head a tad in shame from yesterday's hump-a-thon.

She managed to keep her gasps and startled shrieks to a minimum. She released the smaller dogs into the grassy pen beyond the shelter first, letting them interact and romp around and do their biz before herding them back into their individual cages. No easy feat, since they all tended to want to herd directly into one cage and huddle together. The squirmy, wriggly bodies were a pain in the ass to separate into their individual kennels.

The larger dogs, while a little intimidating and more leg-humpy, were easier to corral since they liked their space and headed to their separate pens without fuss.

She wiped her hands off and was going to the supply closet for the food scoop when she heard Morgan calling her name from the front.

"In the shelter!" she replied, scooping a few more dishes of food before he appeared. And she would have sworn he audibly gulped.

Just for fun, she wiggled her upturned butt a little before straightening, innocent look in place. "Something wrong?"

"Nope," he answered, much too fast. "Nothing. Ah, where's Mara?"

"I let her go when I got here." Something she'd been doing for nearly a week now, but normally she was done and already at her desk when he arrived.

"Oh." He glanced around. "You've handled the dogs already? Or did Mara do that before she left?"

"She took care of Apollo and changed his bandage. I was just up early. Mara said to tell you the leg is healing and looks good, which she also wrote on his chart." She pointed. "These guys have been fed and watered, these guys are still waiting. I'm gonna go take care of the cats, if you wouldn't mind finishing up in here."

"Sure, yeah. Thanks." He brushed past her, his arm grazing her breast in what she was sure was a complete accident. But it didn't stop her nipple from tightening in anticipation anyway.

"Stop that," she hissed at her chest while heading back to the feline area.

"Say what?"

"Nothing!" she chirped. "Dammit," she added, low enough that only the cats now facing her and batting through the cage doors could hear. She opened the first cage and made cooing noises over the first sweet darling, pulling the gray-blue kitten to her chest for a quick cuddle. "You're just so precious, yes, you are. You'll make some sweet, shy girl a wonderful friend, won't you?"

As she placed the kitten in the spare cage they kept for emergencies, she looked down at her shirt and grimaced. "Hopefully your new friend won't mind carrying a lint roller twenty-four-seven."

The cats, unlike their canine counterparts, didn't have temporary names. Since cats weren't known to give a rat's ass about their names, it seemed like a waste of time to bother. Bea shuddered to consider what generic names these cats would have to look forward to. Felix? Garfield?

She cleaned out the litter box and changed bedding and

toys to be washed, humming a little as she went. Replacing the blue-gray kitten, she repeated the process with the other cats, doing a quick check herself to make sure they were all happy and friendly. She wasn't a vet tech by any means, but she could tell when something was wrong or a cat wasn't behaving like its usual self.

When their newest addition, a two- or three-year-old tabby, growled low in his throat at the sight of Milton lying patiently by the door, she took a second to evaluate. As she turned more fully to face Milton, the cat let loose another growl—louder this time, and a warning hiss.

"So, not a fan of the canine species, huh?" She settled him in the cage and made sure Milton wasn't making any moves to come investigate, before taking a pen and writing "No dogs?" on his card with the rest of his information and shot record. She'd remember to ask Morgan later about that one. Wouldn't do to place the cat in a home with dogs if they knew from the start it'd be a disaster.

As she cleaned cages one by one, she watched Morgan from the corner of her eye. It was Thursday, field day, and he'd dressed accordingly. Most days he wore nice slacks and a button-down shirt with a tie, which somehow always was gone by the end of the day. But today he was in old jeans, a chambray shirt, and what Peyton would dub "shitkickers."

With every bend, his jeans pulled tight over his butt, accentuating the worn back pocket where his wallet resided. The denim was old enough the outline of the wallet had rubbed a white square into the denim. And every time he straightened, he had to push his glasses back up his nose. The gesture was so automatic, it was as if he didn't even have to think to do it anymore. The entire package was just so damn sexy and adorable all at the same time.

Glasses, sexy. She smiled a little and traded cats and cages to clean the last one. A year ago she would have thought they were nothing more than an interesting prop. Now she couldn't stop smiling when she thought of Morgan's foggy lenses, and his sweet brown eyes behind them watching her.

The man was crap at hiding his emotions, if he even bothered trying. He wanted her. It was obvious the way he sometimes stumbled over his words and dropped things. And he would sometimes reach out to touch her, in completely normal ways, and yank his hand back quickly like he'd decided against it.

But his want for her didn't rub her the wrong way, as some others did. Maybe because she could almost guarantee he didn't just want a quick roll in the hay. Morgan would romanticize the idea of sex. It wouldn't be sex; it would be making love. He was the kind of man who looked past the physical and wanted more. Had he found something "more" in her?

When was the last time she'd been "more" to anyone?

"Almost done with those cats?" Morgan asked from behind her.

She jumped, banging her head on the open cage door above her. "Son of a bitch!" she howled, and Milton scurried up to see the problem. He barked once at the offending cage door. "Thanks," she added wryly to her knight in shining armor.

"Whoa there, easy." Morgan shut the cage and guided her back a few steps, gentle hands on her shoulders. "Let me look at that."

"It's just a bump." She rubbed at her skull where it hurt the most, but he grabbed her hand and held it away, fingers lacing with hers to keep her from pulling back. "Morgan."

"I just want to double-check. Trust me, I went to med school."

"For animals," she reminded him, but gave in and let him cup her chin with his other hand and angle her head down.

The pose had her nearly cuddled into his chest, the way he held one hand out and cupped her face with the other. It took a lot out of her to avoid moving one half step in and pressing her nose against his chest.

Give a girl a break. Almost two years without any physical contact with a man? She was due a few fantasies, right?

"Ow!" She jerked back, fantasy shattered. "That hurt."

"The dogs never say that." The humor was evident, but she still had to fight hard not to step on his toes. Though in his boots, that wouldn't do much good. "I'll be more gentle, promise."

His fingers rifled smoothly through her hair, and her eyes closed just a minute. It was quite possibly one of her favorite places to be touched, which made no sense at all. But a man who could give a good head massage could make her a very happy woman.

"No blood, not even a bump." His fingers trailed down, just a little, to the underside of her jaw and tilted her face up. She let him, didn't move a muscle when his thumbs traced over her eyebrows, around her cheekbones, and back up again. "Did I put you to sleep?"

Her eyes opened a fraction, unwillingly. "Hmm?"

His face was closer than she'd expected, though that was obvious really. He'd been examining her head. Of course he was bent over her. But he hadn't backed away. Hadn't, in fact, let go of her face quite yet. And she liked his warm fingers there. Almost like acupuncture, the soft touch against her neck and jaw calmed her and slowed her heartbeat until she was nearly putty in his arms.

"I can't believe I'm going to do this," he said softly.

"Do what?" she slurred, just before his lips covered hers.

* * *

Maybe he was an ass for kissing her when her defenses were down. Though, exactly how those defenses had dropped, he wasn't sure. One minute she'd been in serious pain, then the next it was like she was almost drunk on pleasure, from nothing more than his quick examination.

But like hell was Morgan going to look a gift horse in the mouth.

He paused, their lips gently pressed together, waiting for her to slap him upside the head or bite him or something less dramatic to prove her displeasure. But she didn't. She made a soft sound, like a contented kitten who'd found a warm basket of laundry, and stepped into him.

And that's when any thought of holding back became null and void. One hand drifted down her neck to her lower back and pressed her into him. Her arms wrapped around his waist as she accepted the position. As he angled his head to the side to take the kiss deeper, she kneaded his back with her hands.

Oh God, she was going to undo him.

If he gripped her just under her ass, he could spin her around and plant her against the wall with no trouble at all. Her height was a big advantage, and her impractical heels only added to the benefit, bringing her right to the perfect height for kissing. No bending or stooping from his excessively tall height, just a lovely leaning in and melting together.

Or maybe he could find a table. Desk. Floor. Where was the nearest sanitary horizontal space he could set her on and . . .

"Either you have one extraordinary penis with some superhuman perks," she murmured against his lips, teasing the corner of his mouth with the tip of her tongue, "or your cell phone is vibrating."

"My cell phone?" he asked dazedly, then flushed when she laughed.

"If it's not your phone, then I'll have to admit, I've never been with someone whose equipment buzzed."

"Buzz . . . ah, shit. Sorry," he muttered as he broke off and checked. It was his office phone, the one only used for emergencies. Nine times out of ten, his clients either called the office phone, or his regular cell. But a text on this one meant he couldn't just fling it against a wall and continue his impromptu make-out session with Bea.

Fuck, fuck, fuck.

"Something wrong?" She stepped back and twisted her hair behind her ears, a habit that was becoming more common with her now.

He held up a finger and scrolled quickly through the text, then sighed. "We're gonna have to make a quick stop at Three Trees first, before we hit any of the scheduled clients."

"But we're due at our first place in"—she checked her watch—"thirty minutes."

"I know. You'll have to make some calls and switch things around on the drive out there." Damn not having a partner. Damn not having enough time for *her*. He nodded toward the side door. "You ready to roll?"

Bea hustled out ahead of him, Milton hot on her heels. She bent over and reached in her car to grab something, ass straight in the air. It was then he realized she wasn't wearing her usual cute office attire, but something very un-Bea-like. Jeans, no frills or designer holes in sight, and a simple plaid shirt. Of course, the shirt was fitted to her body and tied up in some weird bow at her navel, and the tank she wore under that shirt was displayed nicely. But it was more practical for the barn call day than her skirts and pristine white blouses. The heels, though, were still present.

He sighed as she hopped in the passenger seat of his truck, settling Milton on the backseat to take a nap. "You've really got to stop wearing those shoes to barn calls. Unless you actually like wearing my 'nasty boots,' as you called them last week."

She grinned slowly, and reached in the bag she'd hauled from her car. "Not especially. I'm a quick learner, Morgan."

He shifted the truck into DRIVE and backed out of the small parking lot behind the clinic. "How so?"

"Well," she said easily, "after last week, I went home and did some online shopping." She reached into the bag and pulled out a pair of rain boots with a tan plaid pattern. They were clearly designer, and likely the makers had envisioned beautiful women wearing them while strolling down Fifth Avenue on a relaxing shopping day. Not going from barn to barn standing ankle-deep in mud.

He stared at them a moment before heading out to the main road. "Those are meant for the barn?"

Bea laughed. "Morgan, if you're going to be knee-deep in shit, it can't hurt to make it look good."

Chapter Seven

Bea's nerves hummed continuously throughout Friday. Not just from the anticipation of the Adoption Fair the next morning, and the fact that she'd be up nearly half the night prepping and making sure she had every last detail ready to roll. No, it was that darn Morgan. He was everywhere.

In the exam room when she let patients in. In his back room, when she needed office supplies. Behind her desk, when she scheduled a patient. In the shelter, when she took a quick stretch and wanted to let out the big dogs for a fast run. She couldn't avoid the man.

And she didn't want to. But she needed to, for the sake of her sanity, not to mention her job. How the heck could she concentrate on the all-important task of a successful adoption fair if her libido was busy figuring out ways to accidentally-on-purpose brush against the cute vet's arm, or staring at him for ten minutes before realizing she'd lost track of time?

It was embarrassing, she admitted as she zoned out, eyes locked on the framed poster of a puppy and kitten playing together in a grassy meadow. Jaycee had caught her at least once staring at his ass while he bent over a low file cabinet digging for paperwork. But she played it off like she'd just been staring into space, as she was now, as if she hadn't even really seen Morgan and his nicely shaped behind. Hadn't been fantasizing about squeezing said behind while he was on top of her, thrusting into her, making her moan like her ex-prostitute character, Trixie, on a sex bender and—

The phone rang, and her elbow slammed into the keyboard as she jerked from her mental sabbatical. Crap. She really had to stop doing that.

"Browning Veterinary Clinic, how can I help you?" she answered, amazed her voice sounded as smooth as normal. Her heart was a jackhammer in her chest.

There was a slight pause, and then a tentative woman's voice asked, "Beatrice Muldoon?"

"Yes, this is she." Who the hell would call her Beatrice?

"This is Cynthia Browning."

Who?

"Morgan's mother?"

"Oh! Oh yes, of course. I'm sorry." She laughed weakly. "Afternoon brain lag."

"It's been a while, of course. How are you, dear?"

The tone said she was asking to be polite, but would prefer to move the conversation along. "Just fine, thank you. Morgan's with a patient right now, but I can—"

"Don't bother him," she cut in. "I just wanted to ask you a quick favor."

Ho, boy. "Yes?" she asked, trying not to sound suspicious.

"Could you make sure he eats something for dinner? He's staying overnight tonight at the clinic, and he gets all lackadaisical about eating if someone doesn't pester him from time to time."

She'd just bet he did. "I can make sure he's got dinner before I leave for the night. No problem."

"Thank you. That is a big weight off my mind." She

paused, drew in a breath as if she were going to say something, but nothing came.

Bea counted to five, then asked, "Is there anything else?"

"No, no." The answer was fast, a little breathless. "Thank you, dear."

You already said that. "Not a problem." Bea hung up and leaned back in her chair. What was that all about? Was Morgan a big mama's boy? Or was his mother just having trouble cutting the apron strings? He didn't strike her as the kind of man who needed his mother to baby him.

She checked her watch. Either way, it was definitely time to get some grub. It was coming up on seven, and they'd had an early lunch to accommodate a patient. The clinic was closed, and it was just the two of them until she headed home. Time to eat. She was starving.

After calling in an order to Jo's, and begging Jo to run it over so she wouldn't have to leave, Bea went in search of Morgan.

He was in his office, going over paperwork. She leaned in just a tad and watched the process. His brow furrowed, and his eyes squinted from time to time. Maybe he needed an eye exam, a new prescription. She'd ask later when the last time he'd made it to the eye doctor was. His pen was fast, scratching out words, writing new ones in bold strokes. He had good handwriting, she knew. None of that illegible doctor scrawl crap she always heard jokes about. Nice and efficient, but easily read. Every minute or so, he reached up to touch his glasses between the eyes, like he was pushing them up again, even if they weren't slipping. Habit.

It was cute, really, how absorbed he was in his work. The animals meant everything to him, and he'd jump through fire to save one. Quite literally, she imagined.

When he sighed, stretched his back, took his glasses off,

and massaged between his eyes, she stepped in with a quick knock. "Hey."

He jolted, then smiled wearily. "Hey. You still here?"

"Of course I am. I've got a few hundred flyers to fold and deliver to the newspaper so they'll go out with the morning delivery. And I promised to help get all the supplies prepped and loaded into your truck so all you had to do was load the babies and go tomorrow, didn't I?"

"You did." He smiled and nodded. "Thanks for all the help, by the way."

"It was my idea in the first place. I'm afraid my plan might have made more trouble for you than I anticipated." She grimaced and sat on the corner of his desk, butt barely perched on the edge. When his gaze wandered down her legs and ended at the straps of her very cute Choos, she knew he was slipping out of work mode. Lucky for her. "I feel awful that you got sucked into my scheme. I don't think this was what you had in mind when you said, 'run with it.' "

"It's a good idea," he insisted firmly, grabbing her hand and squeezing. "A great one. All these guys need new homes, and if we can find them in one day with a big push, then fantastic. The timing was a little sooner than I anticipated, but it's solid. And if it goes well, then a repeat performance can definitely be expected."

If. If it went well. That two-letter word hovered over her like a gray cloud. Was that cloud going to move on its way and threaten someone else? Or dump a load of rain on her . . .

When she looked down, she realized his hand was still holding hers. She bit back a smile. "I'm going to need that back sometime, you know."

"Huh? Oh." He let go so fast, her hand smacked the top of the desk with a slap. "Shit, shoot, sorry." He picked her hand back up, clinically this time, examining her wrist and fingers. "You okay?"

"Yes," she said on a laugh. "I'm fine." Without thought, her hand trailed up his arm and to his shoulders, where she rubbed. "You need to walk around and stretch out. You've been bent over your desk for a while now."

"If you're saying something, I don't know what it is. That is magical," he said quietly, eyes closing.

She observed him while her hands worked on his shoulders, kneading the tension away. With his eyes closed and his glasses off, his features seemed both sharper and softer at the same time. No warm eyes watching her quietly, no sexy glint of metal, no sweet smudge of glass. A man relaxed, satisfied. This was what he would look like if she rolled over in the middle of the night and watched him sleep.

And holy crap, where had that come from? Her hands froze, mid-squeeze, and she forced them to relax. But her knuckles were screaming from the effort. When she heard a loud banging, she sprang up. "That's dinner."

"Dinner?" One heavy eyelid slid open, and he gazed at her languidly.

"I ordered delivery from Jo's."

"They don't deliver."

"I know the owner," she said with a wink, then walked out. But when she got to the front door, nobody was there. Huh. She stood for a second, then headed out through the shelter to the back door. Maybe Jo thought the front would be locked since it was after hours, or something.

Wagging tails and a few excited yips greeted her. Other dogs just eyed her sleepily from heads laid on paws. Most of the rest ignored her completely. She hustled to the door, opening it a little.

The back lot, where employees parked, was decently lit,

but no car other than hers and Morgan's was there. And no Jo. Strange. She would have sworn she'd heard knocking. Maybe something had fallen in the storage closet. She grabbed the handle to the heavy door and pulled it shut, then halted when the tiniest of whimpers caught her ear.

The door slammed into her shoulder and she nearly stumbled in her heels. She cursed and pushed at the heavy door, as if that was going to make her feel better. In response, the whimper turned into a whine. There. She wasn't crazy at all. Propping the door open with a brick, she stepped out into the night and searched.

Due to the building's *U* shape, the corners of the back lot weren't as well lit as the center, where the cars were parked, but she did her best to search. Did Morgan have a flashlight in one of the storage closets?

And duh, she didn't need that. She reached in her pocket and pulled out her cell, which she kept in her pocket on vibrate while working. Thumbing through, she found the flashlight app and let the light shine. Not as good as a high-watt floodlight, but better than nothing.

It took her almost no time to find a closed box on the opposite side of the door. It looked like one of the boxes produce came in at the grocery store. Sure enough, as she stepped closer, she saw bananas pictured on the sides; the top flaps were folded in. She approached slowly, then nudged the box with the toe of one shoe.

The whimper started again, insistent, and then in stereo as several more joined in.

"Oh God!" She shoved her cell in her pocket and lifted the lid to the box, uncovering several puppies.

At least, she thought they were puppies. But the hairless little things could have been moles, or rats for all she knew.

"Okay, then . . ." She replaced the lid gently, not worried about air flow as the box had several holes. "Let's just get you guys inside and see what our favorite hottie vet has to say about you." When she grasped the handles and lifted, the whimpers turned to wails of what could only be described as terror. "I'm sorry, I'm sorry, I know. Let's get you in here. I'm going as fast as I can."

Inside, she settled the box on the floor and popped the lid open again in the overhead light. Yup, definitely . . . something animal-ish. There was only one thing to do.

"Morgan!"

Morgan lifted the first pathetic squirming bundle of skin and bone. Bea hovered behind him, anxiously watching as he handled the small pup.

"So they're dogs?"

He chuckled. "Yes, puppies. This one's eyes aren't open yet, so I'd say under two weeks."

"Oh," she cooed. Her arm reached over his shoulder, brushing against his cheek as she used the pad of one finger to rub the pup's head. Then she gasped, reached into her pocket, and brought out her phone.

"Making an important call?" he joked. "Alerting the media?"

"No." The sound of a fake shutter told him she was taking pictures. "I just want a few photos of these cuties. Why would someone dump them and not wait around?"

"I don't know." Anger boiled up in him, enough to have his jaw clenching. "It's not the first time. There's a reason I put up that sign on the back door, about no questions asked, to ring the bell and wait until someone answers since we're staffed twenty-four-seven. Not to just ditch and run. If you hadn't been listening for a food delivery, we might not have heard the knock at all. These guys could have stayed out there all night."

"Oh," she said again, but in a sad tone this time. "What a bastard. Milton, no." She picked Milton up, who'd been sniffing the edge of the box.

"He's fine. Put him back down." Milton strained from Bea's arms toward the puppy in Morgan's hand, whining and snuffling like a pig desperate to find a truffle.

"I don't want him to hurt them." She bit her lip, worried.

Morgan looked at Milton, then shook his head. "He won't. I trust him."

Bea muttered something, but set the dog back down. Milton huffed, obviously indignant at her lack of trust in him, and approached the box. He sniffed, nuzzled the box a little, then peered over the edge.

And stayed that way, tail wagging. He never touched any of the wriggling bodies, but he sniffed and breathed and snorted with excitement. One of the puppies wiggled and slid until he—or maybe she—could almost touch Milton's nose, and his—or her—littermates followed.

"If they can't see him, can they hear him? How do they know he's there?" she asked in wonder.

"Smell. It's the first of their senses to develop. They can barely hear, definitely can't see, but they smell him and want to investigate. Or just find another warm body. The heat aspect is another factor."

"Ah." She didn't take her eyes off the box.

Morgan watched her face as she observed the dogs. Soft. Unguarded. Beautiful. He wanted to go back to that moment the day before when they'd been so madly intent on each other's pleasure they'd forgotten they were in the hallway of the damn clinic. He would have given his eye teeth to drag her to the cot in the back room and strip her bare.

But first things first. "These guys probably need a meal. In the supply closet, there's . . . never mind." He passed the dog into her cupped hands. "You hold him. I'll be right back."

Her eyes widened, but she didn't say no. He stayed for

a moment to make sure she was comfortable, then hurried to grab the supplies.

"So what's the plan, doc?" She was rubbing the pup's stomach with the tip of one finger. Just the sight of that caress, and his body went into lust overdrive.

Great timing.

"Syringe feed for another few weeks. Then wet food, and on to dry." He picked up another of the pups, filled a syringe with the pre-mixed liquid he always kept in stock for occasions just like this, and inserted the dropper end into the side of the dog's mouth. Training took over and he gently released a little at a time while the dog ate. Bea took a few more photos with her phone.

"Since we don't know how old they really are, we'll play it by ear as to when to move on to the food. But for now, they'll need to be fed every few hours for a couple of weeks."

"And who does that? You?" Bea looked skeptical. "You're already here all the time. Isn't this a little much for you to take on?"

"I've got a few foster families. Several of them have fed newborn pups before, so it's nothing new." He warmed at her concern for him. "But I can't call them until tomorrow morning, so I guess these guys are sticking with me tonight."

"I'll do it," Bea blurted out, then looked shocked at herself.

"You . . . want to take them home with you?" He started to say no, they shouldn't be moved tonight, but she interrupted him.

"No, I mean, I'll stay here. With you. And . . . help." She looked down at the other five bodies in the box, then at the one in her hands. "Besides, I have an idea."

"Sounds ominous," he joked. But when she turned her eyes to his, his amusement faded. *Please, God, let that idea*

*have something to do with us picking up where we left off yester-
day.*

"I think . . ." She trailed off as a knock sounded at the
front door. "Never mind. That's probably Jo with our
dinner." She carefully laid the puppy in her hands in the
box. Immediately, he—she?—belly-crawled toward the
pile of brothers and sisters for warmth and comfort.

"Come on, Milton." She stood, using her hands on her
knees for leverage.

Milton sat quietly by the box.

"Milty, come."

He lay down, snubbed snout on his front paws. The tip
of one turned-down ear flicked.

"Looks like these guys have a pseudo big brother,"
Morgan said. "It's okay. He's not going to bother them."

"Yeah, but . . ." Bea looked a little hurt, and Morgan's
heart cracked. Just a nick. But then she shrugged and
headed toward the front door.

A few minutes later, Bea and Trace came back together.
Morgan was on puppy number three.

"You look nothing like Jo," he commented as Bea set
the bag of food on a stool. Milton, ever loyal, abandoned
his new friends to sit by the good-smelling stuff.

"I'm just the errand boy. I was on my way back to the
house for dinner when she caught me and asked me to
make the delivery." Trace sat down at the box and peered
in. "Hello, what have we here?"

"New guests." Morgan handed him a syringe and a
puppy. "Here you go."

Bea hovered behind them. "Should I stay?"

"No, no. You've got stuff to do for tomorrow's adoption fair. Go for it, and then get a good night's sleep." He
didn't look up from the pup in his hands as her heels, followed by Milton's nails, clicked out of the room to the reception area.

"Running that one to ground, are we?" Trace asked mildly.

"There's been progress," Morgan said defensively, then winced. This was Bea's brother. Probably not a great idea to spill details. But the urge to confide in his friend, the friend he'd missed for nearly a decade, was strong. "I'll just leave it at that."

"Whatever, man. All I'll say is . . . good luck." Trace raised his hand to bring the pup to eye level. "Exactly what kind of mix do you think these guys are?"

"All but impossible to tell at this stage. Their coloring should be a bit more defined in a few weeks. But right now, a little bit of everything is my unofficial guess. Hound, shepherd, retriever. Put them all together, and what do you got?"

Trace grinned and held up the puppy again. "Hot dog?"

They laughed at the old schoolyard rhyme and finished feeding the puppies. Then Trace stood and brushed his hands off on his jeans. "I've got bath time and bedtime to get to, so I'm heading out. We'll stop by the fair tomorrow morning to help out if we can."

"Great. See ya." He walked Trace out the front door and locked it behind him, then turned and watched Bea working at her desk.

"Where are the flyers?"

She didn't look up, just clicked something on the computer. "I'll get to those in a minute. Wanted to upload the pictures I took first."

"Okay, then. Make sure the door is locked behind you when you leave." He left her to her job and headed back to the shelter side. He had puppies to get settled for the night.

Stretch, two, three, four. Clench, two, three, four.

Oh God, that hurt. Bea shook her hands at the wrists,

fingers flying limply. Two hours of folding flyers later, her hands looked like the steel claw from an arcade game. She could barely hold them steady on the steering wheel to get her car to the tiny newspaper distribution center and back to the clinic.

As she unlocked the front door and walked in, she heard masculine humming. And not bad, either. She locked the door behind her and followed the sound.

Morgan sat on the floor of exam room two, reading what looked like a textbook. Three cats were draped over his long, extended legs in various poses of languid bliss. A fourth was curled up by the book, tail swishing every so often over the page. The page shuddered with every flick of the furry whip, but he didn't shoo the cat away.

A vet and his harem, she thought with a smile. Most men would love to say they were surrounded by pussy all day . . . but Morgan wouldn't find that joke humorous. "Did you eat?"

He jolted, then looked up. "You're back."

"Of course I'm back." She sat on the chair. Milton trotted in behind her and curled up under her legs, eyeing the cats warily like a ninety-pound junkyard guard dog eying a burglar. *My mommy,* his evil glance said. "I can't leave you alone with those puppies all night. How unfair."

"It's nothing I haven't done before, I assure you," he said, but his smile was welcoming. He started to close the book, then double-checked to make sure the cat's tail was out of the way first. "Now that we're alone, should we talk about . . . that thing?"

"That thing." She tapped one finger on her chin. She loved making him squirm. "I'm drawing a blank."

His face reddened. "You know what I mean. That thing. The thing from the other day. The kiss."

"Oh, the kiss." Bea nodded and scratched Milton's head. "I'm not sure we need to talk about it."

"So, you're not upset?"

"Upset?" She laughed. "Why would I be upset? It was a kiss. A great kiss, actually. You didn't molest me."

He sighed, and she could tell he was getting aggravated at her deliberate obtuseness. And he was just as cute aggravated as he was squirming.

"I just wanted to make sure. I mean, I didn't . . . and you hadn't said . . . but then you didn't stop me so . . ." He ran a hand through his hair, which tilted his glasses a little on the bridge of his nose. She bit back a smile. "I wanted to make sure I didn't have to apologize."

"When did you feed the puppies last?"

He blinked behind his skewed lenses. "What?"

"The puppies," she said patiently. "The ones from the box? When did you feed them last?"

He checked his watch. "About an hour ago. They'll probably be hungry in another two hours or so. I've got the alarm on my phone set."

"Good." She held out a hand, standing when he took it. He stood with her. When she pulled, he followed easily. She led him to the back area where they kept the paper supplies, and the small twin-sized bed his techs slept on when it was their night to do the overnight shift. They stood together, both staring at the tiny bed in silence.

What is she thinking? Am I assuming too much? Should I be a gentleman and stop whatever's about to happen? That would make me an idiot, wouldn't it?

"You're thinking loudly."

He glanced down. She was watching him carefully, but with a small smile tilting her lips. "Sorry?"

"Stop thinking. If you don't want to . . ." She shrugged a shoulder. "It's fine. But I do, and I figured I might as well say it. Cut through the middle, right?"

Did he want to? More than he wanted to breathe. But the long-term effects . . . would she think he wanted just a one-night stand? He'd mapped out a slow, tender courtship in his mind. Easing her into the idea of dating, then of thinking of Marshall as her home.

"Morgan," she whispered. Her hands wrapped around the back of his neck and pulled at him until her lips brushed his. "Morgan, stop thinking so hard. In or out?"

Plans be damned. "In."

Chapter Eight

Bea started to reach for him, then paused. "Those sheets were changed, right?"

He grinned. "It's part of their routine. Strip the bed, put on fresh sheets, pop the ones you used in the washer out back before you end your overnight shift."

"Okay then." She could live with that. She yanked his head down to meet hers in a searing kiss. The kind that sets flames flickering behind your eyelids while they're closed and makes your skin feel like it's too tight for your body. She wanted to scale him, squeeze her legs around his waist, and feel weightless.

He sat down at the edge of the mattress, raised her shirt just an inch, and pressed a kiss to the bare skin revealed. She shivered. He continued the pattern, raising her shirt by inches and following the trail with his lips until he reached the underside of her breasts.

She couldn't take the torture any longer. Bea took a step back, ripped the shirt over her head, and let it fall to the floor. Before he could say a word, she climbed on his lap, her knees pressing into the mattress, her center pressing against the hard, long ridge of his erection. Oh God, if only there weren't clothes between them. This would be a magical position.

Later, she promised herself as he kissed her again. Later,

they could try everything. But first, ring the bell, check the box, dull the knife-edge tension between them so that next time, they could enjoy it more.

"God, Bea," he moaned when she reached back to un-hook her own bra. "You're so beautiful. It's like I can't see anything but you."

She let the lacy bra fall behind her with the shirt and reached for his glasses. "These are probably smudged enough, that's true." She set them on the small table and smiled when he blinked like a sweet pup opening his eyes for the first time.

"You drive me crazy," she mumbled, then kissed him again. She made quick work of the button-down shirt he'd worn, though he didn't make it easy. She had to fight his arms, wrapped around her, to get it off. It was as if he didn't want to let go for even a second in case she changed her mind.

Not freaking likely.

But when she stood up to take off her own pants, he all but gasped. "I think we need to slow down."

"Nope. Not happening." She kicked her heels to the side—sorry, cute Blahniks—and shimmied out of her cropped black pants. The underwear naturally came with the pants, and she was naked. Standing in the back room of a vet's office.

Why was she not appalled by that situation?

Morgan stared, dumbfounded, at her. "I . . . uh . . ."

"Pants, Morgan." She smiled when he barely budged an inch. The man was good for the ego.

"Right. Yeah, pants." He stood so fast he had to steady himself with a hand on the wall. But faster than she could say "What's my line?" he was as naked as she was. And impressive. He managed to hide quite the body under his lab coat and office wear.

Bea ran one hand down the lean muscles of his chest and waist. Not a body builder, not a man used to hitting the weights in the gym. His body was sculpted from lifting hundred-pound dogs onto exam tables and wrangling misbehaving cattle.

As her hand drifted lower and reached around to stroke his erection, she grinned. And yes, he was proportional to his six-foot-three-inch frame . . . everywhere.

"Ho boy . . . okay, you have to stop that." He grabbed her wrist when she gave another playful tug. "I can't let that happen the first time. I'll have to kick my own ass."

She laughed. God, he made her laugh. "Morgan, you're the sweetest man."

He guided her down to the bed and kissed her harder than before. "I'm not sure *sweet* is a compliment in this area."

She cupped his head and sobered her expression. "Sweet is always a compliment. Trust me."

His penis was heavy against her thigh, but she paused. "I'm hoping you're a good Boy Scout and are prepared."

He winged one brow up. "Jesus, Bea. If I were any more ready, we'd already be done."

She snorted. "I meant a condom."

He blushed. "Right. Of course. In my back pocket." He reached around and patted his bare butt. "Jesus. Dammit," he muttered as he crawled off and over to where his pants lay in a heap.

She was never going to make it through without laughing. And what a fantastic feeling. She was already loose and limber, before the lovemaking.

Sex. Not lovemaking. Sex, she reminded herself sternly.

"Ah, there we go." He held the foil packet up like a trophy. "Score."

"You're seventeen again, aren't you?"

"Hardly. I didn't cash in my V-card until I was in college." He grimaced as he rolled the rubber on. "And that's so not something I should be admitting. I'm much cooler now," he added.

"Of course." She nodded seriously, then kissed him again when he settled over her. "Very cool. I only work for the cool kids." She nibbled up to his ear. "Wanna make out behind the lockers after class?"

He growled, settled between her legs, and pushed in without further warning. It was exactly what she wanted. Morgan, on the edge. He pumped into her, moaning with pleasure as she clenched around him.

"Bea, I can't believe . . . I'm not going to make it. Aw, dammit. I'm sorry." He spoke through gritted teeth as he slowed down in an obvious effort to make it last longer.

"I'm a big girl," she assured him, then reached between their sweat-slicked bodies to flick one fingertip over the bundle of nerves at the top of her center. And then she was flying, her own orgasm taking her over before even his.

"Thank you, God," she heard him mutter before a quick warning shout and he collapsed over her.

"That," she said a few minutes later when she could breathe, "was so much more than checking a box."

"What, like a To-Do list? Check e-mail, run to post office, have sex with Morgan. That sort of thing?" He kissed the side of her neck.

"No. Not at all." She smoothed a hand down his back, then grimaced a little. "We're a sweaty mess."

He licked her collarbone. "Yup."

"Morgan!" She pushed at his shoulder. "There's no shower here, is there?"

"Unless you want to use the shower attachment in the dog bath . . ."

"That would be a no." And ick. She waited while he managed to lurch his way to the employee bathroom.

She'd just reached for her bra when he came back. "Don't."

"Don't what?" She held the bra up. "Want it? Trophy?"

"Don't leave." He held out a hand and she stood. It was ridiculous. They were both still naked, in the back room of the vet clinic. But when he pulled her into his arms, she couldn't help but go willingly.

"Stay," he said, cheek resting against the top of her head.

"Fine." She'd stay for another hour or two. Maybe there'd be a repeat performance. And how could she turn that down?

Morgan shifted in an attempt to get more comfortable. Not that it worked, thanks to the fact that they were two tall people wedged into a twin-sized bed. Only so many places for the limbs to go, and right now one of Bea's legs was wedged against his crotch in a not-so-erotic sort of way.

She murmured something, rolled away delicately, then back again. Her breath puffed out, warm and soft, against his chest. His hand smoothed over her baby-fine hair and he wondered . . . just what the hell was he thinking?

The back storage room? Their first time, on a twin-sized bed in the back of his clinic? What a moron.

But she didn't seem to mind. In fact, she'd instigated it. This could be good, or this could be bad.

Good . . . because she was so hot for him she couldn't wait.

Bad . . . because romance didn't matter and you could have a one night stand anywhere.

Good . . . because it gave them a funny story to share in the future.

Bad . . . because she might just remember the vet who had no moves on a bed the size of a cot when she moved back to California, the land of Men with Smooth Moves.

Or, he could just lie here awake all night, making himself crazy.

His cell phone beeped, and he cursed.

Bea mumbled and tried to wrap herself tighter around him.

"We need to get up," he whispered into her ear.

"Five more minutes," she muttered.

"Puppies need to be fed."

That brought her awake. "Oh, right. We have the puppies." She yawned and stretched, and it took everything he had in him to not take one tight breast into his mouth while it was thrust toward him. "You go feed, I'll fix coffee."

"No, you go back home." He kissed her nose. "You're the ambassador of this little function tomorrow. We're counting on you to keep it running smoothly. So go home, get a good night's sleep, and tomorrow you will lead the troops in what will be an epic adoption fair."

She side-eyed him while putting her bra back on. "That sounded suspiciously like a nerdy commercial."

He blushed.

Then she kissed his cheek while grabbing her pants. "I happen to find the nerdiness adorable. Now, go feed the puppies. And if they do anything adorable—"

"They won't. They're too young."

"—then take a picture and text me," she finished, as if he hadn't said a word.

Fine. He'd prop them up doing something adorable, like reading a book. Then she'd laugh at him for being a nerd, and he'd have invested his time wisely. Making her laugh was always worth the time. Plus, it was the middle of the night. What else did he have to do?

She finished getting dressed and opened the door to the main hallway. Milton sprinted in and glared at him, as if he was accusing Morgan of violating his mother.

"Sorry, bud. She said yes."

Bea rolled her eyes and scooped the dog up. "Don't mind him, baby. I'm sorry I had to lock you out. But you're a bed hog and there was hardly any bed to hog."

Milton gave him the stink eye over Bea's shoulder.

Get over it, Morgan mouthed, then realized he was talking to a dog and grabbed his pants before he lost his mind.

"Are you sure you want me to go? I can stay."

"Go," he insisted. "You get your beauty rest—not that you need it—and I'll see you in the morning."

"Okay." She put Milton down and slipped her heels on. He was buttoning his shirt, ready to walk her to the door when she sneaked in another kiss, almost as hot as the one that had landed them in the bed in the first place. It was a good thing his hands were still stuck holding a button or else he'd have started something they shouldn't finish.

"I'll see you in the morning," she said when she pulled back, voice a little husky.

"Yeah," he answered dumbly, then hopped into his shoes while following her out the back door. He watched to make sure she got into her car, got it started, and pulled out before closing himself back in the clinic.

Then, with only the dogs as witnesses, he pumped his fist like a tenth-grade nerd who had just scored with the prom queen.

Nerd status: confirmed.

Chapter Nine

She was going to throw up. She was going to pass out. She was going to . . . grow a pair and stop acting like an idiot.

"Breathe," she whispered, then opened the door to the city councilmen and women. "Welcome!" Her best public-pleasing smile in place, she ushered them in. "Thank you for coming by early to check up on us and make sure we were okay."

"Hardly that. We needed to make sure you weren't going to destroy the building with your horde of animals." Judy Plumber, head councilwoman, sniffed delicately and stepped by her. Bea resisted the urge to trip her, and gave herself points for maturity.

From her quick research into the council—most of which was spent grilling Jo—she knew this woman was a menace to all things good and real in the world. Power tripping was a religion to Mrs. Plumber.

She greeted Bill and Stuart, and the others who comprised the council, all of whom were much warmer in their welcome. And then she stepped back and let them roam. It was eerily quiet, with only their footsteps echoing in the large room. Morgan was back at the clinic with the animals and vet techs, ready to transport when she gave the word.

She had set up rubber mats on the wooden floors so no cages would scratch or dent them. A table was set up for registration and filling out paperwork. And she'd added a list to collect e-mails for those who wanted to be added to the shelter's newsletter. A newsletter they didn't have quite yet, but she would be remedying that. And, of course, also at the table was a hastily put together poster board, science fair–style, displaying the pictures of the box puppies from the night before.

She'd listed their approximate age, that there were four boys and three girls, and a few fun facts she'd mostly made up to be silly and give each pup a personality. Going by what Morgan had said, she also listed the date they would be adoptable, and a quick note to speak to one of the volunteers about signing up to be notified when they were ready to be viewed.

Please, dear God, let this be enough.

Bill walked in a quick *U* around the small pens that were set up, then turned back. "Are you only bringing the smaller dogs?"

"In here, yes. The bigger dogs will be under the awning outside, where there's more space to walk around with them." She held her breath as he nodded absently, then wandered over to read her poster about the babies.

Stuart walked around behind her, then came to a halt next to her. "I'm surprised."

"By what?" She couldn't take her eyes off the wandering councilmen, and their bitchy queen leader.

"You put this together quickly, and efficiently." Stuart eyed her, but not in a sexual way. "You're not quite what you let people think you are."

It wasn't a statement, but she felt the need to respond. "I'm exactly what people think I am."

He raised a brow, but nodded to his fellow members. "No need to stall things. I don't see anything that would cause a problem here. So the hall's yours. We do expect it returned to the original state it was in. No puddles."

Her lips twitched, but she fought to keep a cool, professional front. "Absolutely. No puddles."

He patted a hand on her shoulder in a sort of vague fatherly gesture. "Good luck, Ms. Muldoon."

"Thank you, Mr. Wilde." She watched as one by one, the council members walked out the door. A few gave her smiles and good luck wishes as well. But Mrs. Stick Up Her Fanny said nothing, not even deigning to glance in her direction.

Bea was pretty sure the adoption fair didn't need the sort of luck she'd wish on them, anyway.

She texted Morgan to let him know the coast was clear, and that he could start driving over the babies. Jaycee would be helping him with a second truck, but they'd need to make two trips. And until then . . .

Bea looked down and nudged her faithful companion's butt with the side of her heel. "Just you and me, Milton."

"Are we allowed to join the party?"

She gasped and spun. In the doorway stood Jo, Trace, Peyton, and Red.

"Hey." She held a hand over her racing heart, then cocked her head to the side. "What are you guys doing here?"

"Please. Like we were gonna miss out on seeing this go down." Peyton snorted, then jolted when Red elbowed her in the ribs. She grumbled and rolled her eyes.

Trace kissed her cheek before bending over to scratch Milton's ears. "We wanted to see if you needed some help. Might get a little crazy in here."

"I heard something in the feed store yesterday about discounted pet supplies for anyone who adopted an animal today?" Red winked. "Nice work."

"I heard you managed to get flyers into every kid's book

bag in the elementary school." Trace grinned. "Every kid I've seen the last few days has been begging for a puppy."

Jo raised her hand. "I've put the word out that anyone who adopts today gets a free drink and appetizer on the house."

Bea bit her lip, willing the tears back. "You guys . . ."

Jo bumped her hip against Bea's. "Just doing our job. That's what friends are for."

"And family," Trace added.

Peyton stayed back, more distant than the rest. With her arms crossed, she walked around the room, surveying the setup much as the committee had not ten minutes earlier. She stopped by the puppy poster and read a little. "Trace mentioned these guys showed up last night."

"Someone just dumped them outside. If I hadn't heard the knock . . ." Bea clenched her fists to gain control of her anger. "But I did, and they're healthy, as far as Morgan can tell."

Peyton picked up a clipboard. "The shelter has a newsletter?"

"It will soon." Bea snatched the clipboard back and set it down, nudging it with one index finger to line it up perfectly with the table's edge. "I'm creating it on Monday. Just another way to show off the rotating crowd. Not to mention hint at supplies we're always needing."

"Hmm."

And that, apparently, was as good as she was going to get from her sister. Morgan pulled up, his truck visible through the large windows on the side of the building. "Time to get the fur babies in here. We've got less than an hour before we're officially open for business. Can you help?"

All but Jo—who wasn't overly keen on animals and labeled herself supervisor—helped unload the cages and set the animals up in their predetermined spots.

While Morgan waited for Jaycee's truck, he headed over to Bea and ran a hand down her back. Bea wasn't sure how to handle the PDA. Okay, yes, they'd slept together. But nobody else knew that. And it almost seemed like he was watching to see if she'd accept the touch, or step away and keep it platonic in front of others.

Before she even made up her own mind, she leaned into his side. His arm wrapped around her and pulled her in tight. She caught Trace's side glance from his location across the room, but ignored it.

"You've done great," Morgan said quietly by her ear.

"It's not over. Don't hand out the awards just yet."

"It's just beginning," he acknowledged, and she wasn't sure if she should be pleased by the warmth there, or concerned by any possible double entendres.

Now she did pull back, just a little, and pushed at his chest. "Go get the second round. We can't still be setting up when people start arriving. It would look unprofessional."

"Yes, ma'am." He hovered a moment over her, and she thought he would kiss her. But he just smiled and headed back to his truck.

That was going to take some considering. How far did she want to take it with the handsome vet—who just happened to be her temporary boss? She wasn't here for the long haul, and he was a married-with-two-point-five-kids kind of guy. He'd see a future for them, one that was completely fabricated. Not fair to let it continue if he couldn't separate sex from commitment in his mind.

So they'd chat. She could do that. She was a mature woman. If being in LA hadn't taught her how to handle an on-set romance properly, then she'd learned nothing.

Morgan scooped the fuzzy terrier from his cage and held him up at eye level for the child. "This is Benji."

"Benji," the boy repeated.

"Original," his father said wryly.

"Well, hey." Morgan ruffled the dog's ears. "You start running out of ideas after a while."

"I bet." The man held out a hand and Morgan relinquished the dog easily. The boy's wide eyes were a sure sign he was willing to promise the world in exchange for taking home that dog.

"What is he?" the father asked.

"Mine," his son replied instantly, then grinned sheepishly as both his father and Morgan laughed.

"He's a mutt, like a lot of our guys. But he's definitely got a lot of terrier in him. Terriers require a great deal of exercise to keep them busy. They can get into mischief otherwise," Morgan warned. "He needs an active little boy to play with in the yard and chase balls and sticks with and go for walks. Someone who can crash with him at the end of the day in front of a good movie and pass out because you've run each other ragged."

"I can do that. I can do all that!" The young child bounced in his sneakers.

Yup. Puppy love. Morgan grinned at the dad. "We've got an area outside that's blocked off if you want to let them run around together and see how they work as a pair."

"Sounds good. Anthony, let's give Benji a trial, how's that sound?"

His son nodded like a dashboard bobblehead, following him out the side door to the grassy area they'd blocked off for the smaller dogs.

Bea skipped in on her typical high heels, clutching an adoption form to her chest and beaming. "We've got a taker for Rambo out there." Rambo, a forlorn Doberman mix, who gave Dobermans a wussy name. "A family from—can you believe it—Sierra Hills heard about the fair and drove in to just look. Score!"

He grinned at that. Not just the adoption—which was, as she said, a score—but the infectious excitement in her eyes as she bounced around from family to family, giving advice and tidbits on this animal or that. The excitement she showed when someone signed the final adoption paperwork, making that family feel like they'd solved world hunger by taking in a lovable stray. She took pictures with the new adoptees, informed them they would be featured on the shelter's blog—blog? They had a blog now?—and made each family feel like they'd saved a life. Which, of course, they had.

He resisted the urge to kiss her breathless as she danced up and handed him the paperwork. "Someone's taking Rambo, huh?"

"Yup. And while we're on the subject . . ." She jabbed his shoulder with a finger. "We really need to discuss your terrible taste in animal names."

"What's wrong with 'Rambo'?" The Doberman mix had seemed like a tough guy. Of course, after a few days, he realized he'd given a tough-guy name to a marshmallow.

"It's so stereotypical." She rolled her eyes. "You need to do better. Be more original."

"Tell you what." He dared a quick caress of her hair, running his fingertips lightly over the shell of her ear before pulling back. Her eyes closed briefly. The woman was hedonistic about having her hair and scalp touched. "You can name all the shelter animals from now on."

"Deal," she agreed quickly, then smiled before batting his hand away. The hand that had unconsciously reached in for another quick touch. "Stop that. We're in public."

"I'm not exactly pulling your top up for a quick peek," he murmured, and her eyes glazed over just a little. As if, with only the slightest encouragement, he could convince her to slip into a storage room and—

"Morgan!"

He winced. Nothing broke up a good lusty thought like your mother's voice calling your name. He glanced over Bea's shoulder and found Cynthia plowing through the crowd, waving a hand frantically in the air.

As if he wouldn't notice her, with the big shopping bags and small entourage of his sister, niece, and nephew.

Bea turned to follow his gaze, then her eyes widened. "Your mother, right?"

Christ. "Yes."

Bea's eyes darted around, looking for an opening to escape, he could only assume. But he grabbed her elbow before she could make a quick exit. "Mom, hey." He leaned down and brushed a kiss over her cheek. Meg flashed him a smile, while Andrea and Brent watched the goings-on of the adoption fair with wide-eyed excitement. Kids on Christmas morning, both of them. The adoption fair was where kids went to dream, and parents went to dread.

"What are you guys up to?"

"Just happened to be in the neighborhood," his mother said breezily. Meg, on the other hand, was mouthing the word "run" and rolling her eyes behind Cynthia's back. "I see that, Margaret."

Meg rolled her eyes once more for good measure, then bent to examine the nearest pen's occupant. A sassy Chihuahua that might have some poodle in him.

"In the neighborhood, huh?" He felt a slight, nearly imperceptible tug on his hand, and he stroked his thumb over the soft inside skin of Bea's elbow. Her struggling stopped. "What's in the bags?"

"We happened to run down to the feed store to pick up a few things. You know, just in case a fuzzy somebody struck a certain somebody's fancy." Her head tilted toward the kids, who were excitedly moving from pen to pen. "Meg decided to let them pick out a pet. Finally," she finished, whispering the last word. "But she wanted to see what the cost of one of these buggers would be before taking the final leap. Then we just got carried away with all the cute toys and collars and . . . oh, it was impossible to resist. We can return it all if they don't find someone today."

Andrea's shriek of delight from the corner warned that wasn't likely to happen.

"What kind of animal? Small dog? Medium? Cat?" Bea spoke for the first time, and his mother blinked and assessed her.

"Meg was thinking a cat," his mother said slowly. "Brent is still angling for a dog, and he might get his way eventually. But I know Andrea would love a kitten, and I think that's on Meg's agenda today."

"Sounds like Andrea might be the cat's main human."

His mother smiled at that. "Very likely."

"Is Andrea a quiet child? Does she like to sit and watch TV or read books for long periods? Or is she more likely to want to play and run and wrestle with a pet?"

"Oh, I think there's a good chance she and whatever pet they choose will both be exhausted by the end of the day," Cynthia said with a small smile.

Bea handed Morgan the forms. "I'm going to show her Trix."

"Trix?" He stapled the papers together and let them fall into the file box where they'd collected the forms all morning.

"The tabby, four months old?" She shook her head at him. "He's horrible with animal names. I'm taking over that part," she confided to his mother, walking toward the cat section. His mother followed easily. "I just decided this one is definitely not a Kitty. She's a Trix. And I think Andrea might be the love of Trix's life."

"Maybe," his mother murmured, and eyed him over her shoulder.

And hell. He was in deep shit.

★ ★ ★

Bea collapsed on the chair, staring out at the empty hall. The few animals they hadn't found homes for were already back at the shelter, and all that was left to do was to sweep up, put the tables away, and double-check the bathrooms. But for the most part, she was officially done for the day.

And thank God for it, because her feet were killing her. How was it in a building as small as this, with a town as small as Marshall, they'd been *that* busy?

Because she'd been damn good at her job, that's how. She smiled and let her head drop back so she stared at the high ceiling. Because she'd managed to create something good and real and helpful. She wasn't a blight on society after all.

Morgan's truck rumbled up past the windows, and she tried—she really did—to stand and finish cleaning. But her legs weren't listening. They were rather content where they were. And her feet were content to *not* be in the heels she'd been wearing all day.

"Bea?" Morgan walked in, glancing around the room before finding her behind the table, half-covered by the poster board of newborn puppies. His slow smile sent a ripple of . . . something through her. What was that? Wariness? Anticipation? Some weird mixture of both?

He walked toward her with those ground-eating strides, stopping a foot away. Then he shoved his hands in his pockets, as if he wasn't sure what to do with them.

"You did great."

The words, so simple, made her smile. "Thanks."

He paced down the table to the poster. "This was a good idea. I wouldn't have thought of it."

"We got several people wanting to know when they're ready to be adopted. I've got an e-mail list. Just let me know and I can send out the notification. In theory, we'll be swamped with takers. Those who don't nab one might like one of the other dogs from the shelter."

He picked up the clipboard holding the long list of e-mails. "And the newsletter signup . . . we don't have one, you know."

She smiled smugly. "You will, as soon as I have a few minutes to put one together next week."

He glanced around the room. "The blog?"

"Will be attached to the website at the earliest convenience."

Morgan nodded.

"Welcome to the twenty-first century, Morgan. Time to step up."

"Next thing you know, you'll have a Facebook page set up." When she flushed, he chuckled. "Or you already do."

"It's hidden," she said quickly. "Still needs finishing touches to complete it. It's just, you know, another way to share and advertise. And it's free."

"No need to get defensive. You're doing exactly what I asked. Above and beyond, really." Morgan set the clipboard down and faced her, his hands looping this time in the waist of his jeans. "It was a lucky day when I ended up hiring you."

Bea rolled her eyes and snorted. "Hardly. I'm a crappy receptionist."

"No, not at all. You care, and you're more organized than even I realized. You're scary-efficient, actually. Jaycee wasn't half as good with the tech stuff as you are. Like the program that e-mails appointment reminders? Brilliant. And you're adapting faster than I think anyone thought." When she raised a brow, he added, "The designer barn boots?"

"Oh, right. My boots." She smiled quietly. "I do like those boots."

He held out a hand, and she countered by holding up a

finger. First she slipped her heels on, then she placed one of her hands in his, allowing him to pull her up. He kept pulling gently until her body was flush with his. Her heels put her face just a few inches under his, so if she tipped her head back far enough, her lips could kiss the underside of his chin. But instead she rested against him, just let him hold her while they swayed a little.

It was intimate, the stillness of the room and their two bodies swaying together as if there was music surrounding them instead of stark silence. His breath moved the hairs by her ear, his chest rose and fell beneath her cheek. His body tightened, and she felt the stirrings of an erection, but he made no move to break the simple, almost chaste embrace.

"It was a lucky day," he said again, voice low, the words a rumble against her ear, "the day you sat down in that chair and answered that beast of a phone."

"It's not a beast. You're just not phone-capable."

He laughed silently, just a mere stirring of the air. "There's the truth of it." His hand cupped her chin and lifted enough so he could brush his lips against hers lightly. "Thank you for today."

"It's my job."

He kissed her again. "Thank you."

She looped her arm around his neck. "Am I always going to be rewarded with kisses when I do my job well?"

He deepened another kiss. "Maybe."

"Then I think I'll be a model employee." She opened her lips this time, darting the tip of her tongue to flick against his, inviting him in. Her hips shifted slightly, cradling his thick erection against her groin. If she lifted her leg enough to hitch around his hips, and he—

"Oh dear God, I did not need to see that."

Bea broke off the kiss at the sound of her sister's voice behind her. Oh God, how long had they been going at each other like that with people watching? She blinked to clear the fuzz from her mind before turning to face the foursome standing by the door. "What are you guys doing here?"

Trace grinned. "We were coming back to make sure there were no last-minute details or heavy lifting you needed help with."

Jo leaned against him. "And I was going to offer a round of drinks on the house to celebrate your success. But it looks like you two found a different way to celebrate."

Morgan cleared his throat, but then said nothing, only stood behind her. She glanced back, curious why he was gripping her shoulders so tightly, giving her no way to escape. Then his still-hard cock pressed against her lower back and she realized . . . he was hiding his boner. She snorted, both at the hilarity of the situation and at poor Morgan's discomfort.

"I think we're good. We can . . . celebrate on our own," she assured them.

Peyton plugged her ears and sang, "La, la, la, don't want to hear this, la, la, la."

Red guided her by the elbow to the door. "Come on, honey. Let's go soothe your delicate sensibilities with a drink at Jo's."

Trace and Jo followed, with Jo shooting a thumbs up and a wink over her shoulder before closing the door.

And once again, they were alone.

Morgan grinned, then reached out and captured her arm at the elbow, pulling her back in for another sweet kiss. His thumb drew circles on the thin skin behind her elbow. Her pulse raced in response.

"Come home with me," he whispered as he pulled back a little.

Come home with me. He offered it so easily, though she didn't imagine he offered often to women. He just wasn't the kind. Which would make her acceptance even bigger in his mind. Leading him on to something that wouldn't work long term. Could she be so callous?

"Come home with me." He repeated the request as his lips moved down her cheek, to the hollow below her ear. "Say yes."

His lips caressed, not a kiss but more of a non-teeth nibble. As if he was speaking silent words across her skin.

"Say yes."

No, she couldn't be so callous.

"Say yes."

She *could* be that weak.

"Yes."

Chapter Ten

Morgan heard the rustle of sheets before his mind could register what it meant. Then he smiled, and without opening his eyes, reached for Bea.

He ended up with a pillow instead, still warm from her body. Still smelling like her skin. He was about to open his eyes when light flooded in through his eyelids. "Christ."

"Sorry," she hissed and the light blinked out. "I just had to find my shoes."

Shoes? He sat up quickly. "Why? Does Milton eat shoes?" The dog had, of course, come along with Bea. When she'd shut him out of the bedroom so they could have their way with each other, the dog's whine had all but killed the mood. Not until she'd gone back out there, naked, scolded him and sent him to the blanket she'd brought in from her car and spread out in the kitchen had the whining stopped. And thank God for it.

"Of course not." Her voice told him she was shooting the *Seriously?* look in his general direction. "I couldn't have a shoe-eater on the loose. He would never."

"Of course not." Morgan ran a hand down his face. "You'd be out a fortune otherwise."

"Probably."

He felt the bed sink at the edge and he crawled over to her, looping one arm around her waist—a waist now covered with her shirt—and pulled her back against him. "Back to bed."

"I can't."

"Of course you can. It's not a school night."

She laughed, and hesitated, leaning back against him for a minute. Then she sighed and sat up straight again. "No, really. I shouldn't."

"We will agree to disagree on that fact." His fingers walked around his nightstand until he found his glasses. When he turned on the lamp, a much softer glow than the harsh overhead light, he found her completely dressed, shoes in hand. "Why?"

"Nothing to do with you, cutie." She kissed him quickly on the mouth. "I just need to head out."

"Unfair." He reached for her, but she danced out of reach.

"Plenty fair. You should be nice and worn out now. Back to sleep."

He sighed and swung his legs over the bed. Slipping his jeans on without boxers, he regretted his need to leave the warmth. "I'll walk you out, if you insist."

"I do. But you don't have to get up."

"I do," he echoed, and she smiled.

He waited for her to slip her shoes on, then led her barefoot through his small home. Milton trotted after them easily, the tags jingling on his collar like a merry bell.

There wasn't far to go. He'd designed the place himself, knowing there was plenty of room for expansion if and when a family came along. But for now, a single man who spent little time at home didn't need much space. It'd just be more to clean and heat. As they reached the kitchen, the cold tile had him hopping a little.

"Go back to bed." She kissed his shoulder. "I can get to my car, seriously. It's right there."

"But I'm doing it anyway." As the saying went, his

mama had raised him right. But right now, he didn't want to think about his mother, blissfully unaware of what her youngest child was up to half a mile away at the corner of their property. He wanted to think about Bea, back in bed, naked. Her warmed skin sliding over his and her lips forming the shape of his name while she let go of every inhibition and gave herself up to his loving care.

Morgan shifted one hip slightly to ease the sudden throb behind his zipper. Not smart.

"I insist you stay inside." She put a hand on his shoulder, and he captured it easily with his. "I mean it, Morgan."

"Then I insist you stay inside, too." He brushed a lock of hair out of her eyes. "Why do you need to be back at two in the morning?"

She glanced around, chewed on her lip a little. "I just do. I don't . . . sleep well when I'm not in my own bed."

Lie. Or at least a partial one. He could see it written all over her face. It hurt more than he'd expected, not just that she could lie to him, but that she wouldn't trust him with whatever it was she used the lie to cover.

Then again, they'd been lovers for barely over twenty-four hours. What exactly was he entitled to?

Relationship rules. He hated them.

"Okay then, so let's not sleep." He tugged her hand a little until she would look him fully in the eye. "I want you to stay. I want you to be comfortable enough to stay with me. I want to wake up and watch you still hazy with sleep while I slip inside you."

Her eyes widened, and he managed not to grin at his own ballsy little monologue. He'd never said anything like that to a woman before in his life. Something about Bea just made him bolder.

"Now, will you stay?"

She narrowed her eyes a little, as if calculating, then patted his chest. "I'll think about it."

Good enough for him. He crushed her to him in a kiss. Her hips pressed against his, rolling over his erection in a way that had his eyes crossing behind his closed eyelids. God almighty, she knew exactly how to stir him and make him feel like an idiot.

When one of her legs hitched around his waist, he took the invitation. With one hand on either cheek, he hoisted her butt up until she could wrap the other around him. One of her heels fell to the tile floor with a clatter, startling the annoyed Milton into jumping back. He walked her back to the bedroom, careful around the door frames, and laid her on the bed. And when he came over her, she smiled into his face.

"You know I'll still probably leave, right?" she asked quietly.

"You said probably, not definitely. So I'm calling that progress."

She shook her head in amusement, then kissed his nose and slipped his glasses off. Before she set them down, she used the corner of her pillowcase to polish the lenses.

That little habit of hers drove him crazy . . . with lust. That sweet, unconscious little gesture of caring. It told him she wasn't nearly as unaware of the needs of others as she liked to play at.

He kissed her again, then jerked upright as a sharp set of nails scraped along his lower back. "Dammit!"

"What . . . oh. Milty! No." Her voice dropped low as she scolded the black-and-white pest currently worming his way between them. The dog's jaw rested on her breast, and he stared at her with an expression that said, *Surely you didn't think you could just forget about me, did you?*

"Go to your blanket," she said sternly.

The dog blinked, the tip of one ear flopped.

"Go, now."

He sighed, but did as she asked. As if in final protest, he

farted as he reached the doorway before leaving for the kitchen and his designated spot.

"That dog," Morgan said, "is a more fearsome guard dog than any Rottweiler. If just for the gas alone."

"He has his moments." Bea framed his face and kissed him. "Now where were we?"

He balanced on one arm, using the other to unbutton her shirt and peel the sides away. "Right about here." His fingers traced over the sweet baby blue–colored lace of her bra. A bra he knew matched her panties. She was a sucker for lingerie, she'd told him earlier. Couldn't get enough of the pretty stuff, even when she was sure nobody would see.

He loved that about her. That it didn't take a date, the possibility of a man, to make her want to be beautiful for herself. He leaned down and used his teeth to tease her nipple through the thin lace. "This bra matches your eyes. Deliberate?"

"My eyes are one of my best features," she said on a moan. "Why wouldn't I work with what I've got?"

He nipped just a little harder, which had her eyes flying open before closing slowly again. "Good point." He slid a hand behind her, fumbled just a little, then unclasped the tiny hooks between her shoulder blades so the bra went slack. He eased it away and took the puckered tip in his mouth again, without the lace barrier.

Her hands sifted through his hair, and her hips drove up against his thigh, searching for friction. She was a woman who wanted what she wanted, and she wanted it now.

Morgan was more of a long-term game player. Much like in a game of chess, he derived his pleasure in the now by imagining what it would do to the game twenty moves from now. And what he knew for sure was that Bea wanted him as much as he wanted her. And slowing things down would force her to consider their exchange as more than a few good bounces on the mattress.

But there was a time for slowness, and a time for *oh God he couldn't wait*. Her hand pressed against the side of his temple, her other hand presenting her other breast to his mouth as he clamped down and drew her in.

"Morgan, God. Morgan." Her hands moved down his back, fingertips barely skimming the waistband of his jeans. She couldn't reach them to tug them off, he knew. He was too tall. But that was a damn good thing, since the second his pants were off, he was going to be inside her.

"Now, please." Her moan fired his blood, made him want to crow with pleasure and the thrill of it. But he refrained. He did, however, ease a hand down to her own waistband and unbutton it, pushing the panties down with the pants. Unlike the bra, no fumbling here. She kicked and twisted and aided his efforts until she was completely naked. And her body was a sinful temple he needed to better explore. She whispered his name again, more a question, a plea, than anything. He loved the sound, loved his name coming from her lips.

His lips cruised down from her breast to her ribs, nipping with teeth every so often. Not ticklish. Interesting. He moved down to the inside of her thigh, close to where she wanted him, but not quite there. Her labored panting said she was a woman on the edge. Which he always appreciated. And when he nudged her legs wider and found her wet center with his mouth, locating that pleasure center with the tip of his tongue, she sighed and nearly choked on the next gasp of inhaled breath.

"There. Right there. Faster, please."

Vocal, and absolutely sure of what she wanted. He loved hearing her talk, loved knowing without question what she needed from him. He hummed his understanding, which vibrated through her. Her stomach tightened under his hands and he gave her what she wanted. And her thighs nearly popped his shoulders out of their sockets when she hit her climax and squeezed around him.

Bea couldn't breathe. She tried, but it was like the air was just out of reach and she couldn't draw it in. Morgan's hand crept up from her stomach to her chest, rubbing in soothing circles over her breastbone.

"What's wrong?"

She couldn't answer, and not just because she had no air. She had no clue. It wasn't the orgasm, though God, it had been good. It was . . . panic? Was this a panic attack?

Slowly, she realized she'd started breathing again, but not quite in steady draws. She forced herself to visualize. See the air in, see the air out.

When that worked, surprisingly, she reached for the fly of his jeans. "Off. Let's go, cute vet."

"Cute vet, huh?" His voice held a smile in the dark. "Wanna talk about it?"

And see if she would start crying? Pass. "Pants off. That's what I want to talk about."

He hesitated a fraction of a second, then stood up long enough to slip his jeans off and grab a condom from the bedside table. Captain Prepared. Very considerate that she hadn't had to remind him. Points for Morgan.

But when he slid alongside her, then rolled her over him until her center sat directly over his erection, humor gave way to heat. "You want me up here?"

"I want to look at you and watch you. So yes, I want you up there."

He unnerved her with his way of making things so simple. The man who stuttered and blushed when she gave him sexy glances in the office was in control and cool in bed. Reaching down, she guided him to her and sank down over him. Her back arched in automatic response, her hands reaching back to rest on his hair-roughened thighs. The angle sent him deeper. And then he moved.

Bliss.

Her position didn't give her much room for motion herself, but she squeezed around him and loved the way his hands gripped her hips so tightly. Loved how one crept up her side until it cupped her breast and played with her nipple again. Loved that, as he gained the edge on her in the race for the end, his other hand worked down to her clit and circled the bud with his thumb to nudge her along.

And that was all she needed to explode. Sparks shot off behind her lids. She sat upright while the orgasm took over her body, let it roll through her. Dimly, she was aware of Morgan's own climax beneath her. And then it was quiet and still again.

She slithered down to rest her head on his shoulder. "That . . . was good."

He chuckled and kissed her forehead. "Yup."

After a minute of quiet recuperation, he slid out from beside her and headed to the bathroom. And now was her chance to make a break for it.

Did she want to? Would that hurt him?

And wow, had they already reached a place where she could hurt him like that?

Her head said no. Not after two days. But her heart knew better. He was invested. And she was going to ruin the lovely dream for him.

Best to set the score straight now. She heard the toilet flush, heard running water. She reached down and found her pants, panties still stuck inside, and slipped them on together. The shirt was easy. The bra . . . missing somewhere. She'd get it later.

He opened the bathroom door as she was fixing the last

button. He propped a shoulder on the frame, arms folded, and watched.

"I need to . . ." She gestured toward the kitchen.

He nodded, then grabbed his jeans. It was an odd parody of the scene from an hour ago when she'd tried to leave. But this time, she was getting in her car, come hell or high water.

He didn't try to convince her this time, just helped her out to the car and opened the door for her.

"Thanks, cutie." She kissed his lips lightly. "I'll see you Monday."

He nodded.

She waited, but he didn't add anything to the conversation, so she got in and started the car up. As her headlights flashed against the side of his house, illuminating the shirtless, shoeless Morgan in the process, she had to fight against the urge to throw the car in PARK, toss herself out, and beg him to let her stay the night.

Stupid. Just stupid. She was starting to sound as mentally dramatic as sweet, stupid Trixie, the reformed prostitute of *The Tantalizing and the Tempting*. And that, for the love of God, was unacceptable.

"Milton, we've got to get ourselves together."

He whined in the backseat, pissed at her for the screen she'd put up between the front and back seats to keep him from crawling up to her lap. Morgan had lectured her on the safety of pets in the front seat. And since he was attached to her at the hip, the screen was the only way to keep him back.

"Get over it, bud. It's safer back there, for both of us."

He whined more, snorting a little and sounding like an upset potbelly piglet.

"Nothing doing, bud. I'll spoil you to the end of the earth with sweater vests and dog booties. But you're not riding in my lap while I drive."

He settled down as they turned into the M-Star drive a few minutes later. Convenient, really, how close Morgan was.

Yes. Convenient. Booty calls were convenient, weren't they? That's how she could look at this. She was temporary, and he was a guy. Guys liked sex. Ergo, this would work out in the end. He was a wonderful man, and he'd find a wonderful woman someday and they'd have cute kids and raise a litter of whatever the pet of the week was. But she was headed back to LA, back to the life she knew, back to the only one that made sense.

She pulled up next to the garage, where her apartment was, and climbed out. Milton scrambled out the back when she opened the door and sprinted off to relieve himself. While he sniffed and marked and did his manly leg-lifting thing, she glanced around the ranch.

This didn't make sense for her. She wasn't raised to want this. She was raised to want what she'd had before.

So she'd fulfill whatever obligation she had here. Stick around long enough to annoy Peyton into ripping her hair out. And when she was ready, she'd go back.

Her shoulder blades itched, and she knew it wasn't from her bra clasp . . . which was still somewhere on Morgan's floor. She brushed the feeling off and clapped a hand on the side of her thigh. "Milton, come. Mama needs to go for a quick ride."

Chapter Eleven

Bea watched as Trace walked his horse back into the stables and started the process of unsaddling, hanging tack, and grooming the big gelding. After a quick hesitation, she stepped into the dim lighting of the stable. It was rare enough for anyone to see Bea in the stables as it was, rarer still in the daylight with other people around. Witnesses.

As she passed Lover Boy's stall, he poked his head out and reached for her with his muzzle. She paused and gave him a caress. But when he got feisty, nibbling at her arm, she pushed back. He was begging to be let out, to go for a run. Like the one they'd taken last night. "No, not today."

"Today? That one's always trying to take a chunk outta me."

She swallowed a gasp and turned to see Tiny, one of the older hands, watching her. "I didn't know anyone else was in here."

"Oh, someone's always around." He watched her quietly for a moment. "You usually aren't, though. Did you need something?"

"No." Too fast. "No," she said slower. "I'm fine. Am I in your way?"

He shook his head, reminding her of a saying she'd heard before. Men will never use ten words when one will do.

"I was just . . . looking for my brother," she tried again. Lame. Very lame. But something. She was losing her bullshit skills.

Tiny angled his head deeper back. "With Lad."

"Of course." She stepped away, ignoring Lover Boy when he nickered and reached for her again. *Sorry, boy. Later.*

Trace's back was the first thing she saw, then Lad's bent neck. She watched her brother's slow, even strokes over the horse's flanks and sides as he brushed away sweat and dirt from their early morning workout. They were practically a set, those two. She'd watched them more than once from the main house, though she'd have denied it if anyone caught her. Her brother was good, damn good, on a horse. His time riding the rodeo circuit had been a waste, as far as she was concerned. Busting broncs and riding for eight was a true waste of his true talents on a horse. At M-Star, he was a fantastic partner to Peyton's horse sense and business mind.

"Slumming in the stables?" he asked without looking up from his task.

"Oh, you know me. Bored, looking for trouble." Give 'em what they expect. Then they never look deeper. She stepped up on an overturned bucket—balanced with experience and skill on her high wedges—and watched the horse's front legs. One was steady on the ground, the other bent just slightly, as if the horse was hip-shot like a cocky man. Those legs were unbelievably delicate looking to carry such weight. Not just the horse's own, but another two hundred plus in rider and tack. It always amazed her how perfectly created the animals were to their given task.

"Where's your bodyguard?"

"My what?" She snapped out of watching the gelding's legs and looked at Trace. He was looking at her now from identical eyes to hers and Peyton's. The one physical trait all three of them shared.

"Milton."

"Oh." She smiled. "I dropped him off with Emma and Seth after breakfast. When I left the big house, he and Seth were in a game of hide-and-seek." She grinned to think about it. "Milton was winning."

"No kidding." Trace smiled at the mention of his son. He was a fantastic father. And though Bea didn't begin to understand kids, especially babies, she could recognize when a child was well-loved and lucky.

Must be nice, to have a father so devoted to you and your childhood. And that was pathetic, envying Seth because her brother loved him and spent time with him. *Grow up, Bea.*

Trace finished grooming while she watched. Neither spoke. After he stepped out of the box, handing Lad a treat from his pocket, he brushed his hands and hooked an arm around her shoulders. "Take a walk?"

"Sure." Anything to keep her from breaking out her phone and texting Morgan. She needed a bit of distance there.

He led her out back, behind the stable and workout areas toward the hay fields. They stared for a minute, their backs to the main property, looking out at the vast landscape. No other buildings in sight from this angle.

"Still shocked it's ours?"

"Hmm." She leaned her head on his shoulder a second. "It should have been Peyton's."

"So why don't you just give her your share?"

She huffed out a laugh. "I'm selfish, remember?"

Trace squeezed her arm.

Another minute passed.

"Come riding with me."

"You just finished," she reminded him.

"Finished a workout. I meant a ride. A nice, lazy one. We can give a few of the mares a good stretch."

She chewed her lip.

"I'll saddle your horse for you. All you have to do is go change." He glanced down at her, as if seeing her for the first time. "You're wearing jeans."

She rolled her eyes. "I wear jeans often."

"No, but those are real jeans. Not fancy ones with glitter or artistically torn holes or ones so tight you might split a seam bending over or whatever. Are those . . . are those Wranglers?" His voice held a hint of mocking awe.

She stepped away and punched his shoulder. He let her. "Bite me. I'm sick of my nice clothes being ruined out here when I walk around."

He watched her, inviting her to elaborate.

"Why didn't you offer me one of the geldings to ride?" His brows rose. "Like who?"

"Like Lover Boy." What perverse impulse was leading her down this rabbit hole?

Trace shook his head. "He's too high-strung. I mean, he's not impossible to control, but not for a novice like you. One of the older mares to start."

Jesus. Next he'd put her up on a swayback carnival pony for toddlers. "I can handle him."

"It's not a matter of will, but skill." He shrugged a shoulder. "You haven't been on a horse in years, right? I barely remember Daddy ever setting you up in the saddle. It wouldn't be responsible to—"

"I ride every night."

His satisfied smile told her everything she needed to know.

She screwed her eyes shut and turned to look back out over the hay. Why, oh God why had she taken the bait? Trace was always the best at baiting her. Better even than Peyton.

"Bea-Bea," he said softly. She shook her head. "Bea, don't be childish. Look at me."

She ignored him.

"Come riding with me. In the light. Go get your boots on and let's just go for a good hard run."

She itched for it. Her 3 a.m. run the night before had only taken the edge off her restlessness. "No, thank you. How did you know?"

"I saw you, a few months back. I'd been wondering who had been using my tack, since it had been moved from where I left it the day before. Didn't figure it was you, though."

"Peyton is too small."

He laughed at that. "True. But how about we get you your own?"

The idea of her own tack, her own saddle, both thrilled and terrified her. It was so . . . open. So personal, but so obvious. Like a big neon sign saying *I've been faking it.* "I don't know."

"You can keep it at your place, bring it out when you wanna ride at night." He hugged her. "I don't know why you feel like you need to keep this a secret."

"I don't want to get into it with Peyton. She'd wonder why I don't help out around here."

"Why don't you?"

She elbowed him in the side, satisfied with the *oof* sound he made.

He rubbed a hand over the area. "You're still vicious, Bea-Bea. But I love you anyway."

She went into his hug, happy to have that small weight off her chest.

"You should tell her," he murmured. "She'll want to know, and she'll want to talk about it."

"Maybe." No. "It's not a big deal."

The small hitch in his breathing told her he disagreed, but he kept mum.

For the moment, it just felt good to have her brother with her, and no secrets between them.

Morgan laid out the condiments on the table of his mother's dining room. They were eating in the sacred room not out of a wish for formality, but for simple size. The kitchen table didn't offer enough seating for his parents, him, his sister, and her family. As they'd added people to the mix, they'd been forced into the rarely used dining room out of sheer necessity. And his mother's sewing machine had found its way into his sister's old room, now converted into her woman's cave, as Cynthia called it.

"No placemats, Morgan," she called from the kitchen. "Last time the kids just fought over who got what color. Not worth it."

The kids. He smiled a little, then fought back his own pang of longing. It wasn't worth thinking about. One day, he'd have kids of his own, and he'd be the one rolling his eyes while they fought over stupid crap, like which placemat to take and who wasn't touching who on car rides.

He tried to imagine Bea as a mother. His mind sketched her in a typical outfit of his sister's: loose jeans, one of her husband's T-shirts, and her hair in a haphazard ponytail that usually looked like it was one good head shake away from falling.

Then he smiled. Nope. He knew better. Even at the height of difficult child rearing, Bea would be fashionable. Or as fashionable as practicality allowed. It was just her thing. Some might call it high maintenance. Hell, Bea would likely claim being high maintenance with pleasure. But he just considered it one of her quirks.

He liked her quirks. They made her who she was.

His mother brushed past his stone-still frame and set a basket of dinner rolls on the table. "Why are you frozen in the way? Something wrong?"

"Nope." He smiled and kissed the top of her head as she walked by. "Not a thing."

She wiped her hands on the dishcloth over her shoulder, but eyed him warily while working on the potatoes on the stove. "I've been hearing some surprising things about Beatrice Muldoon."

"Have you?" He sat down at the kitchen table and watched while his mother competently juggled three different dishes at once.

"I have. I heard from Millie Stanler—she's got that old Golden you had to put down last week?"

"I remember." Poor thing had cancer, and was older than Moses to boot. And even knowing it was the best thing for the poor dog, Millie had been a sobbing wreck. Not that he blamed her. He felt a tickle in the back of his own throat every time he put an animal down. He avoided it whenever possible, but it still got to him.

"She mentioned Beatrice was there at the desk after . . ." She stirred a pot of peas for a moment. "Millie said she got in her car and sat behind the wheel and cried for twenty minutes in the parking lot. And when Beatrice noticed, she came out and sat with her. Just sat, then asked about what old Reggie was like as a pup. How long they'd had him, what he liked to play, that sort of thing. Got her through the worst of it to think about him young and healthy again and remember why it was his time to go now."

His heart constricted a little. She noticed, and cared, so much more than she let people believe. "What part was surprising?"

"Maybe that she would recognize Millie needed someone to talk to. Beatrice seems so self-absorbed half the time, like she wouldn't realize if someone was drowning in front of her face. Not a malicious lack of empathy, but just a bred-in-the-bone lack of awareness for others."

Morgan's fists clenched and he started to say something, but his mother went on.

"But maybe even more surprising was that she'd even realize what to say." His mother tapped the spoon on the edge of the pot and laid it aside. "I've known Millie since we were girls, and all I could say was 'I'm sorry' and 'If you need anything, call me.' But that only seemed to make her cry harder. Millie made it sound like Beatrice was her savior that day. That she wouldn't have been able to drive home without their talk."

His hands relaxed a little. "Again, what was surprising?"

His mother shot him a sardonic glance. "She seems to be quite good at hiding this part of her, isn't she?"

He nodded, quiet for a bit. Why was that?

"Seems to me," she continued, not waiting for him, "that a woman who can be that deceptive might not be good for a man."

And there it was. The real reason for the conversation. "Good for me, you mean."

"I love you, Morgan—"

"Ho, boy," he muttered.

"—but I worry about you. Your own heart is too open, too ready to be drop-kicked and torn to shreds. It's wonderful when it's animals. They don't have a manipulative bone in their bodies. What you see is what you get."

He raised a brow.

"You can't say the same for Beatrice Muldoon, can you?" She opened the oven a smidge and checked her roast. "That girl's got secrets. Secrets aren't good for a relationship. It's just not a good way to start things off. That's all I'm saying." Her speech concluded, she turned her back to him and worked on dinner.

No way to avoid it now.

"Mom."

"Hmm?" She took a smaller spoon out and tasted the potatoes, setting the spoon in the sink after. "Needs more garlic."

"Mom?"

"Hmm."

"We're involved."

That got her attention. "Beatrice?"

"Bea. And yes, we're involved. Romantically. I appreciate your wanting to spare my feelings and save my heart from any damage, but you're wrong about her. She's not out to manipulate me. She's a good person. She's a person I trust fully. And wherever our relationship goes, however far it takes us, I'm hoping you respect her and respect us together."

Cynthia pursed her lips, then took in a breath as if to say something. But he was spared from the lecture when Andrea burst in through the back door. "Grandma! You'll never guess what my kitty did yesterday!"

His mother's face immediately lit up as she opened her arms for a big hug. "You'll just have to tell me, now, won't you?" But when she looked up over Andrea's lopsided pigtails, she shot him a look that said they weren't done yet.

"Thank you, sis," he muttered, and headed into the den with his father. The safety zone.

Chapter Twelve

Bea stopped by the main house early the next morning, determined to have a pleasant conversation with Peyton if it killed her. Or Peyton. Yes, if it killed Peyton, they would have a decent, healthy, normal sisterly conversation over her grapefruit and Peyton's bacon fat.

As she walked in, Milton zoomed straight for the dining area to his place under Seth's high chair. The dog was a vacuum. One of the few times he never whined when out of her sight was when he was with Seth. Bea had worried early on that Milton would be too rough with the child. And then, as Seth grew, she worried the toddler would be too rough with the dog. But they seemed to have an easy relationship, full of fun and understanding of each other's limits.

Maybe it was just something the "verbal" crowd wouldn't understand.

"I see the dog, and . . . oh my God." Peyton's voice was sharp enough to cut through steel. "Is that damn dog wearing a freaking bow tie?"

"It's dapper," Bea said, entering the room. "Mondays are dapper days."

"Mondays are Mondays." Peyton stuffed another piece of bacon in her mouth and chewed a little before saying, "You're here."

"Should I not be?" She popped into the kitchen quickly to grab a bottle of water and an apple from the basket on the counter. A grapefruit sounded wonderful, but Emma wasn't in the kitchen and she was too lazy to slice it up herself. She seated herself in front of Peyton, to the side of Seth. "You babysitting?"

"Trace had an early start this morning. Steve hurt himself last night."

"Oh no." Bea frowned before taking a bite of the apple. Steve was their youngest hand, and a doll. He had a puppy love crush on her, which she was flattered by and not at all interested in returning. But it was cute, and he was a sweetheart, as well as a good worker. "Is he going to be okay?"

"Just pulled a few muscles in his back. Didn't start feeling the pain until late last night. Finally had his mama drive him into town this morning for the doctor. He'll be okay, but he needs some rest." Peyton sighed a little. "Puts us in a bind, though."

"How so?" When Peyton arched a brow, she shrugged. "I'm interested."

"He was going with Trace this coming weekend to a small event. It's just a two-day gig, nothing special. But see and be seen, right?"

"Right," she murmured. "Can nobody else go? Tiny?"

"Busy with me."

"Arby?" Their ranch foreman, whom she'd always avoided because he was too wise for her own good.

"Doesn't travel anymore. Claims he's too old." Peyton rolled her eyes at that.

"So then, are you just sending Trace alone?"

"I guess. Red can't go. He's gotta stay back with me since we have another client coming by this weekend, and Red's the connection. I almost thought about pulling out of the event, given how small it is. But Trace said he could handle it himself."

Bea chewed another bite, then played with Seth's food a little. She nudged the Cheerios out of his way so he had to fight to grab them, giggling all the while. She might not get kids, on a basic level, but when she wasn't expected to hold them, change them, or be in charge of their general welfare, she could be amused by them. And as far as kids went, this one was pretty darn adorable.

"I'll go."

Peyton's fork clattered to the plate, still full of pancake. "Sorry, what?"

"I'll go. With Trace. I can probably take Friday off. I mean, maybe half day." She chewed her lip and tried to visualize the week's schedule. "Maybe. Do you think he could leave late afternoon on Friday?"

"No."

"Oh. Well, then I could drive separately, I suppose. Seems like a waste of gas but—"

"No, you aren't going."

Bea swallowed the hurt. "Afraid I'll mess something up?"

"I can't answer that without pissing you off, so I'm going to plead the fifth." With that, her sister picked her fork up and shoveled the bite of carb-loaded pancake in her mouth.

Bea's fingers drummed on the tabletop for a minute. "You said it was a small event."

"Yeah."

"And I take that to mean not many people?"

"Most likely."

"So if I screw up, there's not much I could do to damage our reputation, right?" When her sister said nothing, Bea sighed. "I can just be a helper. Keep my mouth shut.

Hold his space when he's out doing his thing, take names, write down information. I'm good at that much, or I wouldn't still have my job at the clinic. I'm not talking about saddling up and riding out there to make an ass of myself."

Peyton side-eyed her as she snatched Seth's sippie cup in midair before it hit the floor and Milton took off with it. "Why?"

Bea glanced around, shuddering once at the gold-tipped everything in the dining room. Ick. "Because this was my home, too, once. And I'm a Muldoon, dammit. I can do this. I just need the chance to prove it."

Peyton chewed another bite, scowled when Seth swept a handful of cereal down to the floor for the ever-hopeful Milton. "Then fine. Take your chance. But you won't have fun. This isn't a hotel with room service and a spa you can waste your time in. You'll be dirty for most of the weekend, crashing in the bunk of the horse trailer or the back of the truck's cab. You'll be exhausted and you won't know the first thing that's going on."

"Okay." She took a sip of her water to hide her smile. God, they really thought she was worthless. And while she didn't quite have the courage—or maybe just the desire—to share her riding habit with Peyton yet, she was looking forward to seeing the expression on her sister's face when she figured out Bea wasn't so helpless and dainty as all that.

"Just okay? No backing out, no excuses, no begging for a hotel?" Peyton gaped.

"Just okay." She stood up and walked to the kitchen to toss the apple core into the trash. "I can do it."

"I'd like to see that," Peyton said.

Bea let that go. But as she walked by the foyer, her gaze couldn't help snagging on the tacky gold-plated statue of . . . was that supposed to be Satan? She tilted her head this way, then the other, but the art still made no sense. How long had that ugly thing been there that she'd gotten so used to its presence she'd never even considered what it was supposed to represent? Taking out her iPhone, she snapped a picture, then took a few more.

Research time.

Morgan rolled into the clinic parking lot right behind Bea. He watched as she spent the time checking her reflection in the flip-up mirror on her visor, watched her drum her hands on the steering wheel a few times, watched her . . . sing? He grinned. Singing and moving her head around like she was in the middle of a karaoke battle for her life.

Nice.

She stepped out of her car, and he watched the shoes—a sexy navy heel with red polka dots—emerge first. She did know how to choose her footwear. It made a man's blood hum, thinking about her with those heels on. Just those heels.

And this was exactly what he didn't need . . . an erection at his own clinic. He shifted from foot to foot until the ache eased a little.

Milton sprang down when she opened the back door, prancing forth to greet him with a bow tie collar this morning. "He's fancy."

"It's Monday," she said, as if that explained exactly why her dog was wearing a bow tie. He chose not to question the reasoning.

When she reached him, a bottle of water in one hand, purse in the other, her glasses pushed up on top of her head, he simply reached out and caught her around the waist. Her startled look lasted only a second before her lids lowered and she slipped into a sultry, knowing smile.

"Morning, handsome." She leaned in and kissed him lightly. When he pressed for more, she stepped back. "Lipstick."

"Right." Feeling a little like a teenager meeting his girlfriend at her locker before walking her to class, he hurried to get the door. "How was the rest of your weekend?"

She paused as she stepped through the doorway. "Interesting."

Should I have called you? Would you have wanted me to?

Might as well ask her to the prom next. Dammit, Morgan. Get it together. You're an adult. Act like one. "Anything fun going on at the ranch?"

She walked in and set her water bottle down on the desk, dropped her purse in the bottom desk drawer. "Steve hurt his back, poor thing. So he's out of commission for a while. Not that it would normally be a big deal. Seems they have a million hands roaming around at any given time. But there's an event this weekend and . . ."

He watched her mouth, wished she hadn't put on lipstick this morning so he could lean in and take a healthy bite. Soothe that bite with his tongue. Drag her into his office for a real, healthy, down-and-dirty morning make-out session. Best part of waking up, and all that.

"Morgan."

"Huh?" He blinked and looked up at her eyes. They were smiling at him, along with that sexy mouth.

She shook her head a little, then reached for his glasses and polished them on the corner of his still-untucked shirt. Her knuckles skimmed the skin of his stomach before she was through. He resisted sucking in a breath. "I was asking if I could have Friday off."

"Friday off?" He took the glasses and blinked as she came back into focus.

"Or just the half day," she rushed on. "Maybe an hour

or two in the afternoon? I'm going to double-check the appointments and see if I can juggle something around but—"

He kissed her again, quickly, before she could protest. "It's fine. I'm just curious why, if you don't mind me asking."

She narrowed her eyes. "So you really did tune me out earlier. I'm going with Trace. To the horse event thingie. Whatever they call it."

Now he wondered if it was his ears, not his lenses, that needed cleaning. "You're going with your brother . . . to a horse thingie?"

"Event. Whatever." She waved a hand at that, like it was no big deal. Sure, cowboys gathered around and competed in thingies all the time. "The fact is, I'm going. I've told Peyton I would, and so I am. I want to be helpful. This is me being helpful."

He wanted to ask more but wouldn't. She was taking steps, all on her own, to become more a part of the family. This was a positive thing. He waited until she sat in her chair, then kissed the top of her head. "You can take Friday off, the whole day. No problem at all."

She smiled at him, as if he'd given her a gift in a Tiffany's box. "Thank you. I'll juggle what I can appointment-wise to make it easier on you."

"Not a problem." He headed for the shelter, determined to get something done before he had his first patient of the morning.

"Morgan?"

"Yup." He looked over his shoulder.

"Hope you got all that kissing out of your system, because you can't pull that crap in front of clients."

He grinned and gave her a thumbs-up before heading into the shelter and greeting their remaining guests.

★   ★   ★

"I'm going to assume you consider this a grand adventure or some crap like that." Trace pulled into the parking lot of the arena. Bea's back teeth rattled as he hit as many pot holes as he avoided on the rut-filled road to the back, where all the trailers were parked.

"I don't—don't think it's—anything but me he—helping out. I wanted—wanted—oh for God's sake!" She crossed her arms and stared straight ahead.

"Wanted what?"

She shook her head, pointing forward resolutely. This wasn't a conversation to have when she was worried her back molars were going to slam together and shatter. Stupid road.

He laughed, but kept going.

Bea braced a hand on the dash, wrapping the other around the *oh, shit* bar. Through clenched teeth, she muttered, "If the airbag on this piece of junk deploys and breaks my nose, I will never forgive you. My face is my job."

"Relax, this thing doesn't have airbags." She gaped at him, and he laughed harder. "Your job is answering phones at Morgan's clinic, in case you forgot."

"That's my temporary job." She loosened the grip on the bar long enough to roll her shoulders. "My real job is back in LA."

"Which you haven't really seemed to miss much. I mean, you talk about it, but you're not making any moves to go back. Why is that, Bea-Bea?"

She stared straight ahead, watching the dust fly up and surround the truck in a fog.

Trace sighed and pulled the truck carefully into an open spot. "You trusted me with your riding, didn't you? So why not trust me now with this?"

Because it was embarrassing. Failure was always embarrassing. She merely shrugged. Childish, so childish. But she couldn't quite bring herself to admit, out loud, that her acting career was a flop anyway.

They didn't get rid of actresses they liked by pushing their characters down elevator shafts. And the evil identical twin bit? Totally fell through.

Trace hopped out and went around the back to check on Lad. Bea opened the door and started to step out, stopping herself when she remembered. Time to put on the Wellies. She'd worn boots with her jeans, yes. But they were nice, not barn boots. So she quickly switched them for the appropriate pair and hopped down.

The smell hit her first. The overwhelming smell of horses and dry dust and, well, everything else that went along with horses. She dodged a pile of road apples—yuck—and watched Trace lead Lad around to stretch out his legs. "What should I do?"

"You can start unloading the tack, if you wouldn't mind. I need to take him for a quick ride just to get the cobwebs kicked out. Plus, I want to check the layout of the area. Then I'll go put him up."

She started hauling the tack out from its secure place on the side of the trailer. There was a stable, which was where Trace said he would be sleeping tonight, with Lad. Apparently many of the stables came with cots for the cowboys. But she would take the trailer's bunk. The thought was a little unnerving, sleeping in a parking lot by herself. But also sort of thrilling. Like camping, but not.

"Do you want me to get him saddled?" she asked as he led Lad back her way. "Do you need to go check us in or anything?"

"Yeah, would you mind?" He held out Lad's leading rope. "I'll be back soon. These things take all of five seconds to register for, if there's no line."

"I've got it!" She smiled with confidence and waved while he disappeared, then said, "Hurry back," under her breath. Giving Lad a long stare, she fessed up. "Okay, look. Here's the deal. I've been doing this whole saddle thing for a while. I'm good. But I've never worked with you, and you've never dealt with me. So let's get through this with little to no drama and we can cross it off our bucket list, all right?"

Lad blinked at her, as if saying he was completely bored by her monologue.

"Because Lover Boy, while a great horse, isn't quite worth the same as you, monetarily speaking, I mean. He's worth a lot to me, but . . . never mind. Why am I explaining myself to you?"

He wuffed out a breath through his nose, as if to agree, *This is pointless.*

"Fine then. Let's just get to it. You stand there like you are and we'll be done."

As she crouched down to grab the saddle blanket, the shadowy outline of a man came up behind her. "That was fast."

"Is that a compliment?"

She gasped and whirled around, standing up at the same time, nearly bumping into the man behind her. He grabbed her arms to steady her. A few inches shorter than she was, he was still solidly built and had no problem keeping her on her feet. "Didn't mean to scare you."

"Sorry, I thought you were my brother." She stepped back from the man's hold, though it wasn't rough or scary. She just . . . suddenly didn't feel right having another man touch her, even in such a simple way. "Can I help you?"

"You can start by introducing me to this handsome guy." The man reached out a hand, palm up, for Lad to sniff. Bea took the moment to inspect him.

In his late forties, maybe early fifties, he was a man who took care of himself. Not a weekend cowboy, but the real deal. However, he wasn't the kind to just throw on a chambray shirt and a pair of dusty jeans and be ready to go like Red or Trace did. The man dressed in style, if "cowboy" was a recognized style. Jeans that fit his frame well, a shirt that wasn't campy, but also didn't scream "rodeo," and a hat that looked like it'd seen years, but was still clean and presentable. But the boots . . . those were a thing of beauty. Designer, for sure, not something to wear riding out. He was interesting, well put together, and still a real cowboy.

"This is Lad," she said, holding on to the horse's halter loosely. Just in case. She wasn't as familiar with the working horses as she was the ones she could ride. No sense in taking a chance. "He's four years old, and an amazing work of art."

"Work of art, huh?" The man stood quietly, just letting the animal absorb his presence. "I'd say that's probably true. You two make quite a pair, just based on sight alone. How long you had him?"

"Oh, he's not mine. He's my brother's." She pushed some hair back from her face, and the man's eyes tracked the movement. She had a feeling those eyes, hawk eyes, rarely missed anything. "But together, they're magic. His name is Trace Muldoon. We're with M-Star ranch."

"M-Star, huh." Moving slowly, with the grace of a panther, the man moved to Lad's other side and stroked a hand down his neck. Lad shivered in pleasure, tail swishing once. "What kind of operation you running there?"

"Breeding and training. Our trainer, Redford Callahan, is—"

"Red?" The man bent down a little and looked at her from under Lad's neck. "You've got Red with you?"

"We do." Pride, though she'd had nothing to do with the hiring of Red, swelled for her family's ranch. "He stays because he knows a good thing when he's involved in it."

The man chuckled softly. "Nice sales pitch."

"Truth needs no sales pitch." He laughed again at that. "Are you here competing?"

He stepped around to Lad's front again and eyed her for a moment. Then he held out a hand. "Jefferson Montague."

"Nice to meet you, Jefferson." Should she have called him Mr. Montague? He didn't seem like the kind to stand on ceremony. She shook. When he didn't hold her hand longer than normal, she gave him points.

He kept watching her, as if expecting her to say something. What, she had no clue. So she coughed and filled the silence. "Are you going to be here all weekend?"

"I am." He nodded, gave Lad one more look, and stepped back. "I've got to head on back to my own camp. But I'll be sure to watch for your brother and this one out in the ring."

"You do that. I hope we can talk again some more, later!" She shot him a brilliant smile. A feeling of accomplishment warmed her. It wasn't a sale or anything so important. But mingling and keeping your name in people's minds was another part of the game. And this was a part she could play easily.

Trace headed back a few minutes later, just as she was finishing the last cinch on Lad's saddle. "We're all set. We can stay parked here, and his stall is number eleven."

"And you're sure you want to stay with him all night?"

"Positive. The bunk is all yours." He grinned and double-checked Bea's work. She wasn't offended. Anyone would have. Being properly saddled was just too important to trust to others entirely. "Thanks for that. Any troubles with him?"

"Nope. He was a perfect gentleman." She rubbed a hand over the space between Lad's eyes. "Go stretch your legs, both of you. Then maybe I can run and grab some dinner for us."

"I'm all over that." He swung into the saddle easily, tipped his hat, then headed off for a quick ride.

I can do this. I am worth something to this family. With that thought, she walked in the direction of the stadium to find groups of people. Time to mingle and do her part.

Chapter Thirteen

Morgan walked Pepper, the cocker spaniel with a penchant for eating pennies, and his owner to the lobby and left them with Jaycee, who was back to playing receptionist between patients for the day. "Jaycee, Pepper needs to come back in about a week if things haven't, uh, progressed with the pennies."

"Got it!" Jaycee waved to him and he started back for his office. Friday had been mostly cleared out but for the few stragglers who couldn't reschedule, and one penny-loving pooch. All in all, a pretty restful day. Which was fortunate, as he'd had several new guests show up for the shelter via the sheriff and a few good citizens. Time away from the clinic had given him a chance to process them in, check them out, and make sure they were healthy. After a quick quarantine, a round of shots, and a temperament test, they'd go up for adoption.

"Morgan?"

He popped his head back out from his office. "Yeah, Jaycee?"

"There's someone here to see you. I put her in exam room one."

His heart raced at the thought of Bea. *She's out of town, you moron. Get a grip.* He walked out and found a Muldoon female in the room. Just not *his* Muldoon female.

"Hey, Peyton. What's up?" At the jingle of a collar, he glanced down. "And Milton. Hey, buddy."

The dog pranced over and sat obediently for a rub.

"Something wrong with him?" Automatically, he started checking for any tender spots, examining his eyes, checking his gums for anemia.

Peyton blew out a breath. "Hell if I know. He's making enough racket to have me thinking something's wrong."

"Like what? Sharp cries?" Morgan's hands retraced their steps, checking each leg, each paw for sore spots or discomfort. "What's going on, boy?"

But Milton's bug eyes just stared at him with adoration, if a little confusion.

"If nothing's wrong, then he's just an asshole." Peyton tugged the end of her braid, as if she was ready to rip her hair straight from her scalp with her bare hands. "He whines nonstop. He won't eat—"

"It's been less than a full day," Morgan said wryly.

"Have you *seen* that monster eat? The dog doesn't leave a crumb behind. He cleans his bowl with his tongue. Missing breakfast is a big-ass deal."

Silently, Morgan agreed. But when he picked Milton up, the dog allowed it without a single whimper. Just snuggled his cold snout into the crook of his neck and sighed, like this was his master plan all along.

"Maybe he just misses Bea."

Peyton huffed. "Miss someone who dresses him up in stupid outfits and shoes and treats him like a baby instead of a dog?"

"She rescued him," Morgan said quietly. He scratched behind Milton's ears and his stub tail started to wag. "She's his mama, for all intents and purposes. His pack leader. She was the one who saw something in him, took him out of the cage, and gave him something nobody else had before."

A home. He saw from the softening of Peyton's features, she understood. But she refused to admit it out loud. "Well, he needs to stop. Emma is about ready to punt-kick him out the door, and I can't get any work done. Even Seth doesn't want anything to do with him like this. He keeps saying 'doggy no no' and covering his ears." She glared at him. "Do something."

"I'll keep him. It'll be a full house anyway, since I have to take a turn with the abandoned puppies. Their foster parents are out of town this weekend, too." With the docile Boston's eyes closed and his body limp, it was hard to deny him anything. "She comes home tomorrow?"

"Probably Sunday, if Trace makes it through to the end of the events. They'll be done too late Saturday to drive back." Peyton narrowed her eyes and scratched Milton's back. "You little shit. You're just like your mommy. You manipulated all of us to get what you wanted, didn't you?"

Milton unapologetically farted.

Bea turned for the nineteenth time onto her left side, groaned, then rolled to her back and groaned again. The mattress—if you could call the pitiful excuse for padding a mattress—was so thin and lumpy she could feel the bones in her back crying. As she rolled to her right side, she was face-to-face with a cold metal wall.

Not quite the Ritz. The horse trailer in the parking lot of the middle-of-nowhere town was almost worse than her first apartment in LA. And a lot less steady. She put a hand on the wall as the trailer swayed gently with the breeze. All the negatives of a cruise ship and none of the charm.

Rolling to her back once more, she gave up the idea of sleep. There were three viable options here.

One, she could take the truck and go check in to a local motel for the rest of the night. Bea immediately disregarded that idea. It was too much like quitting. And there was no way in hell she was quitting. She wouldn't give Peyton the satisfaction.

Two, she could go see Trace in the stable and stay with him and the horse all night. Not quite quitting, but not exactly ideal either.

Or three, she could call someone and make them talk to her until she was too tired to care *where* she was sleeping or how uncomfortable she was.

She grabbed her phone from her bag.

After two rings, Morgan's sleepy voice answered with a grunt, and a rusty "Hello?"

"Hey-ya, cutie." When he mumbled something, she frowned. "Did I wake you?"

"No. Yes." He sighed heavily. "I think I might have passed out on the kitchen floor."

"Might have?"

"Okay, did."

"What are you doing sleeping in the kitchen when you've got a perfectly decent bed down the hallway?" The thought of his bed sent a pang of longing through her. Not just for his specific bed—though she'd really enjoy that . . . with him in it—but for any bed that wasn't in a rocking trailer that smelled like horse and hay. Firm ground, please.

He didn't answer, but someone else did.

She'd know that pathetic whine anywhere. "What's Milton doing there?"

"How the hell did you...? Never mind. You and this dog have a very odd connection. And I'm babysitting him."

"Aww, you're babysitting my baby?" She grinned at that. "Very sweet. Though why doesn't Peyton have him? She agreed to watch him."

"He apparently missed you so much he brought everyone in the house to their collective knees with his whining and carrying on. He does better with me. Seems to associate me with you." The smug pleasure in his voice was unmistakable. "Smart dog."

"Smart dog, indeed," she said quietly.

"I gave him the pillowcase you used the other night. I hadn't gotten around to laundry yet. He's been sleeping with it on the blanket you left here for him. Your scent seems to keep him from freaking out too much."

"But that doesn't explain why you're sleeping in the kitchen."

"I've also got a box of puppies here. Their foster parents went out of town this weekend, too, and I agreed to take them. They're on wet food now, but they still have to go out every few minutes, it seems like. And then they want to play with Milton, and they get all riled up and—"

"I get the picture." The image of Morgan lying flat on his face on the kitchen floor while a bunch of ragged puppies crawled over his body like a jungle gym had her stifling a laugh. "And Milton is okay with them?"

"He loves them. They think he's the king of the castle, and any attention he shares with them is worth celebrating."

"Sweet. But I'm sorry they're keeping you up."

"I need a mom for the kids. Someone to trade off kid duty," he joked. His laughter trailed off into deep breathing, and she was almost positive he'd fallen asleep.

"Morgan?"

Nothing but the soft sound of breathing and dog snorts.

"Morgan," she said, but whispering this time. If he really was asleep, she didn't want to jolt him back awake. When he said nothing, she ended the call and slid her phone back in her purse. The man was adorable.

But a mom for the kids . . . Was that a subtle poke at her? Or was it just a joke he hadn't thought twice about and she was reading too much into it?

Yes, of course it was. Get a grip, Bea. Being too touchy. She'd blame it on the lack of sleep herself, and being edgy in the trailer alone. Morgan wasn't the kind of guy to play subtle tricks. If he wanted to say something, he'd say it. His natural lack of sneakiness wouldn't let him handle it any other way.

She let the image of him with the puppies and her own dog lull her into sleep, with a smile on her face.

Bea watched as a competitor rode out of the arena and clapped politely with the rest of the crowd. Her hands were dusty, and she coughed to the side at the smell. Lord, she needed a shower. Two showers, and then a bath, with a nice lavender bath bomb and some exfoliating scrub . . . Who knew just being around the arena would coat her in a layer of filth? She'd never gotten so dirty just slipping in and out with Lover Boy for her rides. Must be the excess dust from all the horses running around together.

She sat off to the side a little. Though she'd met others during the day, they didn't know her. And they had their own groups, their own cliques to sit with. A few men had sent her what she could only assume were *inviting* glances, but she wasn't even thinking twice about that. Better off on her own than accidentally leading a man on. That was fine, she didn't mind. Her focus was on Trace and Lad and their showing up everyone else in this next round. M-Star had a reputation to build, and that was the first order of business. Not sitting around making friends.

The bleacher underneath her butt vibrated and she glanced up, shading her eyes a little. The man from the day before, Mr. Montague, was heading straight for her. She bit down the urge to sigh and instead waited politely for him to approach.

"Mind if I grab a seat?"

She indicated the bleacher and he sat, a respectful distance away. Not crowding her, not where their knees could brush against each other. She liked that about him. That he wasn't constantly trying to find ways to touch her, like other men did. "How are you today, Mr. Montague?"

"Oh, you can call me Jefferson, Ms. Muldoon."

"Then it's Bea to you." She returned his easy smile, then watched another horse and rider enter the arena. "Do you have a horse in the competition today?"

He watched her a little, as if he couldn't believe she'd asked that. Was she missing something here? Then he shook his head. "No, I don't."

"Well, good." She grinned and reached down to her bag to grab her sunglasses and slip them on. "Then I won't offend you when I cheer on my brother and root for the others to score low."

"No, that you won't." He chuckled a little, then asked her about her job at M-Star.

"It's not a job, really." Her hands felt a little clammy, and she resisted the urge to wipe them on the thighs of her jeans. "I'm really just helping out while I'm in town. I live out in California mostly."

"Do you show any of the horses? Do any training?"

"That's my brother and Red's area of expertise. I'm more involved in . . . the business side of things. Marketing and advertising. Support staff. That sort of thing." Warming to the idea, she went on. "I'm the marketing director for M-Star." *God, forgive the lie.*

"Marketing director, eh?" He leaned back and propped his shoulder on the seat behind them, spreading his arms out. But again, not touching her or reaching over for some slick, creepy move. "For a smaller operation, that's a new one."

"It's a big part of ranching these days, I think. Maintaining the authenticity that comes with a home-grown operation, while attempting to take on a grassroots marketing approach in a corporate-driven world." Holy shit, had she just said all that?

He nodded absently. "I think you're right. So tell me more."

And . . . shit. "The operations are run by my sister, Peyton." Fighting the urge to roll her eyes, she went on. "She grew up on the ranch, same as Trace and myself. But now the ranch is growing up with her at the helm. She's got a wonderful understanding of the business and of horses in general. And when she brought Red on, it was magic in the making."

"Simple, effective. I like family-run operations. They're more honest, most of the time. Easier to meet halfway."

Bea and Jefferson clapped again as the contestant rode out of the arena. Then Bea let out a huge whoop as Trace entered through the gate. She stood, waving her hands in the air and yelling his name in excitement. And . . . whoops. She sat down abruptly, the metal clanging beneath her feet. "Sorry. I got a little carried away."

His expression said he was amused, not annoyed. "No problem. I understand the feeling."

Bea watched Trace and Lad. Her butt was on the edge of the bleachers, her fingers curled into the seat, her knees bouncing with anticipation. Each motion caused another hitch in her breath. Each quick jolt of the horse's body had her hand creeping up until she covered her throat. And when the announcer called time, she sagged with relief. Being so tense was exhausting.

"They make quite a pair."

"I know it." She couldn't help the stupid grin on her face. Her brother was unbelievable on a horse. She'd have called him a god, but that would go to his head. "He's amazing. And to think, that is the same boy who used to pull my pigtails and call me snot-face."

"When you were kids?"

"Last week."

Jefferson laughed, shoulders shaking. "Another rousing endorsement."

"Well, hey. If that performance can't speak for itself . . ." She shrugged. It was magnificent. Anyone could see. What more could she say? "Thank you for keeping me company, Jefferson." As she stood, so did he. She held out a hand. "I have to go meet my brother now."

"You give him my card when you see him. And here, one for you and for your sister. You need anything, you give me a call." He slipped three cards, plain white with simple black lettering, into her left hand while he shook her right. And then he gave her one more assessing glance.

"I think people underestimate you, don't they?"

She blinked. "Maybe."

"You're more than you seem, even to yourself, I'd bet." He winked, then headed back down the aisle. She watched, mesmerized, as he stopped to talk to several people, shaking hands, clapping a few men on the back, but never fully pausing. People parted to make way for him.

Who the hell was he? Moses?

She shook off the feeling she'd missed a memo somewhere and scooted to find Trace in the back. The cards he'd handed her went into her back pocket for another time. She'd just hand them over later.

But her feet were light as she strode over the packed dirt. Her first horse contact. And she'd brought him in herself. The feeling of worth expanded in her chest.

Morgan blinked and fumbled for his glasses on the nightstand. What the hell had woken him up at . . . three in the morning? He quietly surveyed the room, but all it was filled with was the sound of Milton snoring like a chainsaw at the foot of his bed. How could something that weighed twenty pounds be so damn loud and smell so damn foul?

And why was he in the bed? Morgan nudged the dog with his foot, but the mutt didn't budge.

"Your mother is going to kill me for letting you sleep up here."

Milton was peacefully unaware of Morgan's predicament.

The flash of headlights in his window told him there *was* a reason he'd woken up. And it was driving up to his house now. No need to panic or worry. If there'd been an emergency, he'd have gotten a call from someone. It was likely Bea, back early from the trip and coming to pick up her precious, gassy bundle of joy.

Or maybe, she had thoughts about spending the night. The idea warmed his insides and he slid out of bed, looking for a pair of pants to slip on.

The soft, tentative knock made him smile, until the moment the brain-splitting yipping started. Not Milton, though he gave a low moan of his own. But the puppies responded with a sharp intensity that had him cringing.

He raced to the door, dancing around the wriggling fuzz-butts that were heading straight for the kitchen door to greet the newest thing in their lives. When he opened the door, he did so only a crack.

Bea stood under the weak porch light, looking confused and guilty. "I'm sorry, I didn't think before I came. I just . . ." She blinked, brows furrowing a little. "I just came."

"It's fine. But if you're coming in, you have to be fast. I can't hold them back for long." He opened the door only as wide as he thought he needed, then grabbed her upper arm and hauled her through before shutting it firmly behind her.

Bea's eyes widened; then her gaze dropped to the ankle

biters congregating around her boots and she cooed. "Oh, sweet darlings. Look how big you've gotten!" With that, she dropped on her butt and let the dogs swarm her. Roly-poly bodies tumbled and trampled each other to be the first into her lap. She laughed and gave each some undivided attention, praising them one by one. They were so smart, so sweet, so beautiful.

Milton, predictably, stood off to the side seething and whining while waiting his turn.

Morgan watched, and soaked her in. Her hair was pulled back by an artfully folded scarf. She wore a button-down work shirt that was a little big on her, as if it might have been Trace's and she'd borrowed it. Her jeans had mud streaks on them, and her boots weren't fashionable so much as serviceable.

She was dressed like a rancher. But was it her? Or just a part she felt like playing for the weekend?

And that was uncharitable. The fact was, it didn't matter. She was there, with him, and that was what mattered.

"I thought you weren't coming back until tomorrow."

She glanced up quickly before being attacked on the side by a jealous pup. She picked the dog up and held him at eye level. "You just need to learn some manners, like my own Milton."

At his name, the dog crept forward a step, then two. She scratched behind his ears and his stub tail wagged. With the delicate caution of a cat, he stepped between wiggling puppy bodies until he could climb up on her thighs and press his nose into her neck.

If it wouldn't have been so ridiculous, Morgan would have done the same thing. He was tired of waiting his turn.

"I know, I missed you, too," she crooned and rocked him like a baby. "But that was definitely not a place for you. I don't think it was a place for me, either. But I showed Auntie Peyton, didn't I? Yes, I did."

"Let me get these guys outside for a break and then we can talk." Morgan grabbed the pile of leashes and started clipping leads to collars. They all got tangled up and generally made a mess of it, but they were all secured. He wouldn't lose anyone. Milton never strayed far enough from his side to need a leash. Not out at his house.

Bea watched while he guided the flopping, easily excited batch of puppies outside in hopes they would take the hint and do their business outside. Milton aided in the efforts by providing a good example, watering a bush like a pro. Two puppies took the hint and pottied outside, receiving copious praise and a treat. The rest just played.

Morgan sighed and brought them back up the stairs. Bea was still sitting on the floor, and they swarmed her once more. She scratched bellies, rubbed heads, and gave each one some love before shooing them back into their makeshift pen. When Morgan turned the kitchen lights off, they almost immediately took the hint and fell into sleep. Puppies had two speeds . . . on and off.

Bea scooped Milton up and carried him over her shoulder to the bedroom. Morgan found her struggling to toe off the boots with a curse.

"Damn boots. This is why I wear heels. They're practical." When he laughed, she scowled at him before sitting down to take them off. Milton scampered to the middle of the bed, circled three times, and burrowed into the warm blanket. Clearly, she was making herself comfortable. Morgan stripped off his jeans and let them land back on the floor before sitting on the bed beside her.

"I thought you weren't coming back until tomorrow."

Bea let her second boot fall with a thud and turned to look at him. "I wasn't going to but—" She narrowed her eyes, then sighed and reached for his glasses. Polishing the lenses on the corner of her shirt, she said, "You really need to carry some sort of rag with you."

"You're probably right," he murmured when she slipped them back on. First time he'd seen clearly in two days. "But then I couldn't do this." He reached through her arms to kiss her unexpectedly. She laughed and pushed him back.

"I wasn't going to come back, that wasn't the plan. But Trace was dying to see Seth. Though, as I reminded him, the kid was sleeping."

"Just Trace being a good daddy." He kissed her again, and she pulled him in this time. Her hands crept up his bare chest and looped around his neck. "Will you stay tonight?"

The tip of one finger traced down his jaw, dipping into the cleft of his chin before following the line of his throat and over one shoulder. He shivered a little. She smiled, a knowing, sensual smile.

"I think I can be persuaded."

Chapter Fourteen

Morgan knew in that moment, with the way Bea looked at him, he would have given her the world if she'd just asked for it. Climbed mountains, swum oceans, any other physical cliché he could have thought and mentally mocked himself for later. But when she smiled that siren smile at him, he was completely lost.

"But first, I need to shower." Bea grimaced and stared at her hands. "I'm not feeling quite clean enough for sex."

"So we can have dirty sex." He kissed her before she could complain. "And then we can have clean sex. Variety."

She laughed, but pushed against him and walked to the bathroom.

Morgan followed, helpless to do anything else. When Milton started to weave between his feet, he pointed to the folded blankets in the corner. "Bed."

The dog glared, but did as he was told. Thank God.

He found her staring at her reflection in the mirror, a little horrified, a little amused. She brushed one hand through her hair, then stared at her fingers.

"I used to have pretty hands."

"You still do." He grabbed them and laced his fingers through hers. "Feel this?"

She winced when he rubbed a thumb over a small, nearly imperceptible callous on the tip of her finger.

"That's strength. You're strong. Strong is sexy. Weak is for fools. I would never want a weak woman the way I want you, Bea." He kissed the side of her neck. She smelled a little dusty, a little like she'd spent the day in a horse barn—which, of course, she had. And he found the scent just as appealing and arousing on her as her expensive perfumes and lotions and sprays. Which only meant one thing . . . her. She was what aroused him, in any state.

He reached down and pulled her shirt up and over her head, tossing it into the bedroom. His fingers brushed against her long, lean torso, from just under the bottom of her bra to the top of her jeans. His hands were just long enough, if he spread his fingers wide, for his thumb and pinky to cover the space. He watched in the mirror, and the possessiveness of his hands on her flesh, holding her to him, shocked him.

Bea's eyes closed a little and she leaned back.

"So tired."

"I know, baby. Let me help."

He unbuttoned her jeans and pushed them down. She stepped out of them, almost automatically, as if in a daze now. As if now that her weekend was officially over, her brain had shut down to reboot and would be back online later.

Time to evaluate. Was she even capable of going further? Was he an ass to push for more? Should he just turn on the shower, finish helping her undress, and leave her to it?

Bea answered the silent debate by reaching around and molding her hand over his cock through his pants. And hello . . . game on.

Morgan pushed at her panties while she turned in his arms and latched her mouth onto his. She nibbled and bit and licked while he managed, barely, to get both of them as naked as possible. Okay, yeah, so her bra was sort of hanging off one arm, and her panties were draped around one ankle. But he was about to be a beggar, so he wasn't going to be choosy.

Bea hopped up onto the counter, just beside the sink, and pulled him in between her knees. Perfect fit. Morgan grabbed a condom from the pack he'd bought and stuffed in the drawer earlier in the week—with the intention of replenishing the nearly empty stash in his nightstand at some point. Lucky for him, he hadn't quite yet.

And then he was in bliss, moving inside Bea, listening to her gasps and moans and whispers of his name. She made him feel like a god. Or, not quite, but pretty damn close.

It was over almost before it started, and he would have been embarrassed if she hadn't been coming alongside him. Her back arched away, her head rested on the mirror, and he thought she was the most glorious thing he'd ever seen in his life.

Her hand slipped off his sweat-coated shoulder and landed on the faucet, turning it on full blast and splashing them with cold water.

"Shit!" He jumped, pulling her off the counter with him and setting her down on her feet on the warm bathmat. She leaned against the shower wall and laughed.

Clean up, clean up. He didn't want to clean up while she was still standing there, mostly naked and laughing like a sleep-deprived loon. What to do . . . He snatched the hand towel from the ring on the wall and laid it over the puddle on the counter. Good enough.

"You, get in the shower."

She saluted him, still chuckling, and turned on the water hot enough to steam the small bathroom in under a minute. He winced at the thought of boiled skin, but she only sighed in pleasure when she stepped under the spray. He watched, transfixed, as her silhouette moved behind the shower curtain in a graceful, feminine sort of dance.

It felt almost intrusive, and he broke his gaze away to clean up the bathroom more efficiently, so when she was ready to step out, he waited with a towel.

"I can do that," she said and held out a hand.

But he ignored her and dried her off himself. She didn't put up a fight, only let him gently buff her skin until she was dry enough for bed. Then he picked her up and edged out of the bathroom to the bedroom, where he laid her on the bed naked.

She snuggled down and sighed like she'd never felt a real bed before. "Oh, mattress. How I've taken you for granted."

"Horse trailer not to your liking?" He turned the lights off and climbed in next to her, pleased when she rolled into him to cuddle.

"Absolutely not. I'm glad I did it, so I can neener-neener Peyton for being wrong. But oh, I don't wish that life on anyone."

"It wasn't exactly a third-world country, Bea."

"Close enough." Her voice was quieter, and he could feel her body growing more lax.

"Are you glad you went?" he asked.

"Yes."

In the dark, he smiled while listening to her breathing.

She mumbled something, and he cocked his head to hear better. "What?"

"You called me strong," she said on a sigh, and fell asleep.

Bea opened her car door and waited for Milton to hop in. He settled himself in the shotgun seat like a dignified passenger.

"Get in the back, bucko."

He stared straight ahead.

Selective hearing. The ailment of men. She sighed and slid in behind the wheel. Morgan leaned over, one arm draped over the door, the other propped on top of the car.

"I'll see you over there."

"I know how to get to my own house. You really don't have to follow me there." The thought made her nervous. This was why she avoided spending the night. Because the next morning was always more awkward than leaving in the dark and forgetting your bra or lipstick.

"I want to make sure you get home. And besides, maybe I wanna see Trace, or hang out with Red for a bit." He kissed her before she could argue, then closed her door for her. She wanted to roll down the window and argue some more, but he was already climbing into his own pickup.

With a reluctant sigh, she did some contortionist moves to toss Milton in the backseat and set up the guard to keep him there, put the car in REVERSE, and headed down the short dirt path that was his driveway, onto the main road that would take her to the M-Star entrance in about five minutes.

The puppies were gone, which was a relief—given their penchant for getting up every three hours for a potty break—but also a little sad. Darn things were so cute. And Milton was saddened by their departure, too. He'd sat by the kitchen door and whined for almost an hour after their foster mother had dropped by to grab the rascals early in the morning. Apparently they were charming everyone, even their temporary caretaker, as she'd already picked one out to keep when they were ready to start being adopted.

And now here she was, with a tagalong for Sunday brunch. Because, of course, the second anyone from the family realized he was on the property, it wouldn't be possible for them to hole up in her apartment. Nope. The family would insist she bring him up to the big house for a meal.

And so what? She glanced back at Milton.

"Could you at least fake a little concern for my predicament?" she grumbled.

Milton licked his nose.

"Yeah. Just like a man." She huffed out a breath. "Though I don't know why I expect you to care. You don't even have balls. It's not like you're getting any. You can't really relate to the situation."

Bowing to the inevitable, she turned three minutes later toward the main house rather than her apartment, parking next to Peyton's Jeep. Morgan pulled up a minute later, his truck completing the interesting lineup. Four work vehicles, and then her and Jo's more sporty cars. Because really, when would she or Jo ever be hauling bags of feed?

Bea waited for Milton to hop down, then closed the door and followed the dog up to the porch. Morgan hovered by the hood of her car, as if unsure.

She held out a hand to him, pulling him with her. "Come on. Emma's probably got some sort of amazing meal in there that will make me gain twenty pounds just looking at it."

Morgan slapped a hand lightly on the outside of her hip, jolting her. She looked up into his grinning face. "I doubt that's true. But even if it was, you would be stunning anyway."

She snorted, but bit the inside of her lip to keep from smiling. There was a change from California. A man who wouldn't mind her being something other than her size two.

Okay, four.

And a half.

★　★　★

Morgan stepped into the warm smells of home. He'd always been welcome around the Muldoon property as a
child, hanging out with Trace in the barn or dogging one
of the hands or Trace's father and shadowing their every
move with the horses. Curious boys and livestock, a clas-
sic combination.

But the big house had never been especially tempting to
him. His friend, the young Trace, rarely wanted to be in
there. Rarely wanted to eat lunch with his family, insisting
they do so with Morgan's parents at his house. Or that they
sneak food out and eat in the hayloft. Morgan remembered more than once wondering why he was never allowed in the house.

And then he'd met Sylvia. The woman had the natural
maternal instincts of a dirty sock.

She'd scared the crap out of Morgan, simply from the
hard-edged look she'd carried. The snarl just waiting to
pounce on her lips. The fact that she seemed ready to kick
when someone was down rather than hold out a hand to
help them up. The exasperated glances that said kids were
the most horrifying creatures ever to exist. Trace had escaped outside with his father and the hands. Peyton had
followed.

But Bea . . . Bea, he remembered, had stayed in. By
choice, or by design? Had she disliked her upbringing, or
had she been glad to have her mother's sole attention, despite the woman's lack of caring?

It might have been wrong to think ill of a dead woman,
and one who had met her end in such an abrupt, tragic
way. Nobody wished that kind of a car wreck on anyone.
But he couldn't help wonder how being with her day after day had influenced Bea and her views on relationships,
and life. And he wanted to go back and rescue that little
girl, whether she thought she needed it or not. Wanted so
badly to have insisted they drag her outside to roll around

in the dirt, to have changed her life back then, rather than waiting until now.

"We're here!" Bea shouted as they stepped into the front door, using the bootjack like a pro to wiggle off her boots into a pile by the door with the rest. "I brought company."

Milton sprinted in ahead of them, tags jingling, darting straight for the dining room. The dog rarely left Bea's side, except for one thing. Food. Specifically, bad-for-him people food. For food scraps, he would abandon all pride and beg.

He heard Seth's squeal of happiness at seeing one of the dogs inside the house. A rarity, if he recalled. Dogs were for working, and stayed in the barn. Having a dog inside would have been against Emma's rules of the house. One of the few things Emma and the aforementioned Sylvia would have agreed on.

Bea waited for him to remove his own shoes before walking with him into the dining room. "It's just Morgan."

"Just Morgan," Emma scoffed as she settled a platter of what looked like French toast on the table. Morgan's mouth watered as Emma put her hands on her hips and surveyed him. "Eaten breakfast yet?"

"No, ma'am. I'd be grateful if you'd include me. That smells heavenly." He shot her his best, boyish *pity me, I'm a bachelor* look. Which was true, but still mostly bullshit since he could cop a meal off his own mother any day of the week.

Either it worked, or she was already intending to let him stay. "Sit down and eat a piece. You can have her share. She won't eat any of it." Emma tilted her chin at Bea, who was already sitting down and reaching for the juice pitcher.

"Actually, I think I might have a slice."

Peyton's hand froze mid-syrup grab. "It's got powdered sugar on it."

"It's a carb," Trace added helpfully.

Bea made a shocked face. "Oh my God. No! Never mind then. I didn't realize French toast could possibly be a sugary carb! Thank you for saving me."

Morgan sat beside her and took matters into his own hands. He two-fingered a steaming hot piece from the top of the stack and plopped it onto her plate, then shook his hand. Hot hot hot. "There. You have to eat it now. It's on your plate."

Bea sniffed, but didn't remove it. Instead she started cutting it into tiny pieces so small the baby could swallow three at once without choking.

Morgan grabbed two of his own, some bacon, and a mug of coffee from the carafe. "How is everyone this morning?"

Jo smiled, swinging her jet-black hair over her shoulder. "Oh, we're just fine. How are you two this morning? You both came in together, so I assume that means you—ow!" She backhanded Trace on the shoulder. "No pinching at the table."

Emma set a bowl of fruit on the table and slapped him on the back of the head. "No pinching at the table."

"Damn women." He rubbed his head, then leaned over and quietly said to Jo, "I'll just pinch you later. And you'll like it."

Jo smirked.

"Peyton," Red said conversationally, passing her an orange. "I missed the memo. Should we be more public with our displays of affection?"

"Hell no." Peyton set the orange aside and drowned her toast in syrup. "Don't make me gag." Peyton slid the bottle of syrup to Bea, who stared at it a moment, as if making a very serious choice.

"You can have some syrup. I promise you won't gain ten pounds from it."

She shot him an evil look that swore restitution, then drizzled a thin stream of syrup over the tiny pieces of French toast. It was the most decadent thing he'd ever seen her eat, and even then she didn't go hog wild with it.

"How's the bar, Jo?" Morgan asked, changing the subject.

"Great. We're looking into expanding a little, actually." She beamed, pride in her business radiating from her. "Maybe add some patio seating. I think it'd be a great draw, and not many places around here have that. Completely impractical for the winter months. But for the summer . . ."

"True." Morgan nodded. "I'd be game for a nice lunch on a patio with one of those big shade umbrellas. I might be inclined to get a pitcher, actually, to beat the heat."

"Exactly." She nodded. "That's what I'm hoping. More people relaxing and unwinding. Seeing people right out in the open enjoying a pitcher after work, and getting the idea they need to do the same thing." She wiggled her eyebrows. "Always looking to bring in the moo-lah."

"My woman's got a head for business." Trace kissed her temple, and she leaned into it. Her long ponytail brushed over Trace's arm as he wrapped it around her side to pull her closer.

Peyton mimed gagging onto her plate. Red just didn't look up from his breakfast. And Seth clapped, as if he was a critic watching little theater. Somehow, Morgan doubted *Yo Gabba Gabba!* was this interesting.

Jo leaned around Trace to touch her finger to the tip of Seth's nose, which sent him into a thrilling laugh, playing keep-away with his nose and her hand.

Morgan smiled at them, knowing it hadn't been easy for Jo to be so comfortable with Trace's son. She wasn't a natural kid person, but she *was* a kind person. It had just taken some time and confidence to make the two ends meet.

Did Bea want kids? Morgan stared at the bite of French toast on his fork, dripping syrup back onto his plate. Why did that question suddenly tighten his gut and make it feel like there was no room left for breakfast? He shouldn't be asking himself this yet. It shouldn't matter. They were having a good time, and that was enough for her. It should be enough for him, too.

And even as he forced down the bite of toast, washing it down with a swig of coffee, he knew he was lying to himself.

Chapter Fifteen

B ea took a timid bite of the French toast. *Do not like it. Do not get used to it. Do not crave the sugar.*

Oh my God, this is like an orgasm on a plate.

She took two more quick bites, hoping nobody watched her eat like a starving dog tossed a hambone.

"How was your first rodeo, Bea?"

She nearly choked at her sister's question, and took a sip of juice before she looked up. Peyton's face was bland. No hint as to whether that was sarcasm or not.

"It was much more fun than anticipated." After a moment of mental struggle, Bea put the fork down and grabbed the orange Peyton had set aside. She started to peel, and told herself the citrus smell was just as delicious as the sugary, cinnamon-maple scent from her abandoned plate. "I handled myself pretty damn well. Sorry, Seth. Earmuffs."

Trace pointed his fork at Peyton. "She's right. She kept up. You were wrong. You owe me twenty dollars."

"We didn't bet money on anything," Peyton said.

"Fine. I'll just take twenty dollars then."

She rolled her eyes, but looked back at Bea. "The trailer didn't cramp your style?"

"Well, I wouldn't use a horse trailer as my primary residence. But it wasn't that bad." The small white lie flowed so easily from her tongue, it could have been scripted for her. As was the innocent look she gave Peyton.

"What crap." Peyton took a huge bite of bacon and chewed obnoxiously, as if trying to make Bea jealous of her artery-clogging breakfast choice. "I bet you were whimpering for your Manolos and room service after ten minutes."

She bit into the first slice of orange. The tang woke her senses up a little, and she was refreshed and ready for a good, healthy sibling squabble. Bring it on, sister dear.

"How would you know what Manolos are? I thought the biggest designer name you knew was Old Navy."

Peyton picked up a forkful of French toast and ate it slowly, closing her eyes and savoring the taste.

Bea did the same with her next piece of orange, licking the juice from her fingertips.

Peyton dropped her fork in disgust. "Why can't you just admit you didn't like it?"

"Because that's not true. Don't you dare feed that dog a piece of bacon, Red. He has a sensitive digestive system," she added without looking away from Peyton's face.

"Scary," Red murmured and returned the piece of bacon to his plate.

"She was a help, Peyton," Trace put in. "She helped saddle Lad, and kept an eye on the stuff while I was gone. Anything I would have asked Steve to do, she was up for it. And it was nice seeing a friendly face in the crowd while I was waiting for my round."

"I'm sorry, you let her saddle one of our horses? Are you nuts? She can't even tell the difference between the flank and the forelock!"

Trace opened his mouth, but when Bea shook her head slightly, he closed it again and stared at his meal. Now was *so* not the time to open that can of worms.

Seth, picking up on the mood, started whimpering and ping-ponging his gaze from adult to adult. Jo stood and unhooked him from his high chair.

"Come on, little man. Let's go upstairs for a little play-time. The adults have some discussing to do. Maybe when we come back down, they can all act like mature grownups again." She kept her tone light, but her eyes shot daggers at both her and Peyton.

"She started it," Bea mumbled. Peyton kicked her under the table. "Watch it, shorty. I have a longer reach."

"You better not have talked to anyone important while you were there," Peyton warned.

"Killing the precious Muldoon family name? I think our mother already tried her hand at that one."

The color in Peyton's face bled out, but Bea refused to feel sorry for the comment. "You wouldn't know about that, would you, since you left and didn't come back. Not until Sylvia was dead and you had a shot at some money from the property."

"So sorry for wanting a life to call my own," Bea shot back. "If you wanted to chain yourself here, that's your problem. And money? What money? This place can barely support itself!"

Peyton's palms slammed on the table, rattling silverware. "You don't know the first thing about this place. You've never wanted to."

"You don't know the first thing about *me*. You've never wanted to." God, that felt good.

"Moooooom," Trace whined, "the kids are fighting again."

Emma poked her head in, and they all clammed up like a classroom of naughty kids with the principal making an unexpected visit. The only disturbance was the muffled sound of Seth's laughter from upstairs and some loud toy whirling.

Their housekeeper narrowed her eyes, shook her head, and retreated back to her kingdom . . . the kitchen.

"Now you've done it," Morgan said darkly. "She's never going to bring out another plate of bacon."

"Stuff your bacon," Bea said, picking up the orange peel and dumping it on Peyton's plate. She stood, and Milton scrambled over to follow her. Before she left the room, she turned and said sweetly, "Oh, and Peyton?"

Her sister glared daggers at her.

Bea patted the side of her butt, just behind her hip. "Kiss my flank."

Morgan rubbed a hand over his face and headed toward the stables with Red and Trace, escaping the tension of the big house. Bea had left, pulling on over to her apartment. Peyton had gone into her office, closing the door with a quiet, resolute click of the lock. The *snick* heard 'round the world.

"Was it ever like that with you and your sister?" Trace asked, kicking at a small stone in the dirt.

"We would get into it from time to time. But never like that. We're enough alike that our squabbles were mostly over when we'd outgrown the battle for toys." Morgan shrugged, then stuck his hands in his pockets and gazed toward Bea's apartment. A light shone in the top room over the garage. "Brownings aren't really good at holding a grudge."

"I didn't have any siblings, so I'm playing catch-up on the whole family dynamic thing. But something tells me this isn't going to be solved by walking away." Red walked over to the exercise area to watch one of the hands lead a brood mare around the circle.

"They're more similar than either of them wants to admit." Trace took in both Morgan and Red's faces and smiled. "You don't see it?"

Red was the first to close his mouth and nod slowly. "They're both unmovable as a napping mule and as defensive as a lame mongoose."

Morgan blinked. "That made no sense."

Trace eyed him. "Yeah, next time can you just use English?"

"Instead of asking how things went, Peyton asks in a way that makes Bea feel attacked. And then instead of answering honestly that things went well"—he double-checked with Trace for confirmation, who nodded—"Bea uses sarcasm to deflect the accusation, leaving Peyton not knowing and back to assuming it didn't go well." He sighed. "Which means they'll just go through this again the next time they talk."

"Welcome to my world," Trace muttered. "It was so much easier when we were kids. Peyton and I out here with Daddy, Bea inside with Mama. And never the two shall cross . . . at least most of the time."

"But was that where she wanted to be?" Morgan asked.

Trace opened his mouth, then shut it again and looked toward Bea's apartment. "I thought so. She was so . . . pretty. You know? I remember thinking when they brought her home from the hospital, she was a doll. She was just so untouchable. Like a china doll on a shelf."

"Boys don't really care for babies," Red pointed out. "Of course you thought she was untouchable."

"I didn't mind them. I loved Peyton. She was hot on my heels from the day she was born. We wrestled, we played, she followed me everywhere, and I didn't mind it one bit. We'd roll around in the dirt and hay and come home completely filthy. And Bea would still be pristine and pretty in some overdone white pinafore or dress. I never wanted to touch her, because I was terrified of wrinkling her."

"Did she act like that?" Morgan wondered. "Or did she want you to tussle with her and treat her like you did Peyton?"

"She never followed us out to the barn, so I just assumed that was her personality." Trace shrugged. "Maybe that was wrong, but I was a kid. My world was pretty black and white at that age."

Of course it was. Trace would have been much like his nephew, Brent. He would stand up for Andrea against any schoolyard bully. But have a meaningful conversation? Not gonna happen. Kids had a hard time seeing past the veil of what is to what could be in some situations.

So he would keep peeling away the layers that made up Bea's shell—and he was convinced now a good deal of her bravado was a defensive shell created by childhood—and find out who the real Bea was, and what she wanted to become.

Bea opened her e-mail, then groaned.

Jaycee walked behind, her rubber soles squeaking to a halt. "What's wrong?"

Bea glanced back and came face-to-face with bright pink fabric and cartoon kitties playing with balls of yarn. "Cute."

"Hey, dress the part, right?" Jaycee grinned and ruffled a hand through her black asymmetrical hair, which had a mauve streak running down one temple. It was short enough that she never pulled it back except in surgery, and was a little more punk than Bea was used to seeing on women in the area.

She was young, energetic, and so hell-bent on becoming a full-time vet tech, she could taste it. And she thought Morgan was the big brother she'd never had. Bea loved her.

"Did you ever do any web stuff before, when you were working the desk? Have anything to do with the website?"

Jaycee shook her head, then peered over her to the left side of the screen, where Bea had the clinic's website pulled up. "No, Morgan said he had a web guy who did it, and not to worry about it. I didn't push it 'cause coding and all that crap isn't really my thing, you know? I figured I'd only make things worse." She tilted her head to one side and stared at the screen a bit more. "It is sorta . . . mashed potatoes, hold the gravy, isn't it?"

"If by that you mean boring as heck, yes." Bea clicked through the few pages. "The shelter has such a small portion of the site, and no dogs are listed, so nobody knows what's available."

"I do remember Morgan saying every time he had to change something, he had to use the developer, and it cost. That's a lot of change to put down every time a dog comes through here, or is no longer available." Jaycee shrugged one shoulder, then reached into the bottom drawer of the desk, where Bea had taken to stashing suckers for kids. Grabbing one, she snapped the metal drawer shut again. "Not that it wouldn't be worth it, but it'd be hard keeping up, since the guy only works on it once a month anyway."

"Sounds like a rip-off," Bea muttered, and Jaycee laughed.

"Totally agree. But Morgan, he's too busy to bother. Says he'd rather put his time in with the animals themselves."

Which only made him that much more of a great man. Damn him for that. Bea bit the inside of her cheek a moment, looking over the plain site. It looked like something a middle-schooler would build during computer class with a simple program. "I wonder . . ."

Jaycee smiled a little around the sucker stick. "You're gonna get in trouble, aren't you?"

Bea winked. "Why not? I'm always in trouble for something around here, it seems." As Jaycee turned to head back toward the exam rooms, she added, "Who does your hair? Is she local?"

Jaycee turned back around and ran a hand once more over the inky strands. "You don't wanna go black, Bea."

"No, but I do need my hair trimmed, and a highlight wouldn't kill me. I'm not a fan of having to drive two hours or more just for a simple haircut. But anyone local . . . I need someone . . ." She grimaced while trying to figure how to put it delicately.

Jaycee didn't suffer the same problems. "Younger? Born in the same decade as us?"

"That would be it."

Jaycee grinned and pointed the sucker at her like a teacher with a yardstick. "My friend does my hair. She doesn't work in a shop, just does hair from her house, in a small area she customized in her garage." At the look Bea sent her, she nodded. "I know, sounds a little sketch, but she's amazing. Likes the freedom of working from home, hates paying for booth space. I'll e-mail you her name. She's great. Certified, trained, licensed, and whatever else beauticians need to be damn good at their job."

"Don't say, 'damn,' " Morgan said lightly as he walked by. "Customers might walk in and hear you."

Jaycee rolled her eyes for his benefit, but winked and walked on.

"All set for the day?" Morgan asked, bending over her shoulder to see what she was doing. "The website. Something wrong with it?"

"I was wondering . . ." Might as well give it a try. "I wanted to make a few changes. There are some broken links in here and stuff. Do you have the contact info for the web developer guy?"

"Yeah, somewhere. It should be in the main directory in your book." He named the company, then scrunched his nose. "I usually wait until I have several things to update all at once. Guy charges by the hour and I want my money's worth."

"Makes sense. I just have a few questions. Nothing big."

"Sure, yeah. Whatever you need. Web stuff makes my head hurt. I'd be glad for you to take over." He dropped a kiss to the top of her head while she continued to click through the site and make notes on a notepad. Then he disappeared back into his own office to finish whatever paperwork he could get to before the first patient of the day walked in.

It was comfortable. A little cozy, even. And completely wrong. She wasn't the little missus, coming in to help her husband with his business. Not some bimbo girlfriend the boss kept around either. She was an employee, dammit. A legit employee.

A quick glance assured her Jaycee wasn't nearby. But still. She'd have to talk to him about that later.

Not that she had any ideas of tricking Jaycee. She knew. Bea had no doubt she knew. But she was smart enough, and respected Morgan enough, to keep quiet about the whole thing. At least until there was nothing else to talk about. Small towns . . . the place fed on gossip.

The computer pinged and she swiveled back. Darn web designer guy was fast, for all he didn't seem creative with his work. She opened her e-mail and found not a note from the web designer, but something from Keeley.

Got a hint about a part for you. Made-for-TV movie, but the director's a good guy. He knows your face from T & T. Does other work. Might be a good chance to get your feet wet again, since you've all but slid into retirement at the ripe age of twenty-

six. He has a habit of re-using talent. He likes you for this, he'll use you again. From what he says, you're a "sure shot." Check it out.

Below that was a link to a small blurb in an industry site that listed casting calls, and under that was a name and number to call for *a sure shot* at a reading.

Bea read the e-mail twice, then hovered the mouse over the link. She shouldn't, really. This was a place of business. Reading an e-mail when there were no customers felt like one thing. Job hunting—for all intents and purposes— while on the job was another. She closed the window and faced the row of file cabinets for a minute. Milton nudged her ankle, and she reached down to pet his sweet head before picking him up and letting him settle in her lap a bit.

"You always know when I need something, don't you?"

He yawned and snuggled deeper into her lap.

"This was always temporary, right?" she whispered. "I said that up front. I made it clear. He never asked me to stay on permanently, so he must still be fine with that."

Something low in her gut clenched at the idea of leaving the clinic. How would she know what happened to the dogs in the back? Who would put on another adoption fair? Who would care about Morgan's smudged lenses?

Bea's hand crept back over the mouse, and with Milton falling asleep in her lap, she went to work. Real work. Work she was being paid for.

Morgan waited by his car for Bea to walk out the back door. They'd finished the day, and she'd said she had something to do in the shelter. For whatever reason, he had the suspicion she was waiting for him to leave before she could do whatever mysterious job it was she needed to do. He trusted her, knew she wouldn't ever harm any of the animals. But he couldn't help wondering what the hell she was up to.

Finally, the door creaked open and she walked out, Milton following behind her still-too-high-for-his-taste heels. Those shoes would be damn sexy lying in a heap on his bedroom floor, or scratching his back while he was over her in bed. But at work, they were a hazard.

Oh, not to her. She'd proven more than once she could handle herself in a pair of heels. Though how her feet were never exhausted or swollen was beyond him. No, the real hazard was to his productivity levels. Those shoes did something magical to her legs, and he couldn't think straight when he caught sight of her gams poking out from behind the desk. One shoe was always in danger of slipping off her foot as she jiggled it . . .

"You're deep in thought."

He blinked, surprised to find her right in front of him. "Hey. Yeah . . ."

She grinned. "Was it a dirty thought? Why, Dr. Browning, you are blushing like a ninth grader caught reading *Playboy* behind his math textbook." She patted one cheek. "That is too cute."

He wrapped his hand around her wrist and tugged until she fell into him a little. Milton jumped on his leg, but he ignored the dog. "Come home with me."

She fluttered her lashes a little. "I might." Then stepped back. "But we need to have a talk about your PDA issues."

"My . . . what?" Mind still focused on the mental image of her green shoes falling one by one over the footboard of his bed, he struggled to come back to the conversation at hand. "I have PDA issues?"

"We both do. You for giving it, me for thinking it's not a good idea to take it."

"Oh, come on, Bea." He kissed her forehead between her furrowed brows. "Nobody cares about that."

"Why?" Her voice dropped a little, and he recognized

the warning sign of impending doom. "Did you kiss Jaycee when she was your receptionist?"

"No, but—"

"So why is it different for me?" She didn't give him a chance to answer. "Because we're sleeping together?"

A yellow caution light blinked in the back of his mind. "I don't think many people know about that." He saw it was the wrong answer, though how *Yeah, I kissed Jaycee all the time* would have been the *right* answer was beyond him.

Then again, he was a man, and she was a pissed woman. The odds were, there *was* no right answer.

"So it's because of me. Nobody cares that you're kissing me because, what, it's just expected? Oh, just that Bea Muldoon, back from Hollywood. Taking after her mama, the dead slut." Her voice was rising now, into an octave he would pay good money to never hear again.

That yellow light changed, much like a traffic light, to red.

"That's not it," he said.

"Isn't it? Why would nobody care? Why would nobody give us the side eye?"

"Because people know me here. They probably would assume I was just being friendly. Hell, Bea. It's not like I ran up behind you, flipped your skirt up, and bent you over the desk. It was a kiss on the head." His own head was starting to ache.

"You have to stop." She crossed her arms, which did interesting things to her breasts. "Morgan. Leave my boobs alone and listen. You have to stop. It's not right, and it's not helping my reputation here."

He opened his mouth to argue that, in fact, it likely did a lot of good. People thinking they were in a relationship would make them realize she was settling down, giving

Marshall a chance, creating roots. But he snapped it shut again. Her eyes were telling him more than her defiant, combative posture.

She was scared. Scared people truly thought she was like her mother had been. Lifting her skirts for any man who looked at her the right way. And he wasn't sure how to combat that while still trying to continue the relationship he wanted to be in.

Damn woman and her blocking him at every turn, even with imaginary issues. But he wouldn't ignore her concern, because it was real enough to her.

He glanced around, then ducked his head down a bit. "Is anyone watching now?"

"What? No, but—"

He sealed his mouth over hers for an intimate, searing kiss that had him fighting the urge to lead her back into the clinic, send his night vet tech home, and spend all evening using the overnight cot for his own purposes.

But that would only make her resent him. So he pulled back and smiled at her scowl. "You agreed nobody was looking. Can we compromise?" His hands wandered to her arms, rubbing up and down the soft skin. "I can't imagine going all day being near you and not touching you. But I can be careful and discreet."

He watched the play of emotions cross her face. Disbelief, curiosity, and finally . . . there it was. Acceptance. His heart did a stutter-step in place before beating again.

"Fine." She slid her arms around him for a quick hug before stepping back. "But if Jaycee catches you touching my butt, you're in trouble."

Like Jaycee would care. But he nodded solemnly, a chastened student taking a lecture from the hot teacher. "Yes, ma'am."

"Knock it off." She swatted him, then opened her rear car door to let Milton jump in.

"Come home with me."

She glanced up from starting the ignition. "I can't. I got Steve to agree to change the oil in my car. I need it, can't ignore it."

"Then I'll follow you home. You can pack a bag, leave your car with Steve, and I'll drive you to my place. I can drive you in to work in the morning, too."

Her hand froze on the key still halfway in the ignition. "What would people think about us showing up together?"

"That your car needed work done, we're neighbors, and I gave you a ride?" He shrugged, but really he didn't care *what* people said. That was their prerogative. But he'd take any excuse to have her in his bed overnight.

She must have seen the sense of the plan and she nodded. "Okay. See you at my place." Then she started the car and backed out.

Score one for Browning. He resisted the urge to pump his fist like an idiot and hopped in the truck. Now to make sure she didn't back out at the last minute.

Bea Muldoon was a hell of a lot of work, but damn, she was worth it.

Chapter Sixteen

Bea eyed the clock with disdain.

6:09.

No matter how often she'd had to be on set by five in the morning, she'd never gotten used to mornings. They were not her thing. But something had woken her up before the alarm.

Ah, right. That would be it. Morgan's erection digging into the backs of her thighs. He spooned around her, wrapping his arms over her stomach and breasts as if claiming a favorite toy on the playground. His breath ruffled the hairs at her temple, and his legs hugged the backs of her thighs all the way to her feet.

She waited a moment, then realized he was still deep asleep. His little buddy down below, however, was not. A grin crept over her face. What better way to wake up than sleepy, warm morning sex?

Reaching back, she fumbled a little until she found the hard length of him and squeezed. He exhaled heavily, but nothing more.

She tightened her hand and stroked. Her position gave her little room to maneuver, but she did what she could. Soon, his hips were thrusting into her hand and he was moaning. But still, he slumbered on. Or at least, he never moved above the waist, and his breathing was still deep and even.

She brought one large, masculine hand up to cup her breast. Taking her cue, even in sleep, he managed to squeeze lightly. Men. She smiled. Even in their sleep they were game for a little action.

Suddenly she found herself rolling, legs tangling in the sheets until she was on top of Morgan. His sleepy eyes blinked up at her, and a small grin tugged at his lips. "How long were you going to keep doing that before waking me up?"

"You need to be awake?" She ran her thigh over his erection. "Doesn't really seem that way."

"It's more enjoyable when I know what I'm getting." His hands ran up her sides, over her ribs, and up to cup her breasts again, fingers playing lightly with her nipples. They beaded at his touch, silently asking for more. "You could have let me know this was how you wanted to wake up this morning."

"I figured the fact that we both went to sleep with our clothes off was a good hint we weren't done yet." When he shifted a little, she rose up on her knees. After taking the condom he dug out of the nightstand drawer, she rolled it on and sank down over him with a happy sigh. Her head fell back and her eyes closed as she savored the early morning lovemaking. It was something she'd never really experienced much before, but now she could see she'd been missing out.

Morgan's hand was quick and sure as he continued to play with her breast, and he slid his other hand down to where they were intimately connected. He found her clit and rubbed with his thumb. The pressure began to build, a slow sunrise to match the easy pace they set for themselves. The heat rose in her, filling her, until she was ready to spread her arms out and let it flow from her fingertips.

Flow from her fingertips? The completely overemotional thought halted her in her tracks. She froze, Morgan's shaft nearly out, and wanted to slap herself. This was absolutely not the time, the place, or the guy to be getting all sentimental about. Good sex, good company.

"Something wrong?" His voice was strained, a little frayed around the edges.

She swallowed and looked back at him. Her face smoothed into calm, controlled amusement. "Not a thing. Just wondering how long I can drag you out before you go crazy."

"It's not a far trip. Don't even bother trying. I'm already there." He worked her with his thumb more, and the climax rose in her along with the welling emotion she tried so hard to tamp down. And when she finally burst through the wall and reached her peak, it wasn't nearly as satisfying as it could have been.

Something about spending half the time scolding herself had ruined the moment. She wanted a do-over. The perfect morning sex, ruined by thoughts and emotions and feelings. How inappropriate.

But when Morgan lowered her to his chest, her head nestled in the crook of his arm, she forgot her own lecture, her own warning words, and breathed deeply. A contentment she'd felt very rarely, a stillness, a sort of peace of soul, spread through her. And try as she might to fight it off, her mind relaxed enough to drift back to sleep with the even breathing of her lover in her ear.

Morgan felt Bea get up and head to the bathroom. Something cracked in the dark, he heard her suck in a breath, then mutter a foul curse before uneven footsteps crossed the floor. He cracked one eye open and watched her delicious, naked ass disappear behind the door. She'd waited until the door was closed before turning the light on. To let him sleep, he assumed. Maybe she wouldn't see it the same way, but he recognized the small things she did as the acts of an unselfish woman. Risking stubbing her toe in the dark just so she wouldn't shine a bright light over him and wake him up early. Might seem tiny, and it was in the grand scheme of things. But a selfish woman who thought only of herself—which was exactly what she wanted to present herself as—wouldn't hesitate to light the room up to suit her, and damn anyone else's needs.

He waited until she walked back out, tying his rarely used robe around her waist. The robe had been a Christmas gift a few years ago from his mother, but he just never bothered with one in his own home. Bea was a tall woman, but the robe still dragged the ground a little. The sleeves were rolled back, showcasing just how delicate her hands and wrists were under the chunky dark blue material.

"Going out to get the paper?" he asked.

"I was going to fix breakfast. I can't do that naked. It's unsanitary." She wrinkled her nose. "But it's probably going to be messy, and I don't want to wear my work clothes."

"Fair enough. Is it going to be cereal or a Toaster Strudel?" When she flipped him off on her way out of the bedroom, he laughed.

And then a moment later, he heard her shriek.

He bolted out of bed, mind racing to anticipate the danger. Snake in the house? Something wrong with Milton? Burglar?

He skidded to a halt behind Bea, who stood at the opening of the kitchen, frozen. And in the kitchen . . . aw, fuck.

It was worse than a snake, and a dead Milton, and a bur-glar combined.

His mother.

Bea couldn't move. And apparently, neither could Cyn-thia Browning. Both stood, transfixed by the other's pres-ence in Morgan's house. Some sick sort of dread curled and rolled in her stomach. Like she'd drunk motor oil and chased it with tequila, then decided to swim a mile.

"Mom." Morgan skidded to a halt right behind her and grabbed her shoulders. He pulled her back against his chest. What the hell? He chose now to have an up-close-and-personal moment? As if this situation wasn't already bad enough!

But when she reached her hands back to push at him, she touched skin. Skin where his boxers, or jeans, should have been. Oh holy God. He was buck-ass naked and us-ing her as a human shield.

Shit just got awkward . . . er. Yes, awkwarder. Not even a word, and that was still exactly what this was.

Cynthia's hand came up to her throat; then she turned her back on them, facing the refrigerator. Her dark brown hair, streaked with gray, pulled back in a clip, wavered as her shoulders shook. "I'm sorry, I thought I could sneak in here before you were up for the day. I just need that huge skillet I left here last time I came over to make you food. I have a luncheon and . . ." She trailed off, as if real-izing now probably wasn't the time to explain exactly why she was in the kitchen and her son was hiding his dick be-hind his lover, who was wearing his robe and nothing else.

There was a reason Bea had never been interested in any sitcom auditions.

"So I'll just . . . go now." She edged sideways, back still facing them, arm waving around as she reached for the door. "I'm sorry. I'm . . ." She opened the door, but had to face it to walk out, so she used her outside hand to block her vision like blinders on a horse and bolted for the safety of the great outdoors.

The door slammed shut behind her, and they were both silent for a moment. Frozen in a bubble of horror and . . .

Amusement? Was that why his chest was shaking behind her? She turned and watched his eyes—not behind their glasses as usual—crinkle with laughter. Then he doubled over and let loose a belly laugh so loud she took a step back in startled shock.

"That was funny to you?"

He couldn't answer, what with all the gasping for breath and more laughter.

She nudged him with one toe. "Seriously, how can you laugh like that? Your mom saw me in here at seven in the morning, wearing your robe. And you were naked."

He snorted, shoulders shaking.

"She probably knows we were having sex," Bea hissed. God, this was why people were supposed to live a respectable distance away from their families. So this didn't happen. Ever.

Finally, Morgan straightened and wiped his eyes. "Come on, you have to admit . . ."

"No, I don't. I know what you're going to say and I absolutely don't have to admit anything." Bea sank into a kitchen chair and let her head fall to the table. "How am I ever going to face your mother again? If I run into her in the produce section of the grocery store, I might have to abandon my cart and make a break for it."

"The Hollywood starlet, so modest and prudish." He dropped a kiss to the top of her head, then danced out of the way of her slapping hands. "How about that breakfast you promised me?"

"How about some privacy?" she snapped. "You live with your parents!"

Morgan took down a few bowls and set them on the table. "You make that sound like we're in the same house. I'm not some unemployed slacker who sits in his mother's basement all day sucking down her retirement pay while he plays World of Warcraft and pees into empty Diet Mountain Dew bottles."

"That image will haunt me for weeks," Bea muttered into her hands.

"Good. So you see the difference. This is just a small portion of my parents' land. Or it used to be. I bought it from them, so technically it's mine. And they're almost a mile away."

Bea pointed to a side window without looking up. "I can see their house from that window."

"Barely." A box of cereal landed next to the bowls. "Shredded wheat okay?"

"If I'm eating carbs for breakfast, I like to try and make them tasty."

The shredded wheat disappeared and was replaced by a marshmallowy, sugary, completely adult-inappropriate cereal. "Perfect." She grabbed the box, flipped the lid open, and dug a hand in.

"So, no milk?" Morgan smiled and brought over two glasses and a carton of the cow juice.

"That's dairy. It makes you bloat." She had to talk around a mouth full of faux marshmallows. Fauxmellows? They stuck to her molars and made her want to gag, but in a weird sort of yummy way. Nothing about this morning was right or good or even semi-normal. Why not complete the disaster with empty calories and inevitable cavities?

"I can see why washing down your nine-hundred-calorie, sugar breakfast with a sixty-calorie skim milk serving would completely ruin the meal," he said, clearly not understanding the point at all. Men were irrational idiots. How did he not follow the logic?

"Seriously. How can I ever look your mother in the eye again?" She gaped at him. "Or your father. Oh God. She'll tell him, he'll know what we . . ." She waved a hand between them. "He'll tell his drinking buddies, and they'll tell their wives. And their wives will abuse the PTA phone tree to spread the word that I'm bouncing bedsheets with the vet." HFCS-flavored chunks of cereal bounced on the table as she let her head fall once more to the surface.

"Okay, no more mallow-malt cereal for you." He pried the box away and set it aside. And then he did the one thing that could calm her down even in the face of a true panic attack. He let his fingers wander through her hair, massaging the tension away until she was a puddle of Who Cares on the table. "It won't be that bad. My parents are discreet."

"But they'll tell one person in confidence, who will swear on their great-grandma Nana's canning recipe they won't tell a soul. Which of course they will. Wash, rinse, repeat."

"And so people know we're sleeping together. I know, I know," he said easily when she looked up at him. But clearly he *didn't* know if he could say that so easily. "But if it's going to get out, it's easiest coming from my parents, don't you think?"

"How is that even possible?" Her brain hurt. She laid her head back down, and he went back to scratching lightly over her scalp.

"If the news comes from my parents, it won't sound like an illicit affair. It will sound like we're healthy adults dating. And that's normal and realistic and completely awesome." He grinned when she peeked around her arm. "Awesome for me, I mean. A guy like me snagging you?

Come on. Credit where credit is due. That earns me some cool points."

Why did he have to be so damn adorable? She sighed. It didn't matter to her, really. Eventually she would be gone. Her life wasn't here.

From what he says, you're a "sure shot."

But it mattered to Morgan. He would be the one left holding the bag when she escaped back to California. Was it fair to let people think she was using him for great sex? Or maybe they would think he was using her. Worse for his reputation. After she moved on, he'd find a nice girl who loved Marshall, settle down, and marry her. He didn't need a reputation as a womanizer to deal with.

"Fine." She let her eyes close again and rested her cheek on the cool wood. "Fine. So we're dating." For now.

She wasn't sure if it was her imagination, or if it really happened. But she thought for a moment, she heard Morgan whisper, "Good."

Peyton slammed down into a booth next to the window and tossed her hat on the seat beside her. "You pick the worst times to do this, you know that?"

Bea smiled, a little sharp, but she smiled. "There is never a bad time for alcohol."

Jo slid into the booth beside Bea. "Preach. Amanda?"

The perky waitress, a favorite of Bea's for her quick service and easy way with everyone, scooted over. "Boss is seated," Amanda said. "Time to put my best foot forward."

"Beer," Peyton said quickly before Bea could order. "And if she tries to order something else for me, ignore it."

Bea stared at her sister a moment. Had they truly come from the same womb? "Amanda, I'll have a rum and diet, and a water please. Thanks." She waited while Jo ordered some new drink, which she'd told them ahead of time was the plan. Testing the new bartender on the drink menu. It was why they'd headed to Jo's Place instead of a more out-of-the-way establishment.

"You'll have to let me try a sip of that," Bea said as she placed the drink menu back behind the salt and pepper shakers.

"Have one. Crash at my place tonight. I don't care. That dog is already upstairs right now sleeping on my sofa or in my bed." Jo rolled her eyes. "And honestly, could you have gotten a dog that's any more codependent?"

"Probably not. Wasn't my intention. But he's had a rough life. I can't deny the poor baby now, can I? He deserves a little spoiling." She gave Jo her sad, puppy-dog eyes. "He was skin and bones when I adopted him. Just so malnourished and neglected."

"Okay, okay, stop." Jo slapped her hands over her ears. "He's fine. But if you test out all the new drinks with me, you're not driving home."

"Which is why I'm not. I'm here solely for girl talk."

Peyton blew out a breath and stared out the window.

She eyed Peyton while Amanda passed out drinks and slid away discreetly. That was the good thing about dining with the owner. Best possible service.

"This girl talk isn't code for gossip, is it?"

"No, Jo. It's not. Unless you count mining for gossip about oneself to be the same thing." When both women stared at her blankly, she took the cherry out of her drink and pulled the stem off. "That was confusing."

"Only a little." Peyton took a drink from her bottle.

"I just need to know if people are talking about me." When neither woman spoke, she tried again. "About me and Morgan."

Silence, but for the clink of ice in Jo's glass.

"Me and Morgan dating?" she asked hopefully.

"Oh," they each said together.

Jo added, "We didn't think you were ready to talk about it yet."

"I think it's inevitable."

"Probably." Peyton took another swig of beer, then tilted her head ever so slightly toward another table. Bea took her cue and slid her gaze over without moving her head.

Two women, both who looked to be in their early forties, likely meeting for a lunch date while the kids were in school, were staring at her. Not even trying to be inconspicuous about it, either. Brazen.

"Great," she mumbled. That had happened faster than she'd expected. "How the hell did everyone find out?"

"I heard from Steve," Peyton said.

"Several customers," Jo helped.

"Thank you, Cynthia," Bea muttered.

"Cynthia?" Peyton sat back in surprise. "Morgan's mom?"

"She sort of caught us the other morning. In a delicate situation." Because other women—even her sister—would understand the total and complete embarrassment, she relayed the scene in Morgan's kitchen. With some minor edits.

Jo rubbed her back in a motherly gesture. "It's not the end of the world, you know. People date. Nobody's said anything negative about it. I mean, they usually shut up when I give them a look, because frankly, I don't want to hear it. But some things are unavoidable."

"Tiny said you two were cute together," Peyton added, a slow grin spreading. Of course. Now that she'd found a screw to twist, she was enjoying herself. "I'm pretty sure he was bullshitting about it, but with Tiny, sometimes it's hard to tell."

"Goody. Even the ranch hands are gossiping like hens."

"They've got the best gossip, as far as I'm concerned."

Just then, Janine Stevens walked by the table and did a double-take. "Bea?"

She slipped on her public face, which included the *I'm not feeling great but that's not your problem* smile. "Hi, Mrs. Stevens. How's Alice?"

"Oh she's just great, thank you for asking." Janine beamed. "And you can call me Janine. After my daughter probably scared you half to death with that reptile . . ."

"Alice has a pet python," Bea explained to Jo and Peyton. Peyton merely raised a brow. Jo, more on Bea's wavelength, shuddered. "Alice is adorable. I'm sorry to say, the pet does not match."

Janine laughed, started to wave and walk on, but then bent over the table. "I just had to tell you, I think you and Morgan are a perfect match," she said in hushed tones.

Bea's own brows rose in disbelief. "You do?"

"Absolutely. He's such a sweet man, and he's a fantastic vet. But he cares about the animals more than his own social life. I have a feeling you won't let him get away with that much longer. And besides, if you can put up with Alice's pet, you can put up with anything." Janine winked, waved, and joined the two other women who had been staring earlier.

Bea blinked a moment. Well. That was . . . unexpected. Somehow she'd imagined things would go differently. That she'd be accused of being the whore of Babylon, and lynched for ruining the favorite son.

"See?" Jo looked satisfied with herself. "Shoulda put money on that one. People like you, Bea. People like Morgan. It's a natural fit. Plus, Morgan's a smart guy, and people know it. Calling into question his relationship with you is like calling into question his intelligence. Like he doesn't know what he's getting into. Nobody's going to do that."

"She's got a point." Peyton flipped a thin cardboard

coaster in Jo's direction. "I thought people would make a BFD over me and Red, and it ended up to be barely a trickle."

"True. But you were staying," Bea said easily, then caught the frozen looks on both her friend and sister's faces. "You know what I mean. In town. You were permanent. Red had nothing stopping him from being permanent. I'm not. I'm . . . an extended visitor." Or whatever.

"You could be," Jo reminded her quietly. "You could be permanent."

Bea looked toward Peyton, but her sister was staring at something out the window.

"Moving on." She pasted a smile on her face. "I got a recommendation for someone to do my hair."

"Goody. One of my favorite topics . . . hair." Peyton slid her hat back over her face and slid down in the booth a little.

Bea couldn't help but laugh. A real laugh, this time. Felt good.

Chapter Seventeen

Basset hounds had the best faces. Morgan rubbed the one sitting in his lap under the chin. The dog's droopy eyes closed all the way in ecstasy. Just like Bea's, he thought with a smile, when he rubbed her head. The exact same way . . . except she looked much prettier doing it. She was a hedonist, no question about it.

Thing Two, Thing One's brother, bumped his hand in demand for attention. They were the calmest of his current shelter residents, but when they wanted something, they let you know it.

Morgan was escaping his office during a lull to play with the dogs. It was one of the main reasons he loved his job so damn much. The animals were so intuitive. The shelter dogs most of all, he thought. They'd seen hardship, many of them. They knew pain. They also knew joy. That was the beauty of a rescue dog. They displayed gratitude because they knew what it was to go without, and they didn't ever want to go back to that. Every day in warmth, with a full belly and a good rub behind the ears, was something not to be taken for granted in their eyes.

Except for that one. He watched Milton trot in ahead of his mistress and sit outside the cage. His haughty expression said, *You chose them over me? There's something wrong with you.*

"Hey, bud. Nice tie." Today's collar was meant to look like the collar of a man's button-down shirt, complete with herringbone-patterned necktie.

"Milton says thank you." Bea clipped in behind him and squatted down in her heels. The lift from the back made it look easier to keep her balance. Too bad she was wearing black slacks today. In a skirt, he would have gotten quite an eyeful.

"Eyes up, Morgan," she said with a twinkle in her eye. "Come back to Earth."

"Hmm. Do I have to?"

"Well, you have an appointment in"—she checked her thin silver watch—"ten minutes, so I guess technically you have a bit more time to space out and think dirty thoughts. But I had something to tell you."

"Hit me with it." He let his right hand continue to rub at Thing One's ears while he scratched Thing Two's belly.

"I have a few interviews lined up."

He watched her but said nothing.

"For the receptionist position, I mean. I put the job out there the other day, and I already have some replies. There were a ton of applicants, actually. But only a few who had the skills—at least on paper—to pull off the whole gig."

The whole gig. That's what she was calling working in the office. Running the office, really. She was more than a receptionist, didn't she see that? She thought he didn't know, but he was aware she was redesigning the website in her free time. He'd caught glimpses of it, and knew it was more than he could have ever pulled together with a *Coding for Dummies* book and prayer. She was wonderful with the customers, even those who were cooler to her than they had any reason to be. She didn't balk at muddy paws on her skirt and would let an upset child who'd lost their four-legged best friend cry at her desk. And she continually surprised him with her willingness to take steps out of her comfort zone.

And yet, here they were. Right back at the beginning. She was planning her escape. Because that's what she thought he wanted? No, she knew better. She was a brilliant woman. She was planning to run because it was what she wanted. Or thought she wanted. Needed, maybe.

Brilliant, but complex. Which was probably why he was half in love with her.

"Do you need me to interview them?"

"I was going to do a pre-interview." Bea shrugged and hugged Milton close to her side. He left fur behind on her black pants but she didn't seem to notice. Or she didn't care enough to brush it off. "Why waste your time if they turn out to be a dud?"

"Fair enough." He wanted to shake her, make her snap out of it. Make her see she didn't have to keep going down this path just because it was what she'd originally planned for herself. But that wasn't going to win him any favors. So he nodded as if it was a simple, foregone conclusion, and she was doing the right thing. "Thanks for that."

When she didn't leave, he tried a new approach. "Wanna have dinner with me at my parents'?"

She laughed quickly; then the laugh died down as she watched his face. "Oh, you were serious."

"Yeah, I'm serious. Isn't that what people who are dating do? I have dinner at your place often enough."

"But that's just with my brother and sister and Emma and Red and Jo," she said slowly.

"Right. And they're your family. My parents are my family. I figured it might be nice to start with just them. No need to add in my sister, brother-in-law, and their two hellions yet. They can be a lot to take on."

"Andrea was sweet," she defended instantly. "I remember her from the adoption fair. She took home that gray kitten I loved."

"Yeah, well, quiet maybe. But not around her brother. Put the two of them together and . . ." He mimed his fists ramming into each other. "Boom."

"That's natural. Peyton and I butt heads like a couple of rams." She let her butt slide down to the ground and Milton immediately took up residence in her lap. Morgan didn't even want to think of what dirt and fur she might be picking up on her pants. But she was oblivious. Such a difference from even a month ago.

"That's something you could work on while you're home. Repairing whatever's broken between you."

"What's broken is Peyton's attitude. If it weren't for that, we would get along just fine." Bea stroked Milton's head, and his eyes drifted shut.

"Takes two to feud, sweetheart."

"Stop you with your logic." She didn't look at him.

"If that's what you want," he murmured. "We'll just head back to the topic of eating dinner with my parents. Look at it this way," he cut her off when she opened her mouth to protest. "You can get the whole awkward first-meeting-after thing out of the way in privacy, with nobody else watching. That would be easier, wouldn't it? Rather than Mom catching you at the grocery store picking out cucumbers?"

Heat flushed up her neck, but her lips twitched. "You're being pervy. I can't believe I ever thought you were too quiet and restrained to be pervy."

"That was your mistake," he said cheerfully, tugging gently on Thing Two's tail to get him playing. "Come to dinner. Get it over with. See that you can both be adults about it. And then we can all move on like it never happened."

She chewed her bottom lip a little, then nodded. "But not tonight. I have something to do at home tonight."

"Okay, no problem. Friday?"

"Sure. That works." She stared at him hard. "If you request cucumber salad or something, I'll have to beat you."

He blinked. "I would never."

"Right." She stood, dislodging Milton from his perch. The dog grumbled, but followed her faithfully back toward the clinic side of the building and let the door shut between them.

"She's crazy about me," Morgan told Thing One, who blinked sleepily. "She just doesn't know it yet."

"What the hell could be so important you pulled me away from *NCIS*?" Peyton followed Bea down the stairs with heavy, thudding footsteps. God, she acted like she was being dragged to the electric chair.

"You'll see. I just need your opinion on something." When they reached the bottom of the stairs, Bea turned in a wide circle. God, Mama had disgusting taste in décor. If it glittered or was painted a metallic color, she'd snatched it up.

Elvis syndrome. When zero taste meets disposable income.

Peyton watched her for a second, then did her own slow spin. "Am I missing something?"

"What do you see?" Curious, Bea waited for her sister to take another look around.

Peyton's face scrunched up, like she was thinking. "Is this a trick question?"

"No."

"Okay then." She glanced once more around the entryway, living room, and as far into the dining room as she could. "I see our house?"

Okay, so Literal Peyton was not going to make this easy. "What's in the house?"

"A bunch of ugly-ass stuff."

Getting somewhere. "Exactly. But who picked it all out?"

"Down here?" Peyton snorted and crossed her arms over her chest. "Sylvia, of course. You think Daddy would have given two shits about a miniature fountain with naked babies that spit water out of their mouths?"

"Cherubs," Bea corrected. "They're cherubs. But that's not the point."

"What is the point, Bea?" Peyton watched her warily. "I'm not a big fan of guessing games."

"The point is," Bea said slowly, breathing a few times for patience before continuing, "that this is your house. And the décor is not what you would have picked. It's not your style. It's not this business's style. It shouldn't be any-one's style," she added in a mutter. "And in addition to its being a home, it is also a business." When her sister said nothing, she asked, "Am I on the right track?"

"Yes." Peyton nodded. "Not sure where this track is heading, but you're on the right one."

"The point is, it's intimidating to cowboys to come in here and sit around in a room that looks like Liberace vomited in it." Bea smiled with satisfaction. "You can't do effective business with someone who doesn't even feel they can sit on the pristine white couch or look anywhere because of the 'artistic nudes.' " She broke out air quotes for that one.

"Still right. But what does that have to do with any-thing?"

"Follow me." Bea led her into the office, where she sat at Peyton's desk and opened the browser window she'd prepared just before dragging her sister down the stairs. "See?"

"I see a website with a photo of our naked baby fountain." Peyton peered over her shoulder. "And . . . is that a real price? Like, a no-kidding price?"

"Yes." With morbid pleasure, she zoomed in on the going price for the ugly-ass fountain. "That's what it is currently selling for online. Shipping and handling not included."

"Holy shit. Mama didn't just buy horrible stuff, she broke our bank buying it!" Peyton's fists balled up on the desk next to the mouse pad.

"Before you need your blood pressure medication—"

"I don't have blood pressure meds."

"You might want to consider those. Anyway," Bea said with another click, bringing up the next window. "Recognize that painting?"

"From the dining room. Yeah." Peyton's hands slowly uncurled and flattened on the scarred wood top. "I assume you're showing me all this for a reason?"

"In my off time, when I haven't been working or, well, you know . . ." She waved a hand.

"Playing naughty vet?" Peyton asked with a snicker.

"First off, ew. And second, don't be childish. You're supposed to be more mature than me." She brought up a few more browser tabs to show the other items she'd priced online. "As you can see, this stuff sells for a decent price secondhand. These are all secondhand prices, except for a few. I don't know what Mama paid for it new, but the fact is, we can earn back a decent amount of cash by selling it now."

"So?" Peyton leaned against the desk. "Why?"

"We're cash-strapped." When Peyton stared at her, she added, "Back taxes? I thought, you knew . . ." She shrugged. "You didn't say how much we were in the hole, but I thought at least this might help plug the dam a little while we keep building the business up."

Her sister stared at her for a while. Long enough that Bea fought the urge to pinch her. Old habits die hard.

"Why?"

Bea rolled her eyes. "I just said—"

"Back taxes, yes. I heard. But why did you look all this up? What prompted the sudden, out-of-the-blue interest in saving the ranch?"

Breathe in, breathe out. Murder is a felony. "It might seem sudden to you, but I'm still a member of this family, you know." And when Peyton opened her mouth, Bea cupped her hand over her sister's lips. "Not now. I don't want to get on to that awful not-so-merry-go-round with you. It's boring. The fact is, this is my family home. I've accepted that, I've embraced that, and I'm doing what I can to step up and be helpful."

"Shopping." Her sister's voice was muffled, but calm. Bea took her hand away. "Shopping is what you can do to help?"

Bea grinned. "What else? Go with your strengths, and all that."

Peyton's eyes darted back to the screen. "Can you handle all this? The web stuff, getting it listed, handling the delivery and whatever?"

"Sure can. And I can even decorate the place again, in a more comfortable, appropriate style, of course."

"Out of your wages from the clinic?" Peyton asked hopefully.

"Uh, no. But if you give me, say, forty percent of what I bring in with the sales of the ugly-ass decorations—I mean, priceless treasures—I can make this house a place where your clients, and potential clients, will love to stay and relax and do the horse-chat thing for hours while you impress them with your equine skills."

"Wow. That was . . . quite the pitch. But you can have ten percent. Not forty."

"Thirty."

"Twenty, and not a penny more. I mean it. I'm checking receipts." Peyton straightened and held out a hand. Bea looked at it in amusement, but shook.

"I could have done it for ten."

"But it'll look better with twenty." Peyton shrugged. "I care . . . enough. You're right. We have to think outside the box to get more people in here and returning. So, that's what we'll do." Peyton's eyes wandered over the bookshelves behind Bea's shoulder. "You did good, Bea."

Bea blinked repeatedly to clear her eyes before smiling. "Well, you know I love to shop. It was hardly a chore."

"True enough." Peyton walked out of the office, but paused in the doorway. "And get out of my chair. Your bony butt is gonna make a weird dent in it."

Bea waited until Peyton was long gone before grinning and muttering, "Bite me."

In the early afternoon on Thursday, Bea kicked off her Wellies and stretched her legs in the passenger seat of Morgan's truck. "That was a productive day. Not one emergency."

"It's a record," Morgan agreed, and turned the AC up a little higher. "Don't jinx it, though."

"I know. I just . . . hold up." Bea scrolled through her phone a minute, then smiled.

"Good news?"

"Good news for you. My favorite candidate is still available and willing to come in for an interview today." She scowled down at her outfit. "I'm not looking my best, but that's not the point. So that's one more thing off my list of stuff to worry about."

"Ah. Yeah." His hands tightened over the steering wheel and he stared straight ahead, swerving gently to avoid a hole in the dirt road.

"I know it's a little sooner than either of us expected. But the faster we can get someone in, the faster we can train them." She settled back, pleased with herself. "I think this is going quite well."

Quite well, his ass. He was trying to figure out ways to keep her here, and she had one-way-tickets to California dancing in her eyes. "Dinner at my parents' tomorrow?"

"Have you cleared this with them? It's Friday night, after all. Are you sure they don't have plans?"

He huffed out a laugh. "Right. Would that be eating at Jo's Place in town? Or taking a walk around the land?"

"Good point." Bea ran a hand through her hair. "I don't suppose there's any way I could take a half day tomorrow and run out to get my hair done?"

He nearly said no, because her hair looked fine. But the fact that she cared enough to primp before meeting his folks—again, now as an adult . . . a dressed adult—said it was a bigger deal than she let on. "Yeah. That's fine. No problem."

"Great." She clapped her hands together once and rubbed them gleefully. "It's long overdue."

He bit his tongue before saying something Man Stupid like, "It looks good to me." It was just asking for a beat-down.

"And I'm excited to try out Jaycee's recommendation."

This time, he couldn't hold back. "You're not coming back with blue spikes or anything weird, right?"

Bea smiled. "Of course not."

Whew.

"I was thinking purple."

He dared a look at her, found the smile spreading smugly, and knew she was joking.

God, he hoped.

★　★　★

Bea reached back and rubbed Milton's head, who'd spent most of his day in the backseat stretched out with a rope to gnaw on and his favorite ball. Every so often, he hopped down to investigate the ranch they were at. But the larger animals got his hackles up, and he eventually chose to stay in the truck with the doors open. Damn dog was about as needy as a toddler sometimes.

"I'm thinking about having her look around the shelter first. That'll tell me a lot," Bea mused, back on the interview subject. "Last girl I tried was scared of the bigger dogs. Why she thought a vet's office was the place for her, I don't know."

She continued on, outlining what she would be doing with the candidate, and Morgan let his mind wander.

Dinner with his folks. His dad would like Bea immediately. She was pretty, but he'd see the intelligence there almost as fast. And he trusted Morgan's judgment. If he liked her, his dad would, too. His mom was a harder sell. She wasn't one of those moms who thought nobody was good enough for her baby boy. She'd had plenty of suggestions for wifely candidates over the last few years. But Bea, for whatever reason, his mother just couldn't get behind. There would be some work involved there.

He could handle it. He was a big boy. And if she didn't grow to love Bea, then they would jump that hurdle when they approached it. In the meantime, he would have to pick the right day to bring over his sister and the kids. Then after that, they—

"Morgan!"

"Hmm?" He blinked and took his foot off the accelerator, ready to brake fast if necessary. "What?"

Bea blew out an exasperated breath. "I said, if I like this one, can you meet with her later on today so you can give the sign-off?"

"Oh. Sure, whatever." He relaxed his once-again clenched hands. Fighting it was going to get them nowhere. "What's going on at home? Any news from M-Star?"

"I've started selling off the décor. That was big news. A few paintings are gone. Those things are difficult to ship, but worth the effort." She glowed with pride. "The look on Peyton's face when I presented her with the check those things brought in was worth every annoying minute. Not dead weight anymore."

Of course she wasn't. He grinned that, naturally, she'd found a spot for her to contribute and made it all hers. That was just like Bea. "Proud of you."

She was silent, and he glanced over quickly to see if he'd upset her.

She was blinking hard, staring ahead, her cheeks a little flushed.

He gave her the moment. She'd earned it. But he'd be willing to give her a thousand more if she'd only stay.

Chapter Eighteen

"You cannot be serious." Peyton brushed by Bea to walk into the stable. She ignored the horse heads poking over their stall doors and headed straight back for the tack room.

"Of course I'm not kidding. I'm going tomorrow afternoon to get my hair done. You're coming with me."

Lover Boy stretched his neck out, and she dared a quick pit stop to rub his nose and say hello. Since she'd been sleeping over at Morgan's most of the week, she hadn't had time for a joyride. It surprised her just how much she missed it.

Maybe she needed to schedule in a quick ride some night. She didn't have to spend *all* her time with Morgan in the evenings. In fact, tonight would be a great night to sleep alone. Get a good ride in, feel refreshed, and gear up for meeting his parents tomorrow for dinner.

And God, what a mistake it had been to agree to that.

Lover Boy bumped against her shoulder, a silent *hey, you stopped scratching, get back to work, woman.* She blew him a raspberry, but kept going.

"Bea?" Peyton's head stuck out from the tack room. "Where'd you go? You stopped haranguing in my ear."

She slid gracefully away from Lover Boy, ignoring his snort of annoyance. "Strategizing my battle plan."

"Sounds ominous." Peyton's head disappeared and Bea followed into the tack room. She settled down on an old wood bench and watched as Peyton did a quick catalog of the inventory by turning in a slow circle. Then she sat down on the dusty ground to start examining the equipment piece by piece for wear and tear.

"You could have one of the hands do that, you know." Bea crossed her legs, not wanting to sit in the dust more than she had to.

"I usually do. But people are busy and I had some time. It's called pitching in." Peyton made a mark on her clipboard.

Bea's back teeth ground together. "I'm sorry, I thought I was pitching in. What with the decorating and all. Not quite dirty work, but you haven't tackled it yet."

Peyton sighed and shoved a strand of hair behind her ear. "Sorry. That was bitchy."

Bea held up her thumb and forefinger close together. "Little bit."

"You bring the worst out in me. Always have."

"Is that my fault?"

Peyton started laughing.

"What's so funny?" Bea's feet landed in the dust, stirring the air and making her eyes water.

"We're fighting like we were four and seven again." Peyton searched for a second, then looked over Bea's shoulder. "Can you hand me that hackamore behind you?"

Bea glanced back, reached around and grabbed the looped bit of rope and handed it to Peyton. Peyton's mouth dropped open and her hand went slack around the hackamore. It dropped to the dusty ground with a soft thud.

"What?" Bea glanced back. There were no other hackamores—or other headpieces at all—behind her.

"How did you even know what I was asking for?"

Well. Ahem. "Just a good guess," Bea said, shrugging.

She nudged the rope with the toe of one shoe. "I'm brilliant, you just don't know it."

"What crap. Of course you're brilliant. It's how you always got out of most of the chores when we were kids." She said it so easily, Bea didn't take offense. "But I'm still not going to get my hair done."

Bea sighed. "That's unfortunate. I'm sure Red would have loved it."

"Red met me with my hair stuffed up under a hat and my face streaked with mud. I doubt he's going to mind continuing on in the same vein."

"Oh, sweet sister. You aren't seeing the possibilities."

Peyton's pen stopped its scratching over paper for a moment before it started up again. That small tell showed Bea she'd found a chink in the armor.

"Red loves you. He's gaga over you. It's adorable, it's awe-inspiring the way that strong, hard man goes completely gooey inside over you."

"Morgan does the same thing for you," Peyton said, not looking up.

Bea chose to ignore that, mostly because it was too complicated to think about. "He thinks you are beautiful, covered in mud and smelling like horse crap. But what," she said quietly, "what would he do if you just showed up, very casually, all dolled up?"

That pen paused once more, then started writing furiously, as if it was going to tear through the paper.

"Visualize with me. It's tomorrow night. He's inside, washing off the day's sweat. Thinking about dinner, maybe dying for a bottle of beer. He knows you'll be down at the table waiting for him, that you'll have a nice dinner with Trace and Seth, maybe Jo. Quiet, simple, ordinary.

"And then you walk in." Her voice was a whisper now. The pen was completely still, all pretense given up. "You're not covered in dust like normal. Your hair isn't in a braid.

Your clothes aren't worse for the wear. You're different. You're magnificent."

Peyton stared at her. Her favorite kind of audience: captive.

"Here's the key. He'd love you, just as you are. Covered in mud, no makeup on. But you surprise him. You catch him unawares. You give him something to think about."

Peyton scoffed. "What's there to think about? Am I walking in naked?"

"Quite the opposite." Enjoying herself more than she could say, she settled back. Then immediately wished she hadn't. Ick, dust. Too late now. "You're fully dressed. And not too obvious about it. Nice jeans, the type that mold to your curves and show off everything. A low-cut top. Not slutty, but something to catch his eyes with cleavage when you bend over. Your hair is down, curly and wild, like you just left the bed, and your makeup is subtly done, playing up your eyes."

"Why my eyes?"

Bea smirked. "Because when he looks into them, you can watch him melt like ice cream. He loves your eyes. So use them."

Peyton blinked, as if coming out of a trance. "Yeah, so? Then what? What's the next step in your big plan?"

Bea sighed. "If I have to share what comes next, you aren't doing enough with that handsome man to keep him interested." When Peyton stared at her blankly, she added, "You seduce him, P. Lead him to that bed of yours and do what comes naturally. What the hell else would you do with him?"

Peyton went back to her paper, marking down the number of bits piled in the box in front of her. "Why do I need to seduce him? Our love life is fine."

"But whose love life couldn't be better? That's right. If it's already good . . . what's beyond good? Mind-blowing.

Something to think about." Bea stood up and headed for the door. Then she delivered the killing blow. "You know the best part about the whole plan, Peyton?"

Her sister looked up, aggravated at the new interruption. "What?"

"The next morning, you're going to go back to being covered in dirt and dust, with mud on your clothes and your hair stuffed under a hat or pulled back in some ratty braid. The curls will be gone, the makeup long worn off, the cleavage all buttoned up. And he's going to still love you so much he'd hand you the moon if he could. That's the best part."

She walked away.

Ten, nine, eight . . .

If her sister didn't join her after that pep talk, she was an idiot.

Seven, six . . .

She, for one, would work her tail off to keep Redford Callahan interested. That man was prime beef. Just not *her* prime beef.

Five, four, three . . .

Bea inspected her nails—*two*—as she reached for her car door. *One.* Maybe a quick manicure wouldn't hurt.

"Bea! Wait up."

Bea smiled in the side mirror before turning to see her sister striding after her. "Get in, short legs. I don't have all day."

"Bea. Stop." He watched her flip her hair from one side to the other for the nineteenth time before grabbing her wrist and giving her a reassuring squeeze. "It's fine."

"It's not fine. I should have given it a day or two to settle before doing this. Why? Why did I get my hair done today? It always looks the best a few days out!" Bea rechecked the mirror once more before shaking her head.

"Do I look too punk? It's too short. She cut it too short. She said to trust her, but maybe I—"

"It's not too short." He ran a hand over her head, then circled his thumb at the base of her neck. "And I like that I can do this. Your skin is really soft back here, did you know that?"

She relaxed a little while his fingers sifted through the hairs at the back of her scalp and the top of her neck. Later, she'd probably swat at his hand and say he was ruining her hair. But for now, she let him. And he loved it.

"You don't need to be nervous."

"Shows what you know," she muttered, but her head drooped forward more so he could reach farther up to scratch and soothe.

"They've met you before. You've seen them around town. It's not a secret anymore we're dating." He ignored the way her body tensed up as he pointed that fact out. "So there's nothing to worry about. We're just having supper."

"Your mother caught us in bed."

"No, she caught us in the kitchen." The fact that he was naked and she'd been wearing nothing but his robe was beside the point. Awkward, yes. Worth dwelling on? Not really.

"You're sure this skirt isn't too short?" She fussed with the material, pulling it over her knees a little.

"You look beautiful. Now, we're getting out of the car, and you're going to let me walk you into the house. Okay?" He brushed a kiss over her lips, then another, just to carry the taste of her with him before he opened the door and walked around. She got out, steady in her heels as she linked arms with him.

"Milton okay back at home?"

"He's keeping Seth entertained. Or the other way

around. Not sure which." She smiled a little at the reminder of her four-legged baby. "They adore each other, but Seth isn't a fan of sharing toys. Milton's more agreeable, except with his balls. Those are nonnegotiable. He'd pick a ball over a treat, which is bizarre to me."

"We all have our limits." Morgan opened the side door and led her into the kitchen, where his mother was at the stove. "Hey, Mama."

Cynthia turned and smiled, but the smile was a bit strained around the edges. "Hello, Morgan. Beatrice, nice to see you again."

"Hello, Mrs. Browning." Bea stood, rooted to his side, her voice a little stiff. "Thank you for having me at the last minute. I hope it wasn't any trouble."

"No, not at all. I always cook more than I need to. Bert says I never got used to cooking for two when I was so accustomed to making for four, including the human garbage disposal known as my son." She laughed a little. "And he's right. I always expect that one to come strolling in asking what's for supper."

There was a pause, and Morgan struggled for something to say. Thank God it didn't matter, as his father saved the day by walking in.

"There's the girl." He came over and bear-hugged Bea, lifting her an inch or so off the ground. "I've barely seen you, it seems."

"Hello, Mr. Browning." She sounded winded. "It's good to see you."

"Oh, just Bert is fine. No Mister crap." He slapped Morgan on the shoulder. "Not sure what you're doing with an ugly guy like this, but you let me know if you have a change of heart and I'll—"

"Bert!" His mother's eyes were wide and her mouth was open. "What are you talking about?"

His father winked and headed for the dining room. "Just making pleasant conversation. Come in here with me, Bea, and keep me company. I'd offer to help in the kitchen, but she always blames me for making food disappear. Let's escape and you can tell me all about the trials my son puts you through at work."

"Oh. All right." With a quick glance at Morgan, she followed his dad into the dining room.

God bless you, Dad.

Morgan waited until his father and Bea were out of the room before walking over to give his mother a kiss on the cheek. "Everything okay?"

"Oh, fine. Just fine. You know how I love last-minute notice for company," she snipped, yanking the oven door open fast enough to have him jumping out of the way.

Morgan thought back to the hundreds of times he'd had friends over unannounced and she'd never batted an eye. "So what's really going on?"

"A little notice would have been nice." She let the sheet of dinner biscuits hit the stovetop with a clatter. "But why bother? It's not like I've got things to do in my life."

"Mom. Mom," he said more forcefully. "I get that. It's why I asked four days ago. And you said it was fine. But if you're pissed, be pissed at me. Not her. I'm the one who invited her. And if it's that big a deal, we'll leave. We can come back some other time when it's more convenient. I just thought family didn't throw you in a panic like this."

"Family." She whirled on him, the towel over her shoulder whipping around like a cape. "Family? That girl isn't family. That girl is your date, for who knows what reason. And if you had the sense God gave women, you'd see she's got one foot out of the state already."

"Mother."

She turned back to stir vegetables on the stove. "You're half in love with her, and she's leaving. So which is it? Are

you going with her? Or are you going to watch her disappear and be left here, heartbroken?"

"That's up to me."

She sniffed, and he felt like an ass. But this was the position he was in, and it was time to make it clear.

"Mom, I love you. You and Dad mean the world to
me. But I choose who I want in my life now. I . . . care for
Bea. She's important to me. How important, I'll find out.
But I won't have you telling me what to do. I won't be
belittled for my choice in women. And if you can't manage to handle that, then I just won't come over here as often. Because I plan to spend as much time with Bea as I
can before she leaves." *If she leaves, which she damn well won't
if I have any say about it.* "I would hate for that to mean we
cannot be over here. But I care enough about her to care
that she's comfortable. And if it's awkward here because of
how you feel about us, then we'll stay away."

Cynthia's mouth gaped open a little before she shut it
again. "You're choosing her over your parents?"

"I'm choosing to have my woman respected. You raised
me to expect that."

Her eyes narrowed. "That was low."

"But truthful."

She breathed out shakily, then began placing the now-
cooled biscuits into a napkin-lined bread basket. "I can be
civil."

"Be more than civil, Mom. She hasn't had it as easy as
she wants people to think. She's thirsty for love."

His mother watched him from the corner of her eye. "Is
she, now?"

"Yes. And not just my kind. Family love." He kissed her
cheek again and took the basket from her to take with him.
"Don't worry about me. I have a feeling, if she leaves,
she'll hurt more than I will. She'll be alone. I'll still have
you, Dad, Meg, Simon, and the terrors."

"You fight dirty." She swatted at his hand when he reached for a carrot. "Scoot."

"Yes, ma'am." He snagged a carrot before she could catch him and popped it in his mouth on the way into the dining room.

"Your mother hates me."

Morgan was quiet for a moment, out on the porch while his mother and father washed dishes. She'd offered to help, but his mother had declined and pushed them out the door to wait for ice cream and pecan pie on the glider overlooking their front yard.

Honestly, Bea was relieved. She struggled to breathe when Cynthia Browning was nearby.

"Your silence is not reassuring," she murmured and pushed so the rocker glided once more.

Morgan shifted his arm around her shoulders. Taking the invitation, she let her head tilt to the nook there and breathed in his cologne. Almost as if the scent and feel of him had triggered a chemical reaction, her heart rate slowed and her breathing eased.

So dinner wasn't a runaway success. His father was kind and loved to talk, which alleviated a lot of the strained silence. But nonetheless, Bea couldn't help noticing his mother rarely looked at her, choosing instead to focus on her own plate.

Morgan pushed gently with one hand on the siding to rock them once more. "I think she needs time to process. It's been a while since she's dealt with one of her kids dating anyone seriously."

She just couldn't work up the energy to protest the idea of being serious. Not now, when she was so comfortable against him, sitting on the front porch and rocking easily.

"It doesn't matter," she murmured. But it did. And it

hurt like hell. It was never fun to be disliked, even if you'd earned it. But this seemed like an attack based on something Bea had done in a past life. Or judging her on her profession. Or, God help her, her mother's actions.

"It's okay, babe." Morgan rubbed a hand over her arm. "Forget about it. We'll go back to my place and just relax." He tapped a hand on her chin so she would look up. She did, and found him smiling. "We can eat our dessert naked in bed."

She smiled back, because he wanted her to. Then held out a hand. "Glasses."

He handed them over without question. The routine was becoming flawless now. She used the edge of her skirt to polish the lens, then slid them back over his nose herself and kissed him softly when they were settled.

"Knock, knock." Cynthia stood in the rarely used doorway to the front hall, watching them closely.

Bea jolted away from him a few inches, like a teenager being caught necking in a parked car. But he pulled her back to his side. His point was made quite clearly. He didn't care who caught them, or what his mother thought about it.

"Mom, I think we're going to take off."

Cynthia bit the inside of her lip for a moment, then stepped out and let the screen door close behind her. "Morgan, can you help your father dish up the ice cream?"

"We're—"

"I'll try that again. Morgan, can you give me a minute with Beatrice, please? I'd like to have a word with her."

Bea's stomach clenched. Here it was. The Hussy Speech. As in, *leave my son alone, you hussy.* Maybe she'd get really vulgar and substitute *slut* for *hussy.* Sylvia Muldoon's daughter could deserve no less, right?

Morgan watched her a moment. She straightened and

put on a bland face. She could take it. She didn't want to, but she could. No human shields for her. "Go help your dad. It's fine."

He stood, then bent over to kiss her forehead. "Chocolate or vanilla?"

It was on the tip of her tongue to ask for low fat frozen yogurt as a joke, but she held back the urge. "Vanilla is fine, thanks."

Morgan placed a hand briefly on his mother's shoulder before opening the screen door and heading inside. Cynthia took her time, walking first to the porch railing and staring out over her vast front yard.

"We moved here when Morgan was just a baby. He doesn't remember any other home. And probably won't, if he's still set on staying in the house down the road." She sighed and headed back to the glider. "My daughter is ten minutes away, and my son is at the corner of our property. It's nice, now that they're grown and have lives of their own, that I still get to see them so often. Not every parent is so lucky."

Bea waited.

"And sometimes, that leads to me forgetting they're adults now, capable of making their own choices. Morgan's older now than Bert and I were when he was born. He's a smart man. One of the smartest men I know."

"He's also kind," Bea said quietly. "Dedicated, determined. Patient, even when you don't deserve it."

Cynthia nodded, still looking out at the yard. "You seem to understand him well."

"I think it's the other way around," Bea responded. "He probably understands me better than my own family."

"You're here now. That's something you can change."

She could. Wasn't that what Trace had said? "You have no reason to worry about me, Mrs. Browning."

"The more this evening goes on, the more I think

you're right. But not," she added with a smile, "for the same reasons you seem to think."

What other reasons could there be besides that she wasn't staying?

"I must apologize. I was horrible earlier tonight."

Bea blinked and watched the older woman's face screw up in a grimace.

"I'm not proud of my assumptions, of my thoughts. Nor my behavior. And it shames me it took my own son to point that out. But he was right, God love him. That's what comes of having a smart man around the house."

"Don't you just hate a know-it-all?" Bea asked affectionately, and his mother laughed.

"Isn't he just? Now, I need to know you understand I've realized my mistake. That I want a do-over with you. And that I want you to feel comfortable in my home. I would hate to think you felt anything less than completely welcome."

Her throat closed up for a moment, and it was all she could do to nod.

"And so, you'll come in and stay for dessert." It was said with the firm finality of a mother who was accustomed to getting her way.

"Of course," Bea said. "I'd love to."

"Now, let's go before Bert has eaten all the pie. He's a maniac for pie."

Cynthia stood and held out a hand for Bea. She took the gesture for what it was—a peace offering—and followed her into the house for ice cream and pie.

Chapter Nineteen

Morgan waited until she unlocked the door to her apartment. Something was missing. "No Milton?"

"He's having a sleepover at the big house tonight. Easier, since I didn't know when I was coming home from dinner." She let him in and walked around the small room, kicking off her heels as she did so. They landed in an ungainly pile, as if they'd had too many drinks and passed out mid-step.

Morgan watched the skirt wrap around her legs as she headed into the kitchen. Though the length was modest enough—in deference to dinner with the parents—and the print was traditional, when she moved, it clung to her like wet bedsheets. He doubted she'd want to know that, as she'd tried to dress conservatively this evening. But he could appreciate it, regardless.

"Are you staring at my ass, Dr. Browning?"

His gaze snapped up to her grinning face. She was holding up two bottles of water. He reached for one and downed half of it in one gulp. Christ, she turned him around. "Of course not. That would be objectifying to women."

"Oh. How disappointing." Bea set her own bottle on the counter and started unbuttoning the shirt she wore. "I was actually hoping to be objectified tonight. Just a little. You know, for kicks."

His eyes tracked her fingers as each button loosened, then popped free. "I might be willing to set aside my principles on the matter for the rest of the evening."

She chuckled softly. Gone was the nervous woman meeting her lover's parents for the first official time. And in her place stood a seductress who boiled his blood and made his throat close up with want. "Males are so wonderful. They're so carnal. They see, they want, they act. It's refreshing."

"I'm the only male acting on this want." He jerked her to him when her shirt lay open. Her eyes widened just before his mouth crushed down on hers. He tasted her everywhere he could get his mouth on. Her lips, her tongue, her cheeks, nose, and brow. He worked over to her ear and tugged with his teeth. The low sound vibrating from her throat, as if caught there, made him hard enough to pound nails.

"Christ, what you do to me, Bea," he whispered harshly, pushing at her shirt and her bra until she was naked from the waist up. Her breasts filled his palms so perfectly. The soft globes with their dark pink tips, calling for his attention. He pulled one nipple into his mouth and felt satisfaction at the cry she let out. At the way her hands fisted in his hair, tugging until he felt needle-sharp pain through his skull.

"Morgan," she gasped when he took the other tip in his mouth. "Morgan. Bed, now."

Bed? Screw the bed. He hooked one leg around the back of her knee and jerked so she lost balance. He controlled her fall to the floor of the tiny kitchen area, cushioning the back of her head with his hand, slowing her progress with his arm around her back. She clung to him, and he liked it. Liked sweeping her off her feet—even if it was more of a Chuck Norris move than a Casanova one.

"God, you scared me!" She punched his arm. He held back a wince. The woman was stronger than she looked.

"I've got you." He kissed her deeply, letting their tongues glide around each other before pulling back to look in her eyes. "I've always got you."

She melted. It was the only way he could describe that instant letting go of reserves, of forgetting boundaries, of accepting him and his emotions for her.

He loved her. Knew then he would love her forever. That he would do almost anything—become almost anything—to keep her with him. But she wouldn't want the words. She wasn't ready to hear them.

So he'd show her in action. Show her love by making love. And he started with another kiss.

Bea could barely breathe. Not because he was on top of her, removing her skirt and panties—though that was breathtaking in and of itself. But what she'd witnessed in his eyes that moment before. She'd be an idiot not to know it was pure love. Not lust, not even just plain need. Morgan loved her. And yet he held back from saying it.

He was a patient man. And he probably knew it would send her running to hear it. He was right, she had to admit while her hands fought with the button of his jeans. So for now, she could pretend she hadn't seen it. Hadn't recognized that complex wave of emotion take him over just before he kissed her senseless.

If he didn't say it, she could pretend it didn't exist. They could keep on as they were. Enjoying each other's company, enjoying each other's bed, and working together seamlessly.

She didn't need to admit to herself that he loved her.

But when he slipped into her, moved over her, in her, bucked against her until his back was coated with a sheen of sweat, she knew she was lying to herself on that one. She could never forget the way he'd looked at her in that instant. She'd take it back to California with her. She'd never again see that sort of acceptance in a man's eyes.

The knowledge, the resulting sadness, and the tiny wish that there could be more between them sent her over the edge of her climax, bringing Morgan with her.

An hour later, she shoved at his shoulder. "You have to go."

He barely budged. "No, I don't."

"I mean, I need you to go. I have things to do."

"Can't make me," he grumbled.

She sighed and sat up. The floor—because they'd never migrated to the bed like sensible people—was starting to kill her back. Oh God. She was getting old. "Morgan Browning, don't make me call your mother."

He cracked open an eye. "Like that's a realistic threat."

"I think she knows what we're up to. We weren't playing poker in your bedroom with me in your robe and you buck naked. Besides, I think she and I have reached . . . an understanding," she finished. Because really, what else could she call it? She nudged his thigh with her foot. "Upsie-daisy."

"What in the world do you have to do at"—he checked the clock on the microwave by glancing upside down—"eleven o'clock at night?"

"Girl stuff. Wanna test me?"

"Having had a sister, I can say with certainty . . . no." He rolled over to his side and grabbed his pants. She couldn't resist the temptation, and so reached over and pinched his butt. He yelped and scooted away. "Woman . . ."

She grinned, then frowned. "Don't 'woman' me."

He sprang at her, pouncing like a big jungle cat, covering her before she could blink. "That's what you are. My woman."

My woman. Oh God, talk about Neanderthal logic. And yet, she wasn't correcting him. Her instinct was to kiss his chin and pat his shoulder. "Off you go, caveman."

"If you're sure you don't want company." He kissed her forehead again and stood. "Want me to run over to the big house and grab Milton and bring him back for you?"

Her heart just melted. Oh, this man was going to be the death of her. "Nah. He's probably asleep by now. Waking him would only wake the whole house."

"True."

"Besides, if I leave him over there, he might do something funny, like jump in bed with Peyton and wake her up with a cold nose to the ass."

"Typical." He finished dressing and helped her off the floor. "Then you want me to tuck you into bed? I don't mind sneaking under the covers to keep you warm."

She let him kiss her, let herself extend the kiss and draw him closer before pushing at his chest. "No, I'm good. Thanks for the offer. You go home and get some rest."

He headed for the door, kissed her once more—the man loved kissing more than any man she'd met before—and waited on her porch until she locked the dead bolt. Bea counted to ten, then heard his truck start. Another thirty seconds after she'd lost the sound of his tires on the dirt and she raced to her closet for her riding clothes and headed for the barn. The cool night air, fragrant with the scent of hay, had her tipping her head back to take it in. God, there were so many stars. She opened her arms wide and just let the breeze wrap around her, pulling at the hair she'd pinned back, at the frayed shirt she'd pulled on.

Okay, enough of that. She was a freaking caricature of

Julie Andrews, arms wide and spinning in a field of wild-flowers. She would make herself gag in a minute.

She paused outside the door to the barn, listening for any hands that might be pulling an overnighter with a sick horse. But all was quiet inside, the lights dimmed low for the horses' comfort, but bright enough to see the way. She headed toward the tack room for Trace's tack, but it was missing. She stopped short.

Was he out of town? No. His truck and the trailer were both here still. As was Lad, next to Lover Boy in their stalls. She'd just passed him. So where the—

"Looking for this?"

She slapped a hand over her mouth just as the shriek would have flown from her lips and spun. "Oh my God, Trace. Jesus. Give a girl a heart attack."

Her brother stood at the doorway, holding his saddle over one shoulder. "I ask again, looking for this?"

She crossed her arms over her chest. "No. Why would I be?"

"Bea."

She rolled her eyes. "Yes, fine. If you're going riding, I'm going back to my place for sleep."

He tilted his head to one side. "Check under the blue tarp."

She raised one brow. "That sounds like the time you made me lift up that rock in the garden and a garter snake jumped at me."

"That was fun." He grinned at the memory. "But nothing's alive under there. Just look, and stop being a stubborn ass."

"Fine, fine." She lifted the tarp carefully—they weren't kids anymore, but he was still her brother—and gasped at the saddle sitting on the bench beneath. "Oh my God. It's beautiful." She ran her hands over the stitching. "Whose is it?"

"Yours, you moron. It counts for, like, five birthday presents."

She continued to pet the saddle, then found the tack beside it. "Mine? All mine? Trace, you didn't have to."

"I did, if you were going to stop using mine anytime soon. Now you can wear your own shit out." He winked at her. "Let's go break it in. Come riding."

She didn't hesitate. "Yes. Let's go riding."

Morgan stepped out of exam room two and found Jaycee leading Thing Two, one of the basset puppies, out of the shelter and into the clinic. "Anything wrong with Two?"

She shook her head. "He's getting a new daddy. A guy from a few towns over has been looking for a basset, and fell in love with Thing Two here." She nodded to the man sitting in the waiting room with no leash or animal. "Found us online and came on over. Third one in the last two days."

Three adoptions in two days. Outside of the adoption fair, it was practically a record. "That's great. Has he started all the—"

"Paperwork's done, background check and interview done by me, as you trained me, and I checked with his old vet. He had a basset that died about a year ago. He's finished grieving and ready for a new four-legged friend. His vet says he's a great pet owner and would be a good home for the new guy."

"Sounds perfect." Morgan rubbed the back of his neck to stem the emotion. The rescues weren't his. Not really. And yet, every time one of them left, a little part of him felt like it was being ripped away. "Bea handling everything up front?"

"Like the pro she is." Jaycee passed by and nudged him. "That new website is fantastic."

"New website." He watched as Thing Two bounded toward his new daddy, the man sprawling on the floor with the pup to play and wrestle like a child. "Forgot about that." He headed for the front desk and set papers by Bea's elbow. "Room Two is coming out soon to check out."

"Great, thanks." She didn't look up, only clicked more stuff on the screen, then typed in a few keys.

He should get back to work. But . . . "What's going on with the new site?"

"Went live on Monday. All pets are up on Pet Finder, and calls and e-mails are coming in. I'm just working on how to streamline this so it's easier to manage around handling regular patients. Otherwise, this might end up being a part-time job all by itself." She beamed up at him for a moment before looking back at the screen. "Two more prospective candidates just e-mailed me their applications and are coming in this afternoon. So we'll see."

"Can my web tech guy keep up with all those changes?" God, how much was this going to cost him?

"Nope. So I sent him on his way. He was nice enough, but you were getting hosed on maintenance charges. You need someone on staff here who can handle the maintenance and updates to the shelter page."

"So what, now I have to hire a replacement for you *and* a tech person?"

"Not yet, anyway. I figured it out." She swiveled in her chair and faced him fully. "I did some research on web coding, talked to a few people, checked out a book or two, and now I think I'm on the right track. I might make a mistake here or there, but nothing too lethal, I think."

He blinked. "Wow."

"I know, right?" She bounced a little, then froze, as if remembering she was in public. With renewed composure, she added, "I hope I can train my replacement to keep up.

Once I've got everything in place, it won't be that hard. The initial setup was the worst part. After that, it's mostly removing the adopted dogs and replacing them with new candidates, and remembering to update Pet Finder."

He nodded, like this was all common sense to him. It wasn't. Not even close.

"Have you made a decision on the candidates you interviewed?"

It hurt to admit it, but she'd been right. "I like Nancy for the job."

"I do, too." She nodded, and he felt a small amount of satisfaction in that. But he didn't want Nancy behind the desk. He wanted Bea. Working with him day after day.

He left her to the website updates and phone calls and headed back to his desk. Jaycee followed him. "Need something?"

Jaycee handed him a clipboard with the next patient's information. "Exam room one is ready when you are."

"Great." He set it on the desk and rubbed at his eyes under his glasses. "Anything else?"

"You should fight for her."

He looked up over the smudged lenses. "What?"

"For Bea. Everyone knows you've got the hots for her, and you're seeing each other. And now I know she's got a replacement coming. So what's going to keep her in town?"

He wanted to say it was him, and her family. A nice fifty-fifty split would be healthy. But he couldn't.

"You need to fight for her. Tell her how you feel. Make her understand you don't want a replacement." Jaycee smirked, looking much older and wiser than her twenty-one years. "I mean, you can throw in a bunch of sexy talk if you think it'll help, but—"

"Out," he said, and she laughed and walked away.

Fight for her. Tell her how he felt. And watch her sprint away, screaming.

Morgan didn't have the chance to tell Bea anything, thanks to an emergency call from a ranch owner thirty miles away. A panicked horse, several injured animals, and a huge mess meant he didn't pull up into his own driveway until nearly ten that night.

And he couldn't resist the smile that spread from ear to ear when he found Bea's car parked by his front porch. She must have found his hide-a-key—located so easily in one of those fake rocks his sister had bought him for Christmas two years ago—and let herself in. Fine by him.

He toed his boots off in the kitchen and grabbed a bottle of water. Dinner. Dinner. He mentally surveyed the contents of his pantry before slowly turning back to the fridge and opening it again. There, sitting on a plate, was a perfectly built sandwich of what looked to be ham and turkey. Praise God, and Beatrice Muldoon. He snatched it off the plate with his bare hands and downed half of it before shuffling, sore as hell, to the bedroom.

Bea sat on his bedspread, fully clothed still in simple jeans and a work shirt—his—with her hair smoothed back with a headband. The glow from the laptop screen in front of her illuminated her features with an otherworldly glow in the dead dark of the rest of the room. And her fingers clicked tirelessly over the keys.

"Your boss is a slave driver."

She gasped and shut the laptop with a start. "Oh my God, Morgan. Don't sneak up on me like that."

"Didn't sneak. Made plenty of noise pulling up, slamming the truck door, and rummaging through the kitchen."

She pointed at his hand, still holding half the sandwich. "I see you found dinner."

He held it up. "I did. You know what I need."

"Easy deduction. For men, food seems to soothe many wounds. Everything okay now?" She shifted the laptop over and patted the bedspread.

He sank down easily, then found himself just falling back. He couldn't stop it. His body was giving up the good fight. "Everything but me. Several sprains, a few lacerations from kicks or running into things. But the horses are all going to recover. One of their hands was on his way to the ER, but I think it's just a broken arm. He'll survive."

Bea surprised him by lying down next to him and smoothing a hand over his chest. "How about you? Will you survive?"

"Is that your way of saying I look like death?" He took another healthy bite of the sandwich.

"It is."

"I'll survive."

"Glad to hear it." She settled down and waited silently while he finished the sandwich, then just pulled her closer to hold for a bit.

"What were you working on?"

"Hmm?" She sounded half asleep.

"The laptop you shut when I startled you. What was it?"

"Oh." She blushed a little. Now what could that mean? "I've been exploring what it would cost to expand the building out back. Add more shelter space to take in more animals. And also partnering with local ranches for equine fostering."

He blinked, staring at the ceiling while her words ran through his mind once more. "Equine fostering."

"Well, there's no room for livestock at the clinic, that much is obvious. But think of all those horses that come from terrible situations. Some of them do have a chance at a better, more peaceful life, but there's nowhere for them to recover. They're just destroyed." She sniffled a little, then cleared her throat. "My allergies are killing me."

"Yeah. It's that time of year." He stroked a hand over her hair and gave her a minute.

"Anyway," she went on, voice a little thicker, "the way I see it, there are plenty of places around here that might be willing to foster those animals. Either for the tax write-off—though that bears more investigation—or just out of the goodness of their hearts. Some people live on enough land and have barns and stables but don't even own horses." When he said nothing, still absorbing, she shrugged. "It was just a thought."

"It's a good one. A great one. I've never thought about it before."

"And the other part was just easy. Looking around for estimates on what it would cost versus how much more square footage we would gain, which would equal out to how many more animals. And then what it would take to raise the donations to make that happen."

"More animals at the clinic."

"Shelter," she corrected. "You need to start thinking of them as two entities. They exist as such on paper. I know they're connected by a single door, but they're two different things entirely."

"You're right." He rubbed her back. "But more animals means more work. We're stretched thin already."

"I know. Which is why I looked into what it would take to run the fully functioning shelter as an individual component. Have its own staff—mostly volunteer, of course, with the addition of one full-time manager—and not depend on the hours from the vet clinic workers."

"Holy hell," he breathed. "You've been a busy one, haven't you?"

"It's not done yet. But I think it's something you really should look into."

"I will," he said, sincerely. "You've given me a lot to think about."

"I'm brilliant," she said smugly and snuggled in tighter.

Neither was dressed for bed—or undressed, as he preferred. But it didn't seem to matter, as they drifted off to sleep together in what Morgan considered the pose of perfection.

Chapter Twenty

Bea ambushed Peyton before her morning coffee. It was Russian roulette, playing with her sister's morning routine. She wasn't a morning person—neither of them was, whereas their brother, obnoxiously, got up with the sun. But Bea just had to know . . .

"Well?"

"I hear nothing, I see nothing, I speak to nothing until I have coffee." Peyton brushed by her at the foot of the staircase and headed straight into the kitchen. She grabbed the mug Emma silently held out to her and drank as if she'd just come from the desert and the mug held precious, life-giving water.

"Got any fruit?" Bea asked Emma, who was scrambling eggs at the stove.

"Chick food," Emma muttered and scooped some eggs onto a warming platter before popping it in the oven. Milton camped himself directly by her feet, face upturned, hopeful for a moment of clumsiness to score a second breakfast.

"What does that make bacon and eggs, manly fare?" Bea found a Cutie and went to peeling. Seth loved the tiny fruit he could easily fist and smash into his mouth. Revolting to watch, but it did mean they constantly had the fruit on hand. "Chicks aren't the only ones who want low cholesterol."

Milton trotted over to see what she had, sniffed, and abandoned her for Emma's side again. *Lost cause, buddy. She's not sharing.*

Peyton held up a hand and drained the final drop of coffee before holding out the cup for Emma to pour more in. Their quiet morning routine had Bea missing the days when she lived in her old bedroom. The morning companionship had always been a secret pleasure of hers. Even if the company was intent on picking a fight.

After one slightly more ladylike sip of the fresh cup, Peyton motioned with her hand for Bea to continue.

"Okay. First off, I sold a few more pieces, so I'll have a check for you soon, minus my redecoration fee. Which, by the way, I've already earmarked for new artwork."

Peyton grimaced. "Do I need to ask?"

"You'll like it. It's cowboy chic. Western flair, without being Western cliché." When Peyton nodded, obviously trusting her judgment, Bea went on. "Also, it's been a few days since I've been able to catch you. I wanted to know how the makeover went down with Red."

Peyton's eyes widened over the rim of the cup, but she took another sip. Her hair, back in its customary braid, slipped over her shoulder and onto her back.

"Distraction tactics won't work on me. I see right through them. Did he jump you like a wild animal? Come on, tell me. Did he?"

Peyton spit the coffee back in the mug, choking. Emma gave her one heavy slap on the back, sending Peyton stumbling a few feet forward. "Jesus. I'm being attacked from all sides."

"Just keeping you from choking on your own spit."

"You're a dream, Emma," Peyton said dryly, then set the mug down on the counter. "It went fine."

Bea counted to five, then rolled her eyes. "That's all I get? Seriously? I drag you, kicking and screaming, to the salon and wait with you so you can get made up and surprise your boyfriend and all I get is 'fine'?" Bea scrunched her nose. "Talk about ungrateful."

"What, do you want an accounting of how we went at each other like animals?" Peyton shot back.

"Yes, please." Bea grinned when Peyton scowled. "Okay, maybe not. But confirmation I was right is always appreciated."

"Yes, you were right. His tongue almost rolled out of his head."

Bea pushed to sit up on the counter, ignoring Emma's narrowed gaze at the infraction. "And he had good uses for that tongue, right?"

"Ack!" Peyton covered her ears. "God, make it stop."

"I'd be disappointed otherwise. I have high expectations of Red."

"Expectations for what?" Red walked in, as if on cue, and picked up the coffee cup by Peyton's elbow. He slugged down a few gulps, then held out the empty mug for Emma to wordlessly refill.

"You guys need a change of pace," Bea said sadly.

"We like our routine. Right?" He leaned over and kissed Peyton's temple, who swatted at him.

"Ah, love," Bea sang, then pointed at Red with the last piece of Cutie. "I was speaking of high expectations of you as a lover."

"I . . . ah." He took another sip of coffee, then cleared his throat. "That's . . . yeah. I'm going to the barn now, where it's safe." And he left with the mug as abruptly as he'd entered.

"He's cute when he's flustered." Bea hopped down and tossed the peel into the garbage can.

"He is." Peyton paused, as if considering. "I think I'm going to marry him."

Now it was Bea's turn to nearly choke. "Since when?"

Her sister gave her a purely female, almost feline smile. Bea mentally applauded the satisfaction on her sister's face. "Since he officially asked me the other night, after we went at each other like animals."

Emma turned, dropping the spatula on the counter, which bounced to the ground. Milton pounced on the utensil, licking happily at the rare treat. Bea waited for Emma to scold the dog, or them for talking about sex so openly. Instead, Emma shocked both her and Peyton by folding her older sister into a maternal hug.

"I'm so glad." The older woman's voice was thick with tears. "So very glad."

Bea waited until Emma was done, then went with instinct and took a turn hugging Peyton. Her sister patted her back awkwardly, but it was enough. Then she stepped back and grabbed her left hand. "Where's the ring?"

"I'm not getting one. He sort of did it on the fly . . . I think he surprised himself," she added in a quiet murmur, looking as if she was replaying the scene in her mind. "But I told him if I accept, I don't want a ring."

"You're crazy. Who turns down a ring?"

"I want a horse," Peyton said smugly.

"You're crazy," Bea reiterated. "Seriously crazy." She kissed her sister on the top of the head as she started out, mostly because she knew it would drive her mad. "But I love you anyway. Come on, Milton."

Bea walked out to her car, ready to head into work. But Red flagged her down from the barn before she could unlock her door. She checked her watch, sighed, then grabbed her phone to text Morgan that she'd be a few minutes late.

Sleeping with the boss had its perks.

"Bea, glad you're still here. You've got a visitor."

"A what?" Who the hell would think to visit her . . . Keeley? Bea grinned. "No way." She took off for the barn as fast as her heels would let her, tripping over an embedded rock. Red caught her arm and helped her before she ate dirt. "Okay, walking now."

"Good," he muttered, keeping a firm grip on her arm. "You're going to kill yourself in those shoes."

"I will die looking good. Where is she?"

"She who?"

"Keeley!" She called it out, expecting her friend to pop out from around a corner and scare her to death. "Where is she?"

"Who the hell is Keeley?" Red asked, confused. "Jefferson Montague wants to talk to you."

"Jefferson . . ." Bea halted mid-step. "Who?"

"Says you met a few weeks ago at that show you went to with Trace?"

Bea scanned her mind for a moment, then the switch flipped. "Oh, why me?"

Red shrugged, as if saying *I wondered the same thing.* "He's in the barn, hanging out with Lad."

Bea hurried in, her heels clicking on the clean concrete. It sounded so . . . different from the no-nonsense clunks her boots made when she came in to ride late at night. Lover Boy stuck his head out, but she ignored him and headed for the man toward the back. Lover Boy snorted his disgust at her behavior.

"Mr. Montague." She held out a hand.

He took it and shook once. "Jefferson, remember?"

"Jefferson." She smiled and gave Lad some attention. "What brings you our way?"

"Well, I was passing by, and I remembered you talking about your family ranch. Had to come see what the deal was all about. Plus, I get to harass that one over there." He hooked a thumb at Red, standing a few feet back with his hands in his pockets.

"We're always glad to have a friend swing by." She rubbed Lad's nose and accepted the bump on her shoulder without stumbling. "Business or pleasure this trip?"

"Little of both. But that's the way it works when you deal in horses."

She smiled at that. A real horseman would see it that way. "I can go get my sister, if you want. She's the brains of the operation. Or my brother, though he's probably busy with his son at the moment. I'm sure if you can wait a minute he—"

"I'll take you." He hooked an arm through hers and guided her to the front of the barn, stopping in front of Lover Boy's stall. "This one seemed to have a yen for some affection when you passed by. Friend of yours?"

She stepped up to the stall door, and raised a brow when Lover Boy turned his back on her. "Oh, come on. Really?"

He pawed at the ground once, as if to say, *yes, really.*

"Don't be like that. I can't stop by every single time I walk in here."

He flicked his tail.

She shrugged a shoulder and turned to face Jefferson. "He's not in the mood."

The nip on her shoulder made her yelp in a combination of shock and pain. "Ow, dammit! Now I have horse saliva on my work shirt."

Jefferson laughed a little, and Red stepped forward to pull her away from the stall door, but she waved him off. "I'm fine." She turned to Lover Boy. "You. Are. Glue."

Unphased by the threat, he whickered softly. Jefferson continued to chuckle.

When he nudged the injured shoulder, as if to apologize, she scratched his forelock. "Don't do that again." He nuzzled into her, a contrite child hoping for extra mama snuggles.

"Ugh." But her arms went around the big animal's neck and she pressed a quick kiss behind his ear. "Dumb beast."

Red cleared his throat. "Should I go get Peyton?"

"If you want." Bea glanced around and grabbed a pair of barn boots. "I'm just going to change shoes and show Jefferson around a bit. But not too long, I'm afraid." She glanced at her watch and smiled at him. "I'm late for work as it is."

Red walked up to flank her. "I'll come with you."

"No need." Jefferson easily guided her toward the workout areas. "We're good, Red. Thanks."

Bea's mouth dropped open for a second. Nobody brushed Red off. In their area, Redford Callahan *was* horses. "I really think—"

"I think you're exactly what I need to get the full picture of the operation." His voice was firm, leaving no room for negotiation or argument, but his grip on her arm was still gentle. "Now, we ready to start?"

Oh hell. Peyton's gonna kill me. "Sure, of course. Let's head back this way. Maybe when we get to the arena, Trace will be out and doing a workout with Lad. He can show off for you. My big brother loves showing off." She shot a look over her shoulder at Red.

He correctly interpreted it as *get my brother out here now,* and hurried off.

"Tell me everything you know," Jefferson said easily as they walked up to the fence surrounding the hot walk area. "Including the transition from soap opera star to rancher."

Here goes nothing. "Jefferson, how much time do you have?"

Morgan settled down with the sandwich Nancy—the new receptionist in training—had picked up at Jo's and his laptop, with an article on a new bovine inoculation to read during his lunch hour.

His phone vibrated in his pocket, and he nearly dumped the sandwich reaching for it. Bea, this needed to be Bea.

And damn. His mother. He opened the text—his parents had both learned how to send texts a year ago at his sister's insistence—and smiled.

Bring B 2 lunch on Sunday.

It was a start. Something had shifted, for his mother to issue the invitation unprompted. Either Bea had won her over, or her ideas about what her son deserved had changed. Either way, he wasn't going to say no. He texted back a *yes,* then made sure he hadn't missed another message from Bea.

Damn woman had messaged him to say there was an urgent issue at home and she'd be there late. He'd assumed a fashion emergency, and fifteen minutes. But after an hour, and no call and no Bea, he started to worry. Couldn't be that bad, right? They'd have called him. Someone from M-Star would have called to tell him.

He stared at his sandwich, not hungry any longer. But he needed to eat.

"I'm sorry, I'm so sorry." Bea busted into Morgan's office right as he started to take a bite.

Morgan set the sandwich down slowly and chewed. Bea looked frazzled, red-faced and a little the worse for wear. Her clothes were streaked with mud, hair was sticking up straight on one side, and her breathing was still erratic. He fought down rising panic that she'd somehow been injured. But if she was injured, she wouldn't be moving so fast on those damn heels.

"I didn't want to be late, I promise."

"Urgent, you said. But that was all I got."

"I know, I know. Something came up last minute at home. Ranch business." She sank down into his other chair and all but melted. "That was so not what I expected."

"Nobody's hurt?"

"No, no. Sorry."

His heart returned to normal after a moment. His temper, however, rose exponentially. "It didn't occur to you that telling me there was an 'urgent issue' and no details might lead me to worry?"

She blinked, as if shocked. "No, I'm sorry. I didn't mean to make it sound like an emergency. I just had no time to explain before things . . . got away from me." Her nose scrunched up and she looked annoyed, like even she wasn't sure how it had happened.

Milton nudged in through the cracked door and trotted over for affection from Morgan. He held a ball too big for his mouth, which made him look like a vacuum that had sucked up a balloon.

Bea ran a hand over her hair, smoothing it back down. "On a positive note, it looks like Nancy jumped right in. I might not need the full two weeks to train her after all."

Probably not. But he wasn't about to tell her that. "She mentioned she looked at the notes you wrote out about the website, and knew she couldn't do it." *So see? You need to stay. This place needs you.*

I need you.

Bea shook her head. "I was afraid of that. The good thing is I can keep working on that for a while, as long as I have photos of the new animals. Eventually we can figure out how to handle it."

I want you. Stay. "Sounds good," he choked out, then looked back to his computer.

"Okay then. I'll just . . . go check in with Nancy and start making phone calls." She stood slowly, like she was debating saying something.

Or like she was waiting for him to speak.

I love you. Stay.

She nodded. "Have a good afternoon."

"You, too."

He watched her leave the office, her dog walking ever patiently behind, and knew he was going to lose her.

Somehow, when Bea had thought of Nancy taking over her receptionist position, she'd thought she would have more free time. Time to do things like leisurely set up the last bits of the shelter website. Time to research new apartments in LA. Time to pack.

Instead, she took on a new project. Making the shelter into an individual entity, and then she'd added the equine shelter to the mix. Because she just couldn't leave things the way they were.

Now she sat, in the shelter's back supply area with her laptop, fiddling with the website in one screen while she had a blog with coding tutorials open on her phone. Her shoes were off, her feet were draped over an old box, and her outfit was basically ruined thanks to that morning's excursion around the ranch with Jefferson, whom she'd left in the capable hands of Red and her brother when she finally convinced him she had to get to work.

And why was that so . . . comforting? Fifteen dogs breathing and rolling around over each other, her own dog napping beneath her, and her clothes a mess, all while working on nerd-alert website coding. And all she wanted to do was finish the coding, close up shop, go home and naked-snuggle into Morgan's king-sized bed.

What the hell was happening to her?

The door opened, and instead of the expected Jaycee, Bea saw Peyton walk through. "Bea?"

"Back here." She held up a hand but didn't get up. Too much stuff on her lap to move that suddenly. And she was almost . . .

"Bea, we need to—"

"Shh." Bea held up a finger, typed in a few letters, closed the code, and hit *Publish*. "Time to start asking the blessed baby Jesus for favors."

"Favors for what?" Peyton tilted her head around until she could see the screen. When Bea refreshed, the shelter's website popped up, exactly as she'd imagined it. "Oh, that looks good. Has it always looked like that?"

"Hell no, it has not." Bea snapped the laptop closed and stretched her fingers. "I'd get up and do a victory dance, but I think my legs have cramped this way."

"Hold on the victory dance." Peyton straightened and walked away to a cage holding two littermates still waiting for homes. The fuzzy black-and-tan mutts rolled and played with each other like, well, puppies. "So you talked to Jefferson Montague this morning."

"I did. He asked specifically for me. To head off the Spanish Inquisition, we chatted about the ranch. I showed him a few places, I talked a bit about you and Trace, and then I said I had to go. I left him with Red, and I don't know what happened after that."

"What did you say to him?"

Bea threw up her hands. "I just told you. Stuff about the ranch."

"But what, exactly, did you say?" Peyton pressed. "Think, Bea."

"I'm not an idiot. Don't treat me like an idiot," Bea said through clenched teeth. "I answered questions. I talked about Trace's rodeo career and how you stuck with the

ranch even when things got tough. I talked about how after Mama died, you dragged us both back and neither of
us was ready to come home. But it was the best thing for
all of us. And I told him about my damn decorating plans.
I just kept talking because he kept listening. I don't know!"

Her sister just watched her. "Do you have any idea who
Jefferson Montague is?"

Bea shrugged. "A nice older guy who I met a month
ago?"

"He's a huge name in the horse world. Huge. Bigger
than big. His name is synonymous with winners."

Bea's mind whirled. The guy was the Bill Gates of
horses, and she'd sat there talking about finding western
artwork to hang on the walls and what it was like on the
set of *The Tantalizing and the Tempting.*

"Oh God." Her head dropped to her knees. "How bad
did I screw up?"

Peyton said nothing.

"Okay, that really helps." Bea wanted to curl up in a ball
and cry. "You're making me think we lost the farm."

"We saved it," Peyton said quietly.

Bea shook her head. "What?"

Peyton ran a hand over another cage, scratched behind
the ears of a lonesome golden retriever with a limp.

"*What?*" she asked again.

"He said he wanted to find a family-run business."

"That's not hard to find. Several are."

"One that wasn't too big for its britches. Whose own-
ers admitted their mistakes. A place that wasn't perfect. He
wanted to invest in a family, not a name."

"Which is . . . good?"

"Apparently. He bought two horses today, and wanted
to bring three more for training. And he's already talking
about stud fees and breeding rights." Peyton shoved her

hands in her pockets. "This is the break people in our business die for."

Our business? "You mean your."

"Our." Peyton's mouth quirked. "I figure you reeled him in, even if you didn't mean to. He went on and on how it was nice to just spend time with someone at an event without being bombarded with a sales pitch or impressive stats. That you bragged on your brother because you were proud of him." She grinned. "And that you said nice things about me, too."

"I must have been drunk," Bea said darkly. "Don't get a big head."

"Not gonna. But it helped. He clearly was . . . charmed by you." Peyton tilted her head. "Maybe your whole acting career isn't as worthless as I thought to begin with."

Bea held a hand over her heart. "With compliments like that, how can I leave?"

Peyton took a step back and looked at the two now-napping puppies in the first cage. "I figure you will anyway. Right? That was your goal all along. Now we've got money coming in, and I can buy you out of your portion. Not right away, but soon enough."

The idea appealed, even as she started to deny it. Leave with enough money to relax and not worry about taking awful bit parts in D-list slasher movies or commercials where she scooped cat litter to pay the rent? It would be a cushion to give her enough time to get her through new auditions. Get her face back in front of the people she needed to impress. To remind her agent she was still alive and wanted to work again.

Because it was all about the work. It was all about the fame. It was all about doing what she'd been aiming for her whole life. She needed it.

Like a hole in the head.

Peyton took in her silence, then nodded. "Whenever you need help packing, just let me know."

And then she was gone.

Bea opened her mouth to yell after her sister, but stopped. Why? Peyton hadn't exactly asked her to stay. In fact, she'd offered to help send her off. So why would it matter? Why would she care?

Who would care when she was gone?

Chapter Twenty-one

Later that night, Bea sat down at her laptop in her own kitchenette and sent an e-mail to her agent. The one saying she was ready to chat, if he was ready to take her calls. And yes, apologizing for having gone MIA for months. But really, what the hell else was she supposed to do? Give him weekly updates on her time as a small town vet clinic secretary?

Her screen beeped, and she saw Keeley was calling in on FaceTime. She hesitated, hated herself for the impulse to decline the call, then clicked to accept.

"Hey, girl." Keeley's bright smile melted immediately. "Oh my God, what's wrong?"

"Why would you ask that?"

Keeley pointed at her screen. "You look like someone just shot your dog."

"No, he's fine." Bea scooped Milton up and showed him off to the camera. "See? He's got allergies though, poor thing. Scratches all the time. I might need to take him in to see a specialist, because his meds aren't working properly. And I'm concerned about this limp he has, but only sometimes. If he hops down from the couch, he doesn't use his back right leg for a few steps. I thought he was faking it at first for attention, but then I caught him doing it when I wasn't even facing him, like he didn't think I would notice. So then I—"

"Bea, oh my Lord. Put on the brakes!" Her friend covered her ears, but she was smiling. "It's a dog, not a human baby."

"Shh." Bea covered the floppy ear not pressed into her shoulder. "He can hear you."

"Sorry, Milton. You know you're adorable. But really, stop giving your mother so much trouble. She can't handle the stress. You'll give her an ulcer."

Annoyance tugged at her gut, but she tamped it down. "So what's going on with you?"

"Big news." Keeley beamed. "I'm getting pregnant!"

"Wow." Knowing immediately what that meant, she applauded. "So who is the lucky father?"

"The writers aren't sure yet, but you know what that means."

"Popularity-with-viewers boost," they both said at once.

"I had a small chat with one of the writers, and he agreed. But I had to be sneaky, because I think they were ready to give Marcella an adopted baby from, like, Malaysia or something, so I had to act fast. Too many babies spoil the season, right?"

Bea smiled, happy for her friend. And instantly realized, she wasn't one bit jealous. Not at all jealous of having to claw and scheme her way into the best storylines and fight to maintain viewer popularity. She'd sucked at it. Had never gotten the hang of approaching the right people at the right time. Likely, that's why she'd been killed off.

"And remember when I was talking about that TV movie, in that e-mail I sent you?"

Bea nodded and rotated Milton to drape over her lap. His head lolled and his eyes closed in complete relaxation while she scratched beneath his underbite. *Pet me, minion. It's the only reason you exist.*

"They're changing it up. It's not a movie—they're doing an entire pilot season. And you would be fantastic for it. Seriously, I showed your headshot to the director, and he agreed. I would have considered jumping ship if I hadn't scored the pregnancy. Things were slowing down for me. But now I think it's a great opportunity for you. Seriously, it's a silver platter ready for you."

Bea drew circles around one of Milton's ears.

"Bea? Can you hear me?"

She nodded. "Yeah."

"So? When are you coming back?" Keeley pressed. "You need to jump on this. I can't keep mentioning my invisible friend forever. He's going to start thinking I'm lying about you just going home for a visit with family."

"I don't think it's a visit," Bea said softly.

Keeley blew out a breath, ruffling the hairs falling from her ponytail. "Frankly, no. You all but moved back. It's been a year. You adopted a freaking dog-baby. You got a damn job. A real-people job, like with a weekly paycheck and office rules and stuff."

"It isn't so bad," she said with a smile. Her eyes drifted over to the list of suggestions she wanted to pose to Peyton about the M-Star website. Things she'd learned how to do after coding and updating the clinic's site.

"Time to come back to our world. The non-real one. The *fun* one! There's work for you here."

"But the part isn't mine. We both know that. The director could take one look at me and say no." She'd experienced it before. Humiliating as it was. "Then I'm back at square one, out there in LA with no job."

"Maybe," Keeley agreed with a shrug. "That's our life. Come back anyway. There are a billion parts perfect for you. You're talented and you work hard. And you've got a body to die for."

Nowhere in there had Keeley mentioned enjoying the work. Having a job she loved. A job she wanted to do, that called to her. And maybe that was the reason she'd struggled to begin with.

"I'll think about it."

"Don't think. Do. Come home. Nothing is holding you there. Come back."

She nodded, said her good-byes to her friend, and ended the call. Then she sat with Milton in her lap for another few minutes.

"What do you think, boy? Would you like LA?"

He breathed deeply.

"You might like it. Hell, I bet you'd love it. Maybe we could even get you in some commercials or something. Surely someone will have a part for a slightly neurotic Boston terrier with an underbite and a tendency to limp dramatically."

She smiled a little at the idea. He'd be an adorable spokesperson for the shelter. Why hadn't she thought of that? He was a success story. Talk about cute print campaign fodder. And he would love the attention and praise.

No, not the point. She could simply suggest Morgan use one of the calmer dogs in a quick ad campaign. After the expansion. Which he had to do, because she'd already put so much work into it.

"He didn't ask me to stay," she said softly.

Milton, as if sensing her sadness, snuggled into her body a little.

"Maybe he was more fine with the whole casual affair thing than I was. Talk about ironic." Her head hit the back of the chair. "I don't belong here, do I?"

Of course she didn't. She was raised to be on a sound stage. From the time she was born, she'd been pushed at one thing, and one thing only. Being more than a rancher, more than what she could be in Marshall. Being special.

Pushing back now would be counterproductive.

Acting was what she knew. She was an actress. Just like her brother was a cowboy, her sister was a cowgirl. And Morgan . . . he was a cowboy's vet. There was no changing what they were.

And that shouldn't have hurt, so deep in her chest, like it did.

Morgan was sliding the leftovers he'd taken home from his mother's house into his fridge when he heard the car pull up. He waited a minute, then heard Bea's footsteps outside his front door. He went to open it, and she stood there, illuminated in the porch light. The weak light turned her hair a ghastly orange, and she was wearing simple flats instead of her regular heels.

"I thought you were staying over at your place tonight."

She shivered in the night air, though it was still almost seventy degrees. "I changed my mind. Is that okay?"

"Yeah, of course." He opened the screen door and gave her time to walk through, Milton included, before letting it shut again. "Did you eat dinner? I had supper with my parents, but there's leftovers if you—"

Rational thought left his mind as she clamped her mouth against his in a brutal, needy kiss. She pushed until his back hit the refrigerator. Her hands tore at his clothes, and she made a little sound in the back of her throat as if she was a starving woman in front of a plate of food.

He tore his mouth away long enough to ask, "Bea, what—" before she kissed him again. It was clear there would be no rational conversation until she'd had her fill of him. He felt her feet move around him, knew she was kicking her shoes off when he heard the thud of one hit the tile floor.

And as his hands crept around her waist, then dipped lower to cup her perfect ass in her tight jeans, he realized he wasn't ready for rational conversation either. Not when all the blood rushed below his belt and stayed there.

"Bedroom," he managed when her lips left his to cruise on down to his collarbone.

"Kitchen," she countered.

Well, hell, why not? He took a good grip of her waist and swung her around and up, letting go when her ass hit the laminate. His hand went to the buttons of her jeans, undoing them as fast as he could. When the waistband loosened, she scooted her butt up one cheek at a time so he could slither them down and off.

Her legs clamped around him, pulling him flush up against her as she scraped her teeth over his neck. God, yes. His hands fumbled a little, struggling without sight or room, to get his own pants unbuttoned enough. But she took over, one small hand reaching between them to pull his cock from his pants and stroke it herself.

He nearly went blind with pleasure. But somehow, some way, Morgan managed to keep it together long enough to pull her legs wider apart, position himself, and thrust into her. There was no time, no fucking time, to wait and let them both adjust. His hips moved to their own rhythm, and he was almost a bystander to the process.

Until his climax shattered around him and all he could do was cup a hand around the back of Bea's head to protect it from the cabinets. And then, everything went black.

Chapter Twenty-two

"Bea," he muttered. His voice was distant in his own ears. He let his forehead rest against the cabinet just over her shoulder. "God, Bea. Are we still alive?"

"Mmm," she purred and scratched her nails over his back. She rested her head on his shoulder, snuggling into his neck and breathing deeply. "We really rock the counter sex. Bathroom counters, kitchen counters. Doesn't matter. It's good."

Felt so good. So . . .

He blinked. Blinked again. Right. This was why people mostly made love in a bed. Because it was way too easy to be lulled straight to sleep after a sexual awakening like that. It was more convenient. Everything was right there in his bedroom. Pillows, a blanket, a mattress, everything within arm's reach in the nightstand they needed to . . .

And, shit.

"Bea."

"Yes, Morgan, we're still alive." She said it on a laugh, her voice turning husky with exhaustion.

"We forgot the condoms."

"Mmm. Right." She kissed his neck and scratched some more. "I'm on birth control, and clean, if you trust me."

"Of course I trust you." Why would she ever think he wouldn't? "I am, too."

"No surprise there. Which I mean in a good way," she added when he tensed. "You may act like a Boy Scout, but you're an animal when it counts, Dr. Browning."

His cock, before as sleepy and sated as he was, zinged awake at that one. "Keep talking like that and we'll never make it to the bedroom. I might just slide you over to the table this time."

"Like I said, an animal when it counts." After a quick nip of teeth, she leaned back and smoothed a hand over his hair. "Glasses."

He handed them over, blinking rapidly while she used her shirt to wipe the smudges away. "Why is it whenever I try that with my shirt, they come out worse than before? And when you do it, they're perfect?"

"Hidden talents. I can also sing the alphabet backward. Learned it for a bit part on a cop drama. My little act got left on the cutting room floor."

"Cute parlor trick." He slipped them back on and kissed her nose. "Should we take this party into the bedroom?"

She bit her lip, then shook her head. "I need to go back."

He grinned a little. "So this was, what, a sex-by?" When she didn't laugh, he added, "You know, instead of a drive-by?"

One corner of her lips turned up in the weak imitation of a smile.

"What's going on?" he whispered and kissed her temple. "Tell me. Let me help."

She tilted her head so he could keep kissing. "Just a lot on my mind."

He pulled back and hitched up his pants. If it was Serious Conversation time, he wasn't going to have it with his dick on display. "So lay it out. Let's run through it together."

She chewed on her bottom lip, then hopped down and pulled on her pants.

"Bea." His voice was growing hoarse from holding back everything he wanted—needed—to say. "Talk to me."

She stared at him while finishing the last button. Opened her mouth, then closed it again and shook her head.

"Fine. I'll go first." He gripped her shoulders. "I love you."

"Keeley found me a part," she said at the same time.

Her eyes widened. "You what?"

"Keeley who?" he asked simultaneously.

"Stop that," they said together.

Bea shook her head and stepped away, facing the refrigerator. "Okay, that's enough of that."

"I agree. Who the hell is Keeley?" He wanted to reach out again, touch her again. Feel her warm skin under his hands and hold her to his body. Feel her mold around him, hug him like a vine on a tree, like she did when they slept in his bed.

"Keeley. My friend from back . . . back in LA. We were on the show together. She . . . well, she mentioned it before and I thought it was nothing. But she has a friend who's starting a new series. And not a soap this time. A legit TV series."

He let that sink in for a moment. "Right. And it's . . . good?"

"Good?" She ran a hand through her hair, skewing one of the bobby pins holding it back from her face. "It's fantastic. It's . . . what small-time people like me hope for. Of course, a series always runs the risk of being not picked up after the pilot, and then there's the theory that you could be replaced if the network decides it. And then . . ."

Morgan watched her pace, ticking off reason after reason why this could, in fact, be the worst thing ever for her career. But he'd heard it in her voice the first time. The ache there, for something more. And he knew in that moment what he'd feared all along.

He waited until she paced by him and gripped her shoulders. She jarred to a halt and glanced up, surprised.

"It sounds good. Great, even."

She stared. "Seriously?"

"Yes." *No. I'm a liar. Stay with me.* "I'm happy for you."

"I don't have the part," she rushed to say. "It's not like this is a done deal. But it's . . . an opening, I guess." Her eyes drifted to the right.

"Openings are good."

She didn't look at him. "You said you loved me."

He closed his own eyes and squeezed her arms gently. Couldn't take that one back now. "I did."

"Did? What does that mean?"

He pulled her to him, rested his chin on the top of her head. Sighed a little when her arms wrapped around him. "It means, I think you're going to slam-dunk whatever hoops you have to jump through to get this part. It means I think you've got a real shot at happiness in LA. And it means I want you to grab the chance."

"You want me to go." The words were muffled into his shirt.

"I want you to go."

His hands wanted to fist in the back of her shirt, to keep her with him, keep her from walking out his door, walking away forever. He would get down on his knees and beg if it would work to keep her in Marshall, with him.

And he would feel like the world's worst douche for it. If she wouldn't stay by her own choice, then staying because he begged would be worse than her leaving. Because she'd still leave, eventually. But she would leave feeling resentment for him and his manipulations to keep her.

If she was leaving, he wanted it to be with peace.

She pulled away slowly, as if she was moving underwater. Her eyes were a little red, but he wasn't sure if that was from pressing against his shirt or not. "Thanks, Morgan. You . . . you've done so much for me."

"I gave you a job." *And my heart. Still yours, if you want it.*

She laughed a little, but it was a dark sound. "Not a job. That was . . . an opportunity. I'm not Bea the Hollywood Fuck Up anymore. I'm not the washed-up actress they had to kill off her soap because she couldn't bring life into the character anymore. Stupid character," she mumbled as she sat on the floor to pull one shoe on. "Stupid rehabilitated prostitute."

"I didn't just hand you the job. You deserved it. You're good at it. And I'd fire Nancy in a second if you still wanted it." It was as close as he allowed himself to coming right out and asking.

Bea shook her head and pulled on the second shoe. "She's good. She'll be a good addition. And I can e-mail whoever you set up as manager of the clinic those plans and research I did."

It hurt. He never thought a broken heart would physically hurt. But somehow it did. His chest felt carved open.

She stood and clapped one thigh for Milton. He raced into the kitchen so fast, his paws skidded on the tile and he bumped the fridge. She picked the dog up like a baby over her shoulder. Then, in a final slash to his heart, she grabbed the collar of his shirt to tug him down and kiss his cheek.

"Thanks," she whispered, and headed out to her car.

The taillights of her car disappeared, and he sank down to the same tile Milton had just skidded over. He'd probably screwed that up somewhere. Somehow in the grand scheme of relationships, he'd gone wrong. Or maybe he was just wrong, period. Wrong to think they belonged together. If they did, she'd have wanted to stay.

He scrubbed a hand over his hair, then fixed his glasses as they were knocked askew. Now was when he really should have his own Milton to crawl in his lap. Morgan let his head fall back to hit the counter with a dull thud.

The last few weeks, he'd spent imagining what it would be like to have Bea permanently at his side. Now he had to go through the ugly process of erasing the dreams and replacing them with reality.

Reality sucked.

Bea started a trash bag first. Knowing what she wanted to throw away would be the easiest. From there, well. She'd have to figure out how to pare down her wardrobe.

The thought made her want to throw up.

Okay, the entire idea of leaving made her a little ill. But like hell was she admitting that one to anybody else. So, she'd toss all blame onto her shoes.

The numbers of which were apparently reproducing more effectively than Peyton's brood mares. She sat down on the carpet, surrounded by pairs of shoes, and wondered . . . had she really worn most of them more than a few times since she'd been back in Marshall? She had several favorites that went with the majority of her outfits, but the total number of pairs she'd owned . . . This was completely impractical.

"Oh my God," she whispered. "I just used the word 'impractical' when discussing my clothes." To apologize, she immediately picked up the nearest pair of Louboutins and stroked them gently against her cheek. "I'm sorry. That was stupid of me."

Milton walked over to her, stepping gingerly between

the heels and sandals. When his front paw landed in a fire-engine-red pair of stilettos, she laughed at the sight. Milton was disgusted and shook his paw to rid himself of the offending shoe.

Trace's voice called out from the porch. "Bea, you in there?"

Ah. A distraction. She hopped up, shoes scattering as she ran for the door and threw it open. "My favorite brother."

"Only brother. For a little bit longer, anyway, until Red makes Peyton an honest woman." He stepped in and glanced around the room. "Did you get robbed in reverse?"

She took stock of the progress she'd made on deleting things. Which was none. "That's as good an explanation as any."

He glanced at the trash bag in her hand, then at the boxes she'd stolen from the back storage corner of the exercise arena. "Donating things?"

Might as well get this over with. "Packing. Or trying to. Not doing a very good job of it. My stuff seems to be growing every time I close the closet door."

Trace took the bag from her hands and set it aside. Then he just pulled her in for a hug. Bea's arms snaked around him, and she buried her face in his chest.

"Bea-Bea," he murmured by her ear. "You don't have to go."

"Yes, I do. I need to get on with it. I've been hiding here, and we all know it. It's just nobody had the balls to say anything. Or they just didn't care."

His cheek rested on her head and he rocked her like a baby elephant rocking with its mama. "Not true. Nobody wants you to go."

She huffed out a breath, but it sounded a little watery and got caught in her throat. "Peyton does."

"Peyton might have, once," he corrected. "But she doesn't now."

"Bullshit."

He rubbed her back in circles. "Regardless, nobody is kicking you out. So why are you going? What's the rush?"

She pulled away and wiped at her eyes. Allergies, of course. Lots of dust flying around with all the organizing of clothing. "Keeley—my friend from the show—said there's a good chance at a part on a series for me. I talked to my agent late last night." She'd taken advantage of the fact she knew she'd get zero sleep after leaving Morgan's house and had woken him up. Displeased, but at least glad to hear she was alive, he'd done some searching and had called her first thing in the morning. Keeley came through, and her agent locked it down. She had a reading scheduled for next week. They were holding mass auditions for the role but would wait to make a decision until they met with her.

"That's not why. Try again. And be honest with yourself this time," he said. The tone was a gentle reproof, the same as when he was correcting Seth's behavior. That should have annoyed her. Instead, she felt guilt rise up and choke her.

"No," she whimpered, and scooted to the kitchen for a bottle of water. Trace gave her space.

A minute or so later, she came back through. "I can't. I don't have a job here anymore. I gave it up, Morgan's all set at the clinic, so he doesn't need me."

"If you think that man needs you only as a receptionist, you've got a hole in your head the size of Texas." Trace took the bottle from her and had a sip himself. "Bea-Bea, you're smarter than that. The man's half in love with you, and you're half in love with him."

"Not half," she whispered, eyes closed.

Trace put his arm around her again, and she let her head fall to his strong shoulder. "Trace, I'm a mess."

"Yeah."

She nudged him in the ribs with a knuckle. "I don't belong here."

"You've always said that, even when you were a little kid. I used to believe you. I think you used to believe you, too. Now neither of us does."

Home run, Trace Muldoon. But still . . .

She concentrated on breathing for a minute, battling back the panic and fear that threatened to rise in her chest. She tamped it down until it was nothing more than a dark spot under one of the pretty Jimmy Choos she had no real need for.

Or, well, actually she did need them. Now that she was going back.

"Let's go for a ride."

"Now?" She glanced at the clock. It was midafternoon.

He grinned, as if knowing what she was thinking. "Most of the hands are out working on the cattle right now. And a few are transporting a horse, so no one's around the barn. Peyton's having lunch at the big house. It's safe. I'll just go saddle up and walk out to the back. Get dressed and meet me downstairs in twenty."

One more ride for the road. She'd never have time for riding out in LA. Might as well. "Yeah, okay. See you in twenty."

Bea let Lover Boy have his head. Trace kept easy pace with her on Lad, and they simply rode. Rode against the wind so it rushed into her face, blew her hair back, stung her eyes. And it was exactly what she needed.

Trace veered off a little, and she followed, giving Lover Boy the pressure he needed with her legs to make the turn. When Trace slowed to a walk by an old silo, she squinted. And then he disappeared behind it.

"Trace?" She nudged Lover Boy on ahead. "Is this the part in the ride when you disappear and a crazed psycho with a chainsaw for a hand comes after me?"

"I'll have to look into that chainsaw thing. Might be efficient." Peyton and Ninja, her horse, rounded the silo, with Trace right behind.

Bea's eyes widened, then narrowed. "You bastard. What the hell is this, an intervention?"

Peyton eyed her critically. For a moment, Bea straightened in the saddle, improving her posture and form. And then immediately slouched again. Hell if she was going to pretend Peyton was giving her a freaking riding lesson like she was a five-year-old on her first pony.

"So . . ." Peyton finally said.

"So?" Was that defiance in her voice? Or just bitterness.

"You ride."

"I ride," Bea mocked.

"You ride like hell," Peyton added.

Bea opened her mouth with another sarcastic comment, then closed it. "What is that supposed to mean?"

"It means you ride like you were born doing it. Which I damn well know you weren't. So who taught you? Some stunt rider in California?"

Bea rolled her eyes. Figured. "Yes. Some big, burly stunt man took me in and showed me his Western ways," she bit off.

"Bea," Trace said quietly. "We just wanna know."

"Then how about we get down from the saddle? I feel like a cliché up here having it out." She swung down without a word, landing softly and looping the reins over Lover Boy's head. Trace dismounted as well and held out his gloved hand for them.

"I'll watch them. You guys go."

"I only want to say it once," she said.

"I can hear. Just, go."

Peyton was already crashing through some tall grass that came up to her sister's waist. "She does that to annoy me, doesn't she?"

"Probably." With a gentle push between her shoulder blades, Trace sent her off to follow her big sister.

Chapter Twenty-three

"How long?" Peyton asked when Bea finally caught up. Her sister had short legs, but she could move like the wind. Bea rested her hands on her knees and breathed for a second.

"God, you've been here like a year, and you're still sucking wind walking?"

"Thanks for . . . waiting. You could have . . . slowed down," she gasped. "How is it you have legs that short and you move that fast?"

"Focus, Bea." Peyton pinched the bridge of her nose. "Have you always been able to ride?"

"Since I was about six." She shrugged when Peyton's mouth dropped open. "What?"

"There's no way. A six-year-old can't teach herself to ride."

"Remember that hand we had back then? Caffy? He came in before Tiny."

"Cafrey," Peyton said quietly. Her eyes scanned over the edge of the tall grass, as if she was trying to bring his image to her memory. "His name was Cafrey."

"But when he started, I was only about four. I couldn't say Cafrey, so he was Caffy to me. He never minded."

"How the hell did you even meet him?" Peyton shook her head like a dog removing water. "This makes no sense.

You were a toddler. Cafrey wasn't one of the main hands. He was there for a few years, then gone. He wouldn't have spent time in the main house. How would you have—"

"I used to sneak down to the barn after everyone was in bed." She grinned at the memory. It had been so simple to wait until everyone was asleep, slip down the stairs in her nightgown and a pair of Peyton's old boots, and race to the barn to look at all the pretty horses. To touch the ones that would bend their heads over the stall doors and say hello, especially the gentler brood mares and older geldings. To feel like she was free to ride . . . if she could.

And then Caffy caught her.

"He knew I wanted to ride, and knew Sylvia, crazy ass that she was, would never let me. I think he saw my desperation to have something outside of her." Bea closed her eyes for a second against her regret. "So he taught me when I would sneak out. I'm sure Daddy would have skinned him alive if he'd found out. But he didn't, and it was fine. He taught me how to saddle the horses, though it was too hard for me at that age. But I got older, figured out how to saddle my own horse, and could take off when I wanted to."

She stretched her arms out, eyes still closed. Her fingertips brushed over the edges of the grass. "God, it was like, the definition of liberation to me as a kid."

Peyton said nothing, but when Bea opened her eyes again, her sister was staring at her, arms crossed.

"Why did you hide it? Why didn't you ask for lessons with Trace? He would have been old enough by then to show you how to ride. Or even Daddy, when he wasn't busy."

"Which was when?" Bea shot back. Peyton nodded after a moment, acknowledging the hit. "Daddy wasn't really keen on spending time with me. It was almost like he and Mama had an unspoken agreement. Daddy got you and Trace, and Mama got me. Split custody, without the split."

Peyton blinked, as if it had just dawned on her. "You think Daddy didn't want you?"

"Not that he didn't want me, but . . ." She held out her hands, palms up. "Didn't know what to do with me. I was raised as Mama's china doll. It's what I knew. Daddy had no clue what to do with a priss like me."

"Neither did I," Peyton admitted. "You confused the hell out of me. You were so . . . white."

Bea choked on a laugh.

"I mean, you were always wearing white. I rolled you over once, when you were a baby. Just playing a game. You laughed, you loved it. And Mama screamed at me for getting you dirty." Peyton grimaced. "You really were like a doll. One of those stupid collectable things you put in a glass case and never touch. I started figuring you didn't want to play, because you were always inside and never followed us out."

"Mama kept me in." Kept her from so much. "She told me once she'd had one girl, but Daddy stole her. So I was her do-over."

Peyton's eyes widened. "That woman was insane."

"Basically," Bea agreed easily. Who knew better than the one stuck with her? "I mean, don't get me wrong. I'm not about to go walking around like you do all the time, looking like you rolled in a pig pile," she added, and Peyton scowled at her. She grinned back. More solid ground there. "I don't really get the whole ranching business. I don't want to get it."

"That's not true," Trace said quietly from behind. She gasped and turned. "Sorry, just had to check and make sure you weren't going to kill each other."

"Not today." Peyton shrugged. "Just filling in some gaps that we all seemed to miss as kids."

"My childhood wasn't a gap," Bea snapped. She didn't want their pity. Yeah, she missed out on doing some of the things she'd wanted to do. But she wasn't suffering.

"Is that why you went into acting?" Peyton kicked at a stone, which barely made it a foot before being stopped by a clump of weeds.

"I went into acting because . . . it seemed natural." She couldn't explain it. Not the way she wanted to. It was too difficult to form into words. "It was what I had been doing my whole life anyway, so it was an easy shift. And I think I was good at it, which only made it easier to keep going. And it got me away from her. It was good work."

Until they didn't want her. And then she realized it was more freeing than disappointing. But to keep up the façade . . .

God, it was exhausting even thinking about it.

"I'm not living a double life or anything. It's not like I'm freaking Wild Horse Annie. I just like to ride. And I'm not as grossed out by the stables as I might have pretended." Immediately she regretted the admission when Peyton's sharp grin spread.

"So you can start mucking out a stall or two. Be useful."

"Don't get your hopes up for free manual labor." She plucked the tips off several strands of grass, held them out in her palm, and let the wind take them. "I'm heading back."

"Back to the house?" Peyton glanced at Trace, who had moved back and was staring up at the sky like he wasn't at all eavesdropping. What bull.

"Back to LA. Back to work."

"You work here. You've got the job with Morgan. And we can always pay you minimum wage to muck out a stall." Peyton smiled, but the smile was hesitant, as if she wasn't sure how it would go over. "So stay and put your sweat into the place."

"I do. But you haven't noticed anything I've done in the main house." Her temper was starting to rise, in direct correlation to her frustration. "You didn't even notice I stepped up and went with Trace to a show when I had no clue what I was doing there."

"I noticed." Her sister's quiet voice threw a bucket of cold water on her overheated temper. "I'm grateful. I don't know that I say it often—"

"Try never," Bea added.

"But I mean it," Peyton finished through clenched teeth. "Stay. We have . . . stuff. Stuff to work out and shit to fix." She kicked another rock, watched it barely roll to the same weed patch.

"I have an audition back . . ." She couldn't call it home. Not right here, looking at her sister, who was all but begging her to stay. A sister who had never begged for anything. Before today, Bea would have bet her life savings that Peyton would never have wanted her around for more than five minutes. "I have an audition," she finished.

"So go, and come back." Trace kept staring at the sky, like that made him invisible.

"Go check on the horses," Peyton said with a shooing motion. She waited until Trace rolled his eyes and tromped off back toward the silo. "He's going to miss the hell out of you."

"I'll miss him. Maybe you, too." She grinned when Peyton raised a brow. "Come on, things can't all change."

"Do you feel like this is just something you have to do? Why are you leaving us? Why are you leaving *him*?" her sister added, with such emphasis Bea couldn't possibly pretend to not know whom she was talking about.

"Some people are meant for this lifestyle. I just don't think I'm one of them. I wasn't raised to want this."

"You were raised by a narcissistic bitch with delusions of grandeur." Peyton bent over to pick up a rock and heave it. The stone whizzed through the air until she couldn't see where it landed.

"And look how I turned out? Is that the punch line?"

"You're not any of that. You're selfish sometimes, but you're not narcissistic. You can be bitchy, but you're not a bitch. The delusions of grandeur . . ." Peyton tilted her hand back and forth. "Maybe."

Bea flipped her off.

"The point is, you're not our mother. She was . . . a piece of work. She was selfish to the bone, she was a liar, a cheat, and was never a good mom, either. Maybe that's breaking a commandment or something to say it, but it's true. And if she made you feel like you couldn't even learn to ride a freaking horse as a kid, she deserves about as much consideration in the afterlife from us as she gave us when she was alive."

"None?" Bea guessed.

"Just about." Peyton took her hat off and rubbed the back of one wrist over her forehead. Her braid flopped around between her shoulder blades, and her shoulders were hunched over, as if she was about to bend at the waist to catch her breath. She looked . . .

Defeated.

That couldn't be true. "Is the ranch okay?"

She looked up, surprised. "More than. We're not out of the woods, but we're aiming in the right direction, and we can feel the sun. It's going to be okay," she said fiercely.

And Bea believed her. "So you don't need me."

"Maybe I just want my sister."

Bea blinked rapidly to hold back the tears. *No. No, no, no. Not now. Don't do this to me now.* "I . . . Peyton." She turned away and covered her face with one hand. "Don't you dare take another step toward me."

"Or you'll what, beat me up? You're a stick. I'd kick your ass in a minute." Peyton wound one arm around her.

It was the closest they'd come to a hug since Bea could ever remember. "Morgan loves you."

"I know," she whispered.

"It's gonna kill him when you leave."

She said nothing.

"But don't let that be the reason you stay. You have to stay for you. Is it gonna kill *you* to leave?"

It just might.

Peyton squeezed her a little. Their difference in height made the position awkward, but more friendly than they'd been in years. "Just keep an open mind, okay? While you're packing up your four hundred pairs of shoes and shit, just think about it. There's work to be done here, work that has your name written all over it."

"If you're talking about manure," she warned.

"I was talking about the shelter." Peyton considered for a moment. "But if you really want a crack at manure . . ."

Bea swatted her sister's hat so it flew several feet in the wind before landing. Peyton cursed and kicked out, but Bea jumped away with a laugh and sprinted toward Trace. Juvenile, but they'd skipped this step in the sibling process. And she wasn't above being immature when the situation called for it.

Bea let Peyton and Trace set the pace for home—which was meandering with a side of boring sauce—because she just didn't have it in her to race. Sorry, Lover Boy, but you got your run in earlier. Now she needed time to think.

Or not think. Bea closed her eyes and let the gentle sway of the horse beneath her saddle lull her for a moment. If she wanted to, she could just fall asleep right there, sitting upright. Let it all go and take a nap.

Naps solved everything.

Of course, when she fell on her head from the saddle, she would wake up and find nothing was solved at all. She was still leaving a family she'd barely connected with. She was leaving a job she'd all but created with her own imagination and passion. And she was leaving love.

Bea fisted one hand around the reins, then forced her hand to relax. Love. She had to say it, didn't she? Love. Four letter word. And she was smack in the middle of it.

But so was Morgan. So if she was going to suffer, she'd suffer with someone.

No, actually she wouldn't. He would move on. Because he was one of the best men she'd ever known, and someone would snatch him up in a heartbeat. Meanwhile, she would be in LA reading scripts, being shot down for parts, and—God forbid—going back to a crap job to pay the overpriced rent. Even if the series worked out, there was no telling if it would be there the next day, or the day after that. Or if she would get killed off again.

Morgan would be there. Morgan loved her. Morgan wanted her. And she wanted him. And the job. And her family. And Marshall, God bless its ass-backward country heart.

If a neon sign had crash-landed at Lover Boy's feet, she wouldn't have been more startled.

"Oh my God."

Peyton turned around, a smug smile on her face. Trace looked a tad more concerned. "What's wrong, Bea Bea?"

"I have to go." She blinked at them, but their forms faded and blurred until she had to blink some more to clear the tears. "No, I can't go. I screwed up. He must hate me."

"Oh, please," Peyton said dryly. "Biggest load of horse sh—"

"Peyton," Trace muttered. "Bea, can you use more words? I'm not understanding what's going on."

"Just go," Peyton advised. "I'll catch him up on the way home."

"I have to go home, too," she pointed out. "I need my car."

"You've got a mode of transportation." Her sister pointed to her horse with a smile. "Use it. Show him what you've got."

Bea froze for a moment, Lover Boy halting beneath her in response to her tension. "Seriously?"

"Less than a mile across that field." Peyton pointed to the left. "Unless you don't think you can handle the ride. On second thought, you'd better come back. We'll get Milton up to the big house for the night, you can rub down your horse and pretty yourself up and . . ."

Peyton's words faded behind as Bea wheeled Lover Boy to the left and kicked him into a gallop across the field for Morgan's place.

Morgan sat at the kitchen table, laptop in front of him, open to the shelter's webpage. Every day, the thing seemed to grow. Some small new feature, a little detail, a new design feature. Already, it was the most functional and user-friendly site they'd ever had. But Bea had taken it above and beyond what they'd needed. Now it was an attraction. Something to bring people in from farther than they'd ever reached before to look at their dogs.

He shut the laptop with a snap. He had to stop doing this to himself, punishing himself. It was like the guy who couldn't change his sheets for months after a breakup because they smelled like his ex. Not quite as creepy, but no less pathetic.

Coffee. He needed coffee. Morgan reached for the coffee filters, then paused. Caffeine was likely what he didn't need right now. His eyes hovered over the top of the fridge, where he kept the few bottles of alcohol he owned—mostly unopened. Nope. Not there either.

Back to bed, then. He'd do better tomorrow, pretending to be a functional, not-heartbroken adult.

He made it halfway to the bedroom when he heard Bea's voice outside, shouting his name. To hell with pride. Morgan took off like a shot, sprinting to the side door and flinging it open.

He was nearly convinced he'd drunk himself into a stupor and was hallucinating things when he found Bea, in dingy jeans and a simple Western shirt, sitting atop one of the Muldoon horses like she'd been born riding.

"What . . ." He licked his lips and tried again. "What are you doing here? And . . ." He was losing the ability to string together coherent sentences.

"And why am I riding a horse, when I hate barns and animals and all that?" Bea grinned down at him, apparently enjoying his lack of speech. "Long story. I'll catch you up a little later. Suffice it to say, I'm not quite the equine hater I sort of led people to believe."

She dismounted and walked the horse to his porch rail, where she loosely looped the reins. He could pull away if he needed to, but the pressure would keep him in check otherwise. Then she held out a hand. "Walk?"

He glanced down at his sweatpants, bare feet, and bare chest. "Um."

She laughed. "Go get dressed, and then take a walk with me. I have things I need . . ." She bit her lip, looking a little uncertain. "Things I need to say."

Was this the last good-bye? Her final attempt to make things even between them? Good luck with it, because they weren't even. He loved her, wanted her, was going to be broken without her. And she was walking away for a career she didn't even like in California.

No, he thought as he tugged on a shirt, nearly popping a seam in the process. She couldn't just tidy this whole thing up with a simple good-bye speech. He wasn't going to have it. If he had to get down on his knees and beg her to think it through, he would. Pride be damned. He could mend that. His heart . . .

That was a break too deep to think about.

Bea dragged the heel of her riding boot through the dirt, making a square, then intersecting lines to create triangles. What the hell was Morgan doing in there? She was supposed to be the primper, not him.

His footsteps thundered down the porch stairs and he grabbed her wrist in a firm grip and started walking. She was tall, but she struggled to keep up with his long-legged strides away from the house and toward the open land that separated his place from his parents' home.

"Morgan, wait. What are you doing?" She shook her arm, and he immediately let go, but then bent and hoisted her over his shoulder. "Jesus! Morgan! Caveman much?"

He merely grunted, but she didn't think he was being funny. He was just that empty of words.

So she would enjoy the ride. Really, staring at his cute butt wasn't all that bad a view, and she wouldn't be busting ass to keep up with him. Who was she to look a gift ride in the mouth?

After he'd gone another few yards, he dumped her back on her feet with zero notice. She stumbled, but he held her steady, at arm's length. When she took a step toward him, he held her back.

"I have to say something."

She blinked. "Maybe you should let me—"

"No, dammit." He raked his hands through his hair, knocking his glasses nearly off. He caught them and slid them back on, hopelessly smudged. She could see his thumbprint right in the middle of his left lens. Oh Morgan. "You're going to listen to what I have to say first. It's important and I won't be pushed aside."

Wow. Forceful. Not Morgan's style at all. She took a step back and swept an arm in front. "Go right ahead." This, she had to hear.

Morgan paced away, then back to her. He opened his mouth, closed it, and paced away again. She barely managed to wipe the smile off her face when he did another abrupt turn toward her.

"This?" He waved a finger between them. "This is important. This is something that doesn't just show up everywhere. We are important."

She bit the inside of her cheek.

"So you saying what you're about to say? Not happening." He shook his head with authority.

"Okay." She used her best *I'm the student, you're the teacher* voice. "What is happening?"

He seemed taken aback that she didn't fight him, but recovered quickly. He held up a finger. "One? You're not going anywhere. You're staying right here, in Marshall. Visit LA when you need to. But you belong here now."

She waited patiently. His cool façade slipped a little more when she didn't interrupt.

"Two, you're not quitting your job."

"But Nancy has my job now," she pointed out calmly. "That would be disrespectful and downright wrong to take it back from her."

He grimaced, as if seeing the truth there. "Then we'll figure something else out."

"Not going to keep me, like a sugar daddy?"

He scowled. "No, and don't play the 'simpering starlet' role. I know better. You don't want to live off me any more than you want to leave. You're fulfilling some predetermined role and it's annoying me. So stop."

Now that . . . she had to gather herself. God, she'd thought he got her, but he more than got her. He wanted who she really was. Who she wanted to be.

"Three," he went on, as if she hadn't just had the last in a long line of epiphanies for the day. "Three is, you marry me. Because I love you, and you love me, though you're going to make me fight to get you to admit it. But you're worth it, so I will fight. And that's what people do when they're in love. They get married."

"Could you look any more pissed about it?" *Flatter a girl, why don'tcha?*

"I'm pissed that you're making me propose out here in an empty field with my barn boots on and nothing around us when I could have taken you somewhere nice with candlelight and wine and—"

She held out a hand to stop him. If he was going to start getting truly upset, she couldn't do what she wanted to. "Morgan, I appreciate your forthright list. But I came here to say something, so I'm going to say it now."

He muttered something, but she couldn't hear what.

"One," she said, taking a page from his own book. "I'm staying in Marshall."

He looked like he wanted to argue with her, but then her words registered. "Staying."

"Yes. I have things I want to accomplish here, not the least of which is dealing with my family." She smiled a little. "We're a really screwed-up bunch. But we can be better."

He nodded silently.

"Two, you're giving me a job. But not Nancy's. She's good at it. I'm going to keep working on the website, because I've come to find that I'm picky about it. And I don't mind coding." Huh. That sounded practically nerdy of her. "But I'm also going to be taking on the job as full-time administrator for the shelter."

His head tilted to the side, and his lips twitched a bit. "Are you? That position doesn't actually exist."

"It does now. Or it will, as soon as you sign off on it. And you will," she added with a pointed look. "And three . . ." She breathed deeply and closed her eyes. When she opened them, Morgan was standing right in front of her.

He looped his arms around her and pulled her tightly against him. "Three?" he asked, voice husky and full of emotion.

"Three is, you're going to marry me. And you're going to hate it sometimes, because I'm high-maintenance. And I'm going to hate it sometimes, because I'm selfish and I want what I want when I want it."

"You're not selfish," he whispered and kissed her temple.

Bea wrapped her arms around his waist and let her ear rest against his chest. His heart thumped erratically beneath. "I am. I'm selfish and sometimes I'm entitled and I'm pushy when I don't get my way—"

"Easy there, that's my fiancée you're talking about." He tilted her chin up to brush a kiss against her lips. "Was this what you were coming over to say before I interrupted you?"

"Yes." He kissed her fully then, tongue sweeping in until she forgot to breathe and had to pull back. "I can't promise I won't get bitten by the show bug sometimes. I might miss it."

"So you fly out to LA for something. Commercials or whatever. Right?" He shrugged. "I'm not going to tie you up in the barn if you need to try something new. As long as you're coming back home to me, I'm happy."

"Good." She looped an arm around his waist when he guided them back toward his house. "Because I have this plan to advertise for the shelter. A commercial spot, local

TV. See, I want to try my hand at directing now. Isn't this a great plan? I've already got the whole thing mapped out. It involves Milton, in a shark costume, and a baby duck. Maybe a Roomba . . ."

He kissed the top of her head. "Sounds great."

She sighed when Lover Boy came into view. "I have to return him."

"Like hell you do. I'll call Trace. He'll come get the horse in a few minutes."

"But Morgan, I . . . ah!" She shrieked and laughed when he lifted her in his arms to walk up the porch steps.

"Just practicing for the wedding night." He kissed her again. "I love you."

"I know." When he nipped her ear, she laughed. "I love you, too."

She had love, and her family. And she was determined to carve out her own space in the place she'd been running from for so long.